'This baby changes everything for you and Jack.'

'I know,' Lucky told her sister. 'We're already separated. What's a baby going to do to us?'

'Lucky, it *is* possible to raise a child without a man around.'

Lucky didn't respond. At this point she didn't know exactly what she wanted. But despite his annoying quirks, she loved Jack and didn't want to raise their child alone. He'd never allow that anyway. He'd demand to be part of his child's life.

'You'd better tell him as soon as possible,' her sister said.

'I will,' Lucky replied, but with little conviction.

'Lucky, do it. Don't make things worse by having him find out some other way.'

'I will, okay?' And she would, but she dreaded it because she knew how Jack would react. He'd be thrilled. He'd want to move back in. But not for *her*. Not because he wanted to be with *her*. Only for the sake of the baby. And when that happened, she'd never be able to trust his feelings again.

This pregnancy might destroy any hope she had of saving her marriage.

Available in April 2003 from Silhouette Superromance

Mr and Mrs Wrong
by Fay Robinson

The Baby Doctor
by Bobby Hutchinson

The Secret Son
by Tara Taylor Quinn

The Baby Cop
by Roz Denny Fox

Mr and Mrs Wrong

FAY ROBINSON

SILHOUETTE®
SUPERROMANCE™

*First published in Great Britain 2003
Silhouette Books, Eton House, 18-24 Paradise Road,
Richmond, Surrey TW9 1SR*

© Carmel Thomaston 2001

ISBN 0 373 71012 7

38-0403

*Printed and bound in Spain
by Litografia Rosés S.A., Barcelona*

Dear Reader,

In my story, *Mr and Mrs Wrong*, Jack and Erin Cahill love each other, but their differences result in a separation before their first wedding anniversary. Jack has secrets from his past that he's unwilling to share. Lucky—as Erin has been nicknamed by her family—must let go of hurts from long ago if she and Jack are to have any chance of making their marriage work.

Lucky is a bit eccentric. Of all the characters I've created, I believe she's my favourite. To do justice to her, I paired her with someone very special. Jack is a strong, sexy cop who adores her but doesn't always understand how her mind works. That makes for some interesting conversations—and trouble.

This book contains drama and laughter, suspense and romance. The setting is special to me—the Black Warrior River, where I spent many wonderful days of my childhood.

I very much enjoyed writing this story. I hope you enjoy reading it.

I'd love to hear from readers. You can write to me at PO Box 240, Waverly, AL 36879-0240, USA. You might also want to visit my website at http://www.fayrobinson.com

Sincerely,

Fay Robinson

For my mother, who was fearless.
And for Casey, who never minds listening
to my crazy ideas.

ACKNOWLEDGEMENT

My deepest appreciation to the following people
for their help with research questions:
Buck Sanders, logger; Larry Hood, forestry manager;
Julie Merced and the Autism Society of Alabama;
forensic investigator Jim Sparrow and the Alabama
Department of Forensic Sciences; Larry Nichols of
the IRS; Cindy Taylor, private investigator;
Robert Seidler, game warden; and the members
of the P-rock research list.
Any errors in this material are mine and not theirs.

CHAPTER ONE

HE SHOWED UP without warning on a Thursday night. He said he'd left his boxing gloves behind when he'd moved out and needed them, but they both knew he kept them in his locker at the gym.

Lucky undid the latch on the screen door and the one on her heart and invited him in—again. Last time, the supposedly missing object had been his extra pistol. Before that, a basketball.

In the four months since Jack had taken an apartment in town, putting their eleven-month marriage in question, they'd searched for a "favorite" shirt he'd never worn and for tools he didn't use. They'd turned the cabin upside down looking for a first-edition Hemingway he didn't own and for a burglary-case file he'd never have left lying around. The only things they'd ever found were the zippers to each other's pants.

"Whoa!" he said with a start, getting a better look at her. "What the hell did you do to your hair?"

"Whacked it all off, obviously."

"No kidding."

She waved back a moth that tried to follow him onto the porch, then flipped on the lights at the pier to draw the insects down to the water and away from him. The mosquitoes never bothered her. Like all the creatures who called Alabama's Black Warrior River home, she'd accepted them as a natural part of life.

But Jack was already slapping at his skin, so she handed him the canning jar she'd learned to keep by the door. It contained a mixture of herbs and 190-proof grain alcohol. She'd inherited the recipe for the insect repellent from her granddaddy thirteen years ago, along with this cabin and eighty acres of sur-rounding bottom land.

Unscrewing the lid, Jack took a sniff. "You didn't brew this in a whiskey still out here somewhere, did you, runt?"

"If I had, don't you think I'd be drinkin' the stuff, instead of making bug juice out of it?"

Chuckling, he dipped his fingers in the jar and dabbed a few drops of the liquid on his neck, face and below his rolled-up sleeves. He wore his dress clothes from work and, after chasing bad guys all day and being out in humidity over ninety percent, ap-peared wilted and tired. His tie was askew, and beggar lice and other bits of plant material clung to the hems of his pants. He needed a shave.

The gun he usually carried was probably locked inside his car's glove compartment, but the empty shoulder holster by itself was enough to give him a dangerous look.

Much about Jack was dangerous, mysterious even, including his background. That was one of the things that had attracted her to him in the beginning. These days, though, the unanswered questions about his past only irritated her.

"So what's the deal with your hair?" he asked. "Did you have one of those hissy fits your grand-mother talks about?"

"A hissy fit is when you're mad. I wasn't mad."

"What were you?"

"I don't know. I felt like cutting it off, so I did."

She fingered it. Three nights ago, during a depression over their crumbling marriage, she'd suddenly decided—after a lifetime of wearing her hair to her waist—that it had to go. The first crude snips she'd made with sewing scissors. A beautician had taken off most of the rest the next morning while trying to repair the damage Lucky had done. With the weight gone, it was no longer forced to behave, resulting in a riot of brown curls.

"Pretty awful, huh?" she asked him.

"No, not at all. Shocked me at first because you look so different, but it's cute." He reached out and playfully ran his fingers through it.

She let out a breath, exasperated. Never in a million years had she imagined he'd like it. Maybe she'd even lopped it off to spite him; she wasn't sure. Where Jack was concerned, she had a hard time being honest with herself.

"But…you told me a million times I looked good in long hair."

"You did. But this suits you, too."

"Cal says I look like I had a brawl with 100,000 volts of electrical current."

He chortled. "Want me to hurt him for you?"

"No, silly." She tried not to smile.

"I could maim him slightly," he teased. "Lock up one of his knee joints so he'd have to hobble around for a few weeks."

He could, too. She'd once watched him take down three suspects in a robbery and never even draw his weapon.

"Better not," she said. "As much as I'd love to see him in pain, he's the only brother I've got." She waved for him to follow her. "Come inside. It's a bit cooler."

"Have any beer?"

"I think so."

The front room was a combination den and kitchen and even had a bed for nights when no breeze came off the river and the tiny bedroom became an oven. The old ceiling fan rattled overhead but barely stirred the air.

Her treasures—bird feathers, turtle shells, fossils, snakeskins and other objects she'd found in the woods and water—covered the walls and nearly every surface. Photographs littered the couch and chairs, leaving nowhere to sit.

"Things are a mess," she said.

"When *haven't* things been a mess?" He headed for the kitchen area.

"Try calling first to let me know you're coming. I might clean up."

"Like that would do any good. You need to throw away or burn some of this junk. The place is worse than a nature museum." He opened the refrigerator, leaned in and started moving things around in search of a beer. He jumped back abruptly. "Damn! There's a dead animal in here in a garbage bag!"

Oops. She'd forgotten about him. "That's an otter."

"What's it doing in the refrigerator?"

"The poor thing drowned in one of my fish traps. I put him in there until I can give him a proper burial."

He turned back with a pointed stare. "You're going to have a funeral for an otter?"

"Not a funeral, Jack. Don't make me sound like some nut. I don't feel right simply tossing him in a hole in the ground since I caused his death, so I'm going to find a nice box for him."

"Dead animals don't belong in the refrigerator."

"The next time I buy a chicken, I'll remember that."

"I'm serious, Lucky. Stuff like this shouldn't be in the house, and you know it."

She made a mental note not to let him in the bathroom if she could help it. He'd have a stroke if he saw what she was keeping in the tub.

"Let's not argue, please."

"Fine. It's your place. You do what you want." He slammed the fridge door. "I'll pass on the beer until after the eulogy."

Lucky bit back her retort.

He wandered over and took a cursory glance at the prints on the couch. "What's this stuff?"

"Leigh asked me to frame two or three of my photographs to hang in her new office, now that Dad's vacated it."

"I'm surprised he's taking his retirement so well. He seems really happy."

"When did you see Dad?"

"He and Cal and I played golf the other day. He looked better than I've ever seen him. More relaxed."

"I think he'll enjoy concentrating on his weekly column and leaving the day-to-day hassle of running the newspaper to Cal and Leigh. Besides, Leigh's managed the editorial side of things for a couple of years, anyway. She may as well have the title."

Lucky picked up some of the photographs. "I like the ones of the hummingbirds. The sunrise reflecting in the water is pretty good, too, but what do you think of this one? It's Mr. Byrd, the old man who squeezes lemonade down at Turner's drugstore."

"I like it. Shows all the character lines in his face." He chose one from a stack she'd developed that afternoon. "I'd skip this ugly thing, though. What is it?"

"A cicada. They're courting right now."

"That must be the racket I heard when I drove up."

Racket. She thought of it as music.

He picked up several more prints and this time studied them. "These are pretty incredible," he said, making her smile. "It's a shame the public only ever sees your news photos. If you had your own studio…"

The smile vanished. "Don't start, Jack."

"Come on, Lucky. At least think about it. You'd get exposure for this area of your work. You could set your own hours and you wouldn't have to be out at night. I don't like you driving around here in the dark. It's too isolated."

"I'm three miles from downtown! And as far as my job goes, I couldn't make a living freelancing. I'd have to worry about paying rent, getting equipment, setting up my own darkroom and buying chemicals—"

"Okay, I get it."

"Not to mention having to hire someone to answer the phone and handle appointments."

"I said I get it."

"I like being able to take personal photos at my convenience, and Dad lets me use the *Register*'s darkroom after hours for nothing. That saves me a lot of money. I'd be foolish to quit my job there."

He squeezed his forehead with one hand, his usual gesture of frustration. "I said okay. You've made your point."

"Then please stop nagging me about this."

"I would if you'd stay out of trouble. Your name's already crossed my desk twice this week. What were you doing in the middle of that domestic dispute on Carver Avenue Monday afternoon?"

"That was purely accidental. I was taking photos there when the woman's ex-boyfriend showed up drunk and tried to break down the door."

"Situations like that can get you killed. What if he'd had a weapon?"

"Good grief! The story was about her *doll* collection. How could I have possibly known there'd be problems from that? You act like I get myself in trouble on purpose."

"Sometimes I think you do. You thrive on the thrill of it."

She started to respond, then let the comment slide. No, she wouldn't talk about this anymore. Not with him. She had a job she loved and did well, and he was wrong in trying to tell her what she could and couldn't do.

She crossed her arms and didn't say anything. He tried to discuss it further, but she refused. Finally he gave up and dropped the subject.

He asked her about bills that needed paying. She asked him about her traitorous dog, who preferred to live with him. They talked about the weather, if she thought it might rain by morning. The conversation was stupid, purposely noncombative. But at least they weren't arguing.

When they'd exhausted every "safe" topic, they stood staring at each other.

"Well…" He absently scratched his dark head.

"Well…" She looked away, no longer able to meet his gaze without feeling foolish. Her cheeks grew hot. Other places grew hot. They were about to engage in something she didn't want—sex without commitment—and she couldn't figure out why.

Because…the only time they got along was when they were horizontal. Much as she hated to admit it, that was the sad reality. He accused her of being too independent, and maybe she was. But he was too dictatorial. The one thing they had in common was their overpowering physical attraction to each other.

The anticipation thickened. She shifted from one bare foot to the other. Her pulse rose and her heart thumped so hard she imagined he could hear it. One of these nights she'd refuse to give him what he'd come here for.

But not tonight.

"I guess we should look for those boxing gloves before it gets too late," she told him, playing the game. They never spoke the rules out loud or even acknowledged there *was* a game, but the result was always the same. "Where do you think you left them? The storage room?"

"The bedroom."

Her face turned an even deeper shade of red. He was anxious tonight. He'd skipped a couple of the usual steps.

She swallowed her nervousness. "Okay, let's go look."

The room was tiny, dominated by the double bed, with no space left for any other furniture except a trunk she'd picked up at a garage sale and used as a table. A half-size closet built into one wall held the jeans and shirts she wore to work, the drawer under it her underwear and shorts. Her few good dresses for church hung from a hook on the back of the door. That was it. Nothing else could fit.

She made a pretense of going through the closet, anyway, even getting on her hands and knees to peer under the bed with a flashlight.

"I don't see them. You sure you didn't take them with you?"

When she stood, he moved closer and pressed himself against her, enveloping her in his arms. He was already aroused. "Now that I think about it," he said, sliding one hand inside her shorts, "I guess I did."

JACK PROMISED HIMSELF he wouldn't do this again, because it only made the situation harder on Lucky and on himself, but his determination had deserted him the instant she'd appeared at the door. In its wake remained an aching desire that only touching her could erase.

He nuzzled the crook of her neck, catching the scent of sunblock and the metal left on her skin from the iron-contaminated groundwater. Sexy. He didn't know how, but it was.

Lucky could smell like fish, or the vinegar she sometimes put on her sunburn, and still excite him to the point of pain. But it was the breathy little sounds of pleasure she made when he touched her that always did him in. Like now. They bubbled from her throat to heat his blood and erase whatever good intentions he'd had when he arrived.

He continued to stroke as he undressed her, taking time as he removed her top and bra to kiss the freckles on her shoulders and the line her bathing suit had made across her tanned back. Slight of build, with few curves to speak of, she wasn't the ideal of beauty, and yet she *was* beautiful. To him, anyway. She possessed the kind of beauty that exists without effort or artifice.

Big brown eyes...a quick smile...even that thick drawl of hers put a twist in his gut. The new hairstyle flattered her wholesome good looks; he thought it made her resemble a water sprite.

He sat on the side of the bed and took off her shorts, sliding them down slender hips and legs until she faced him in nothing but neon-purple panties, a pair of red lips printed above the crotch. Outrageous. But that was Lucky. He peeled them off and tossed them aside.

Given her history, it was a miracle she'd even remembered to put on underwear. She often forgot it and her shoes, or she got distracted while dressing and ended up wearing something crazy, like one rubber beach shoe and one fuzzy house slipper.

Right now only the nails on her right hand had polish, and two of her left toes. She might have done it purposely. Then again, she might have spaced out in the middle of painting them and not realized she hadn't finished. With Lucky you were never quite sure.

The bed was too small, the room too hot to be comfortable, and the air, as always, held the unpleasant odor of mildew. Outside, a tugboat—or towboat as Lucky called them—chugged upriver toward one of the inland docks, its horn blaring. The pilot checked his position by flashing a search beam back and forth between the banks. With each swoop, the light penetrated the curtains and illuminated the bedroom.

Jack wiped the annoyance from his mind as he hurriedly shrugged out of his own clothes and pulled Lucky down to lie with him. He concentrated, instead, on the taste of her mouth. Sweet. And on the taste of her breasts. Even sweeter. When he entered her it was better than the fantasy he'd been having for the past couple of nights. The fantasy about this very thing...

He began to move with almost cruel slowness, long, controlled strokes that had her writhing beneath him. Again and again he took her to the edge of madness, then withdrew.

Why couldn't she care as much about him as she did her damn river? He'd expected her to follow when he'd made his ultimatum and rented a place in town. She hadn't. Over him, she'd chosen mud, fish guts and noisy insects.

Still, fool that he was, he couldn't stay away from her. And he couldn't move back. Even if his pride allowed it, they had other problems that proximity alone wouldn't resolve. Still...anything was better than this sham marriage they'd created.

The tugboat passed, the sizzle of the bugs again invaded the room, and he and Lucky climaxed in near-perfect unison. When he could breathe once more, he took his weight off her and gazed into her eyes. They were dark, unreadable.

"Move to the apartment with me."

"No. You come home."

They'd both spoken the same words a hundred times before.

"This isn't a home, Lucky. It's an undeclared disaster area. When we married, I never expected you'd want to live here permanently."

"My family—"

"Hell, I know. You don't have to tell me. I have it memorized." Her family had settled this bend in 1837 and a Mathison had lived here every generation since. The original log cabin had long ago fallen in to decay, but this ridiculous place, erected near the same spot by her late grandfather, might as well be the original, considering its condition.

When the winter rains came, the river rose, sometimes to a level that threatened the whole area. The dam downstream couldn't always handle all the runoff.

Jack hadn't lived in Potock long enough to see a flood, but he'd heard the old-timers in town talk about how bad the floods could get. This bedroom told the story. The walls had water stains all the way up to the window casement.

Despite that, and even though she knew he was uncomfortable here, she refused to live in town, even for part of the week. They'd tried it for a month and even *he'd* had to admit the running back and forth had been inconvenient.

So he'd given in and suggested they build another house on the river—a decent house—but this land was too low, and Lucky wouldn't hear of selling it. They were at a stalemate.

"You have to commit to this marriage if we're going to save it," he told her.

"*I* have to commit?" She sat up, so Jack did, too,

propping his elbows on his raised knees. "*You're* the one who ran out of here at the first sign of trouble—like a coon with hounds on his tail." Her hick accent had thickened with her indignation. "*You* left *me*, Jack. Not the other way around."

"Because I felt like a visitor here, or one of your specimens, packed up and put on the shelf to take down every now and then when you felt like it."

"I *never* treated you like that."

"Yes, you did. After giving up everything in Pittsburgh, including my career, to move down here and be with you, I still didn't get a commitment. You live the way you want. You do what you want. I expected compromise when we married, but I didn't figure I'd be the only one doing it. Hell, we've been married nearly a year and your photo credits in the newspaper still say 'Mathison' instead of 'Cahill.' How do you think that makes me feel?"

"This is about my job again, isn't it."

"Only partly."

"It galls you that I won't quit just because you decreed I had to. Admit it."

"Yeah, it galls me." And he wouldn't apologize for it. He worried about her. She ran around at all hours and alone. And she had a bad habit of getting in the middle of the stories she photographed.

"Let me see if I have this right," she said. "You hate my job. You hate my home. You hate my lifestyle. I guess I should count my blessings that you get along so well with my family."

"You're being catty now."

"And you're being unfair. You complain about how *I* treat you, yet I can't ask you a few simple questions about your past without you shutting me out. That infuriates me.''

"You know everything there is to know. My parents died in a car accident, and I've pretty much been on my own since I was sixteen. End of story.''

"That can't be all. How did you take care of yourself? Don't you have any other family?''

"Not anyone who matters. I have an older cousin I lived with until I finished school.''

"You never told me that. Why haven't you ever mentioned him?''

"Because we've lost touch. I wasn't that close to him, anyway. He gave me a room to sleep in and that's about it. I paid for it a thousand times over by working my ass off in his hardware store after school and on weekends.''

"You don't have any grandparents? No other cousins? Aunts and uncles? Surely there's *someone*.''

"No. The army was my family after high school.''

"What was your childhood like? I find it very odd that you never mention it unless I bring it up. It's as if, I don't know, it never happened. You don't even talk about your life before you lost your parents. Why is that?''

"Because there's nothing to tell. We were an ordinary family.''

"But why was—''

"Let's concentrate on the present, okay? Nothing else is really important.''

She slumped and shook her head. "See? You're closing up on me again. You do this every time and it makes me crazy.'' Tears formed. "I'm terrified of what's happening to us, Jack. We're not making any progress toward getting back together. We're not

communicating. We talk, but we never resolve anything.''

"Then let's not talk.''

"We have to. I have things I need to tell you.''

"Later. Let me hold you.''

He kissed her and brought her back down to lie
with him spoon-fashion, his front pressed against her
warm backside.

It was always the same. They made love, she cried,
and he went back to his apartment to lie awake and
feel guilty about her tears.

He'd tried to stay away, but he couldn't. An hour
didn't pass when he didn't think of her. And
nights...God, nights were hell. In the dark, the regrets
of his past closed in; demons with faces and names
he'd tried to forget rose up to assault him, and only
the hot pleasure of Lucky's hands on his flesh drove
them away.

Maybe he *would* bite the bullet and move back in.
Living with her, even in this hellhole, was better than
living without her.

He held her for a long time, until her tears ceased
and her breathing began to slow. Quietly he eased
from the bed, but she stirred at his movement.

"Don't leave yet,'' she said without opening her
eyes, her voice sleepy.

"I'm only going to clean up.'' He patted her
gently. "Don't you need to?''

She yawned. "In a minute.''

Padding to the bathroom, he flipped on the light,
grabbed a towel and headed for the bathtub.

"Wait, Jack, no!''

Lucky's panicked cry reached him at the precise
moment he pulled aside the shower curtain and saw
movement below.

CHAPTER TWO

IN THE GRAY of early morning, cops and firefighters wearing protective gloves searched the railroad tracks, their yellow slickers like strokes of paint on a neutral canvas.

Lucky checked her light meter, then framed a test shot in the viewfinder. She'd lose the effect of the slickers with the black-and-white film, but the rescue workers seemed ghostlike in the mist and that, along with the overcast sky, helped convey the somber tone. The composition suggested the horror of the officers' assignment without actually showing it.

But she didn't have the right perspective yet. She slid carefully down the steep grade of the track to where she, police and fire personnel had parked.

With the permission of the fire chief, she climbed on top of one of the pumper trucks and reevaluated the scene. From this slight overhead angle, she could include more of the track. She could also sneak a contributor to the tragedy—the Top Hat Gentlemen's Club—into the bottom right corner of the frame.

Despite the fancy name, "The Hat," as it was more commonly known, was little more than a shack; it owed its popularity to the two-dollar drinks served from midnight to closing and a waitress named Ginger. She'd posed for *Playboy* ten years ago, but her chest still had its fans.

The victim had apparently left the club drunk last night, decided to walk rather than drive, but passed out on the tracks, instead. The three-o'clock freight express to Birmingham had ended his life. Lucky had found the body when she crossed the tracks on her way to work.

Satisfied that she had a good photo for the front page of the Sunday edition, she braced her left elbow against her body, held her breath and squeezed off several shots, bracketing the exposures to compensate for the wavering light levels.

"Hey, Lucky," called one of the police investigators. Deaton Swain picked through some weeds along the bank about ten yards away. "I dare you to get in the cab and turn on the siren."

"I'll pass."

"C'mon, Lucky, don't be a girl."

"I *am* a girl, Deaton. Haven't you figured that out in all these years?"

"Yeah, but you're no fun anymore."

"I grew up, Deaton. You should try it. We're too old for pranks."

He shook his head. "I'll never be *that* old."

Lucky finished up and rewound her film. She climbed down and stuck her camera, meter and film in the bag on the rear compartment of her Blazer.

With these two rolls, a couple waiting at the office and the roll she'd taken yesterday of the twelve-pound squash, she'd have a full morning in the darkroom.

Off in the weeds, Deaton was starting to whine.

"Oh, man, enough of this." He yanked off his gloves. "I'm outta here. Let the uniforms handle it." After making his way down the bank, he came over and plopped down on her tailgate. "God, I hate these messy cases. And I do mean *messy*."

"Me, too. Give me a ribbon-cutting or a town-council meeting any day. At least those don't involve dead people."

Deaton snorted.

"Well, usually they don't," Lucky qualified. "That one time was a fluke."

"Not for you. How many bodies does this make for the year? Three?"

"Four."

He seemed to think about that. "I remember the kid who crashed his car out on River Road and the old lady who died of hypothermia last winter during that freak ice storm, but what was the third one you found?"

"The floater. You remember. I was fishing for Channel cat and pulled him up, instead. The big guy."

"Oh, yeah. Wasn't wearing a ski vest."

"Uh-huh."

"Stupid idiot. Ought to be a law against fat people going in the water, anyway."

She didn't comment. Deaton couldn't possibly mean half the things he said. She'd known him since kindergarten, and he was just as crazy and amusing as he'd been back then.

"Damn, Lucky, that's four bodies in seven months. That's got to be a record, even for you. What's your total?"

"Seventeen. Eighteen if you count the one before I started working for the newspaper. Nineteen if you add the one out of state."

"Seventeen locally in how many years on the job?"

"Twelve."

He shook his head. "I'll bet this stuff doesn't go over too well with the captain."

No, it didn't, but she wasn't about to discuss her personal life. People speculated enough on the reason she and Jack were living apart.

"Where is he?" she asked, instead. "He's usually one of the first on the scene."

"We had an earlier call and he took it."

Good. After the fiasco with Jack last night, at least she wouldn't have to face him in person this morning.

Or maybe she would. His unmarked police sedan turned in the service road and came around the barricade the moment she counted her blessings.

"Ah, hell," Deaton said, hastily jumping to his feet.

Lucky took a deep breath to fortify her strength, but her already queasy stomach did a major somersault.

Jack was a formidable presence when he was in a good mood, but when he was all business—like now—he seemed even bigger, his shoulders broader. Lucky felt both overwhelming joy and deep sorrow at seeing him. She'd gone thirty years without losing her heart, but then this man had come along and stolen it within seconds.

One minute she was single and accepting of it, if not content, and the next—bam! She'd looked into deep-brown eyes and started dreaming about wedding vows and waking up next to him for the next seventy-five years.

Regrettably Jack had proved to be more interested in the *idea* of marriage than the reality of it.

As he approached, he didn't take his gaze off her. Even as he spoke to Deaton, he didn't look away. "Swain, have you secured this scene?"

"Yes, sir."

"Then why is there a newspaper photographer inside the perimeter?"

"Uh, that's Lucky."

"I recognize her," he said dryly, the comment so ludicrous she wasn't sure how he kept a straight face.

She cleared her throat. "I called it in, Jack. I was already here when your people arrived."

His expression didn't change, telling her he already knew.

"Wait for me," he ordered. "I'll be back in a minute."

He motioned for Deaton to come with him, and they walked off several yards, then stopped. Jack's posture suggested forced control as he listened to a rundown of the incident and the procedures followed by his department since their arrival.

He asked Deaton if he'd requested an investigator from DFS, the Department of Forensic Sciences.

"No," Deaton told Jack. "I didn't see a need to call. The death isn't suspicious and we have an ID on the victim from Lucky. Some old guy named Charlie Bagwell. Plus, we found his wallet. His car's still sitting in the parking lot of The Hat with a flat tire. Guess he was too drunk to change it last night and started walking. He only lives a mile or so up the road in that subdivision on the other side of the tracks."

"Collect the evidence and don't speculate. Call

DFS and get someone over here. Have them take possession of the remains. I don't want the funeral home leaving with them."

"Yes, sir."

"Did you get photographs before you moved anything?"

"Uh...no."

A few seconds passed before Jack spoke again. "Get them now. And get a video of both the scene and the car. Impound the car. I also want you to send someone over to the man's house and make sure he's not sitting at his kitchen table eating breakfast."

"I'll go myself." Deaton hurried off.

Jack turned and walked back to her, his face grim. He mumbled an expletive under his breath.

"If I caused trouble, I'm sorry," Lucky told him. "I grew up with Deaton and most of these people out here, and they're used to me being around with my camera. They trust me to keep out of the way."

He shook his head. "It's not your fault. Did he bother to get your statement?"

"Yes."

Jack looked at her more closely, and his expression softened. "Are you okay? You're pale."

"I'm fine."

"You don't look it." He lightly rubbed the back of his hand against her cheek. "And you're distinctly green around the gills. What's wrong?"

"It got to me, I guess."

"I've never known you to let this stuff bother you."

She shrugged. "I suppose it's because I knew the man."

"Do you want to sit down?"

"No, I'll be all right." She prayed that was true. She'd hate to embarrass herself by throwing up. Usually she could eat, drink, smell or look at any gross thing and not be bothered. A cast-iron stomach came with the job, and he knew it from experience.

"Can you tell me what you saw?" he asked. "You can come down later and give an official statement."

"I didn't see much. I came through about six o'clock on my way to the office and glanced down the track. At first I thought the train had hit a cow again. When I realized it was a human, I called 911."

"Are you sure of your identification?"

"Reasonably sure. He cut some trees for me a few years ago, and I've run into him a few times since. Yesterday afternoon he crossed the street in front of me and waved. I noticed his shirt—pink flamingos and palm trees on a yellow background. Your victim over there has on the same shirt. I can't imagine there'd be more than one of them around."

She told him how he might get in touch with his daughter, an old school friend of her sister Shannon's. Lucky thought his wife was dead, but she wasn't certain.

"Jack, I…" She hesitated, hating to bring this up, but feeling as if it had to be repeated. "I promise I don't intentionally get in the middle of things. Deaton said you were on another call. Did you leave it because of me?"

"Not entirely, but yes, I wanted to make sure you were okay. Besides, we haven't found anything on the other call. They can handle it without me."

"What was it?"

"A bomb threat at the box factory. Probably called in by some joker who didn't have anything better to do this morning. Chief's out there leading the search, so he can reach me if I'm needed."

"Does he know I reported this?"

He nodded. "Yeah, he asked me what it felt like to be married to the 'Body Magnet.' That's what people are starting to call you."

She slumped, her misery increasing. "I know."

"People at work kid me at least once a day that you're part bloodhound. The sheriff's department has a pool on when you'll find the next body in their jurisdiction. I'm told it's up to six-hundred dollars."

"I heard."

"I don't get it. Why does this happen to you? When there's trouble, you always seem to be part of it."

"I'm out taking photos every day, and I cover the whole county. My chances of being involved in any given incident are a hundred times, maybe a thousand times, greater than the average person's. It's perfectly understandable."

"Is it?"

"Of course it is."

The argument was an old one. They'd had it many times. The irony was that the thing that had brought them together was now one of the things that kept them apart.

Last year she and her oldest sister, Leigh, had gone to Pittsburgh to be bridesmaids in their cousin's wedding, and Lucky had found body number fifteen in the bathroom off the lounge of the Holiday Inn. Jack Cahill was the investigator on the case.

The attraction had been instant, the courtship wild and brief. Phone calls nearly every night. A couple of weekend trips to see each other. He'd come down to meet her family and visit Potock's police department.

When the local chief, Rolly Akers, inquired if Jack was interested in relocating permanently and heading the revamped detective division, the offer had seemed like a gift from God. They'd married nine days later in the office of the probate judge.

And she'd never been happier in her life.

Until her new husband discovered she was a tiny bit eccentric. Her odd propensity to attract things that were no longer living wasn't an asset, either.

"If you hadn't rushed out mad last night," she told him, "*you* might've been the one to pass through here first thing this morning and find the body."

"Forgive me if I have a major problem with snakes in my bathtub."

"They weren't poisonous."

"And you think that matters?"

Yes, it mattered, and she told him so. She'd caught the water snakes to photograph, had built an enclosure by the pier where she'd planned to put them at first light. She'd needed a way to keep them wet and contained until morning, and the bathtub had been the logical choice.

"This isn't the place to talk about our personal problems," he said. "I've got work to do."

"So do I."

"I want your film. I need the photographs you took before my unit got here."

"I didn't take any."

He held out his hand. "Come on, Lucky. I don't have time for games. You shot at least a roll before you called it in. I know you. You recorded every gory detail."

"I did not!"

She tried to act indignant, but he saw right through it. He snapped his fingers with impatience. "Give it to me. No screwing around anymore. This isn't funny."

"No! It's newspaper property. Leigh would skin my hide. You'll get me in trouble."

"I'll make you prints and bring them over."

"No, I'll make *you* prints and bring them over."

"I need them for evidence."

"And I need them for the Sunday paper."

He pinched his forehead. "Do you have to argue with me about everything? You're too damn much work."

His words wounded her gravely, and he had to know it. She teetered between anger and despair, settling on despair.

"I didn't mean that," he said immediately.

"Yes, you did." Her voice quavered.

"No, not the way it came out."

"Yes, you did, and that's the root of the real problem between us. You married me thinking everything would be easy, that *I'd* be easy. You created this fantasy about the perfect life. House. Kids. Job. Extended family. A wife you could control. But then you found out you'd married a woman who refuses to fit your fantasy."

"That's oversimplifying it."

"Maybe, but it's still accurate."

"I don't want to control you, Lucky, only protect you."

"No, you want to change me, because deep down you don't really like who I am." She walked to the back of the Blazer and reached into her bag. "Here."

She slapped the film into his hand. She pushed up the tailgate and closed the hatch. When she walked to the driver's door, Jack tried to stop her, but she ignored him and got in.

"Sweetheart, wait," he said through the open window.

"The sad part is I'm stupid enough to still love you."

"I love you, too. That's never been the issue."

She wouldn't even dignify his comment with a response. If he loved her, he would never have left her. He'd accept her for who she was. She cranked the engine and put the vehicle into gear. "Move if you don't want to get run over."

He didn't budge.

"Move or I'll show you in front of your officers what a hissy fit *really* looks like."

He took a step back and raised his hands in surrender. She drove off, spewing dust and gravel behind her.

By the time she got the hundred yards to the barricade and went around it, she was weeping. Hiding her sobs from the uniformed cop was impossible, so she didn't try.

The clock in the dash said it wasn't even nine, and already it had been a horrible day. She blotted her tears on the sleeve of her shirt and tried to control herself, fumbling in her purse for sunglasses.

If she went into the office with red eyes, she'd have to answer a million questions, and she couldn't handle that now. What she'd rather do was go home, sit on the pier for the rest of the day and feel sorry for herself. Unfortunately she had too much work and a noon deadline.

Worse than that, she'd have to face Jack again in a little while. It would take him about two hours to get that film over to the police lab and have it developed—and discover she'd given him photos of a twelve-pound squash.

THE BUILDING THAT HOUSED the *Register* had begun its life before 1870 as a pickle factory. Some days Lucky could still smell the brine that had once saturated the hardwood floor.

She loved every square inch of the place, from the elegant antique doors at the front to the ink-stained concrete in the pressroom.

She particularly loved the second floor, her own private domain. Storage took up most of it, but she had a fair-size darkroom, a bathroom and a "parlor" that overlooked the street. The natural light in the front room, filtered by the beveled glass in the windows, was exceptional.

The office was already bustling when she arrived. The newspaper published twice weekly, on Sundays and Wednesdays, so the composing room did computer pasteup for those editions on Monday and Friday mornings.

She'd called Leigh on her cell phone earlier to tell her about the train accident and the bomb threat. Pushing through the doors, Lucky headed straight for the stairs with only a wave to the office and advertising staff and down the hall past the framed copies of front pages with historic headlines:

Local Man Commands Shuttle
Plant To Bring 300 Jobs

Her favorite page was at the end. The banner head-line of this special edition, from July 5, 1973, said:

Lucky Child Found Alive

She'd read the story so many times she knew it from memory. The reporter had written:

A three-year-old, who fell from a boat last night and spent more than five hours floating in the Black Warrior River, sustained only a slight case of hypothermia and no serious injuries, doctors at Riverside Community Hospital said this morning.

Erin Renee Mathison, youngest daughter of newspaper publisher Matt Mathison and his wife, Ruth, of 103 Brighton Street, was pulled from the river at 3:45 a.m. near the Gorgas steam plant on the Mulberry fork, some two miles from where she fell overboard.

The girl tumbled from her family's pontoon boat at about 10 p.m. Monday while watching the Independence Day fireworks display with her parents, grandparents and three older siblings.

Sgt. Albert Cummings of the Walker County rescue squad said the child was wearing a life vest and had learned to swim as an infant. "But it's a miracle she didn't drown or get run over by the flotilla," Cummings said, referring to the annual lighted parade of boats. "She's one lucky kid."

As she went by the frame, Lucky rapped lightly on the glass, something she'd done every workday as long as she could remember. Over the years she'd discovered that luck came in both good and bad varieties, and while her superstitious ritual might not help, it sure didn't hurt.

Leigh's office was next to the stairs, and she called out as Lucky passed. Lucky stopped, turned and stuck her head around the door frame. "What?"

"I've rearranged the front page for you. I need three or four shots."

"Give me an hour and you can clip the negatives you want me to print."

"What do you know about this? I need to put together a quick story."

Lucky came in and gave her a rundown of the facts while Leigh typed them into her computer. They usually couldn't cover breaking news with any success or compete with the big papers out of Jasper, Birmingham and Tuscaloosa. Aside from Leigh, they had only one other full-time reporter. Correspondents, called "stringers," sent in news from outlying communities.

The *Register* carried in-depth features, follow-ups of events and local stories the dailies had no interest in pursuing. But often, like today, they had exclusive photos.

While other small newspapers were being swallowed up by chains or going bankrupt, theirs flourished because they gave readers news they couldn't get easily anywhere else—names of hometown people serving in the military, the lunch menus for the schools, profiles of new people in the area. That meant residents subscribed to both a daily paper and the *Register*.

Their dad had been a good editor and publisher, but Leigh had a better instinct for what readers wanted. With input from Cal, who'd completed his master's degree in marketing last year, Leigh had dramatically increased readership and profits.

Unlike the two of them or Shannon, Lucky hadn't gone to college, but her photos helped keep them in the black, and she was proud of her contribution.

"That's all I know," Lucky told Leigh, finishing. "I wouldn't print a name until you get it officially. I might be wrong. And I don't know how long it'll take them to notify family."

"I'll call before we go to press and see if we can release the name." Leigh kept typing as she talked, reworking the information into a story. "If you get in a bind processing, get Cal to give you a hand. You can hold the rolls Eddie and I left. They're for Wednesday. And the stuff you took for the food page."

"Okay."

"Whose case is the train accident? The Yankee with the fast feet?"

Jack, she meant. Leigh was the only one in the family who believed Lucky had made a mistake marrying someone she'd known for just a few months. Their parents, grandmother, Cal and Shannon were all crazy about him.

Leigh's opinion about marriage was tainted by a rough divorce four years ago and lack of child support from her ex-husband. She didn't even know his whereabouts. Most men were beasts, in her eyes, not only Jack, so Lucky didn't take offense at her barbs.

"You can try Jack and see if he'll give you what you're missing," she told Leigh, "but I wouldn't hold my breath."

"I'll call the coroner. Jack still living in town?" she asked casually.

"For the time being. We're working things out."

"Uh-huh." She stopped typing and turned in her chair. "If that's true, how come you've been crying again this morning and look like death warmed over?"

Lucky took off her dark glasses, dropped her camera bag on the floor and sat down in a chair across from the desk. Nearly eight years separated her and Leigh, but despite that, they were very close. Lucky had never been able to hide much from her, not like with Shannon or Cal.

"I'm scared Jack and I are trying to repair something that can't be repaired," she told her, "and I don't know what I'm going to do."

"Things aren't going well, I take it."

Lucky told her about the argument and her swap of the film, making Leigh roar with laughter. "It's not funny," Lucky said. "My marriage is going down the drain."

"I'm sorry, kiddo, but I'd give anything to see his face when he finds out what you've done."

"I'm sure you'll get a chance. No doubt he'll be in here later to raise hell."

Cal walked through the door carrying doughnuts. "Who'll be raising hell?" He extended the open box across the desk.

"Jack," Leigh said, taking her usual lemon-filled.

"Big Guy? What for?"

"Lucky pulled a fast one on him." She related the story. "You can run interference when he shows up, since you two are so chummy."

Cal shook his head. "Oh, no, you're not putting me in the middle of this." He offered Lucky a doughnut, but she got a whiff of the sweet smell and declined, unable to hide her grimace. "Your stomach still bothering you?" he asked. "You look pretty green this morning."

Lucky shook her head, stood quickly and grabbed her bag.

"Stomach?" Leigh asked. "I didn't know you were really sick."

"I'm fine. A little two-day virus or something."

"Two days!" Cal said with a snort, opening his stupid mouth again. "You've been pukin' for a week. You splattered all over one of my best shirts."

"That was *your* fault, goofball. You shouldn't eat tacos for lunch and then breathe on people."

"Ha, ha. Seriously…you need to go to the doctor and find out what's wrong. You're hunched over the trash can or running to the bathroom nearly every time I see you."

Leigh's eyes widened and an unspoken question passed between the sisters. Rather than answer, Lucky looked away.

"Go have a checkup," Cal added. "I'm worried about you."

Lucky gave him a soft punch in the arm. "You're sweet to worry, but I'm feeling much better now. Whatever I had is going away." She backed toward the door. "I'd love to stay and gab all morning, but I've got a ton of film waiting for me, so I'd better get to it. See you two later.'' She turned and hurried out the door and up the stairs before Leigh could question her.

In the darkroom she put on an apron and a new pair of long rubber gloves. She made sure her skin was covered and the vent open, then mixed the chemicals. She'd only gotten as far as getting the developer in the film tank before Leigh banged on the locked door.

''Let me in, you rascal. I want to talk to you.''

''I'm busy. Go away.''

''Not on your life. Now open the door.''

Lucky ignored her.

''Okay,'' Leigh said after a few seconds, ''you're forcing me to call Jack and ask him what's up.''

Damn her. ''Hold on a second. I'm coming.''

She switched off the lights, loaded the film and screwed on the lid, tapping the tank on the counter to remove air bubbles. She set the timer and agitated the tank. ''Okay, come in,'' she said, flipping the light back on and unlocking the door.

''Are you pregnant?'' Leigh asked without preamble.

''If I said no, would you believe me?''

''No.''

''Then yes, I'm pregnant.''

Leigh sat down hard on the stool, obviously stunned. ''When did you find out?''

''Three weeks ago—or I suppose it's four now.''

Leigh went wild. ''A month! You've known for a month and haven't said anything to *me?*''

''I wanted to tell Jack first.''

''Oh, God, Lucky, how far along are you?''

"About eight weeks. Nearly nine. I figure it was the basketball."

"The what?"

She waved away the question with her hand. "Nothing. A...game between me and Jack. It's not important."

"Does he still not know?"

"Not yet. I've tried to tell him several times, but talking calmly about anything isn't one of our strengths."

Plus, the news had hit her like a bomb. She'd been too overwhelmed to think logically about how to handle it. She wanted a child, but not now. She hadn't been married a year yet, and a third of that, she and Jack had spent apart.

"Cal didn't suspect, did he?" she asked. "If he lets something slip..."

"He's concerned you're sick, but clueless about the reason. Nothing's wrong, is there? He's right, you *do* look green."

"Other than my blood pressure being elevated, I'm healthy as a horse. The doctor said the morning sickness should go away pretty soon. She gave me a prescription for vitamins and told me to drink ginger tea to settle my stomach. The most important thing is she warned me I have to reduce my stress. That's ironic, isn't it? The pregnancy is what's giving me stress."

"Should you be fooling with these chemicals?"

"They're safe. That's the first thing I checked. As long as I don't bathe in them, they can't hurt me or the baby, but I am taking extra precautions."

"I guess we should start looking for help, someone to do some of the shooting and processing for you. I've been thinking about that, anyway. I've put too much of a burden on you the last few months, with Dad retiring and me feeling my way along as editor.''

Lucky had known this was coming. "No, you haven't. And I don't need any help."

"We'll definitely need someone when you go on leave, so we should think about hiring a trainee or a part-time person. And you'll probably want to stay home with the baby for a few months, maybe even the first year."

Lucky didn't even want to think about that right now. "We have plenty of time to work out the details. I'll face those problems when they get here."

"And what about your other problem? This baby changes everything for you and Jack."

"I know. That's what worries me. We're already separated. What's a baby going to do to us?"

"Lucky, if the marriage isn't working and you're not happy, then, for God's sake, file for divorce and save yourself a lot of grief. It *is* possible to raise a child without a man around. I'm doing it and getting along fine. In fact, you'd probably be better off without him, if you want my honest opinion."

Lucky didn't respond. At this point she didn't know exactly what she wanted. Maybe her sister was right. Leigh was certainly better off without Keith. The bastard had demoralized her, cleaned out their bank accounts and taken off with her best friend.

But Jack wasn't Keith. And despite his annoying quirks, Lucky loved him and didn't want to raise their baby alone. Jack would never allow that, anyway. He'd demand to be a part of his child's life.

She thought she heard a noise, so she peeked out the door to make sure Cal hadn't followed Leigh and might overhear them.

"If you're worried about Cal, don't be," Leigh said. "I asked him to put together some projected advertising figures for the remainder of the year. That should keep him busy for an hour. He's absolutely orgasmic about being able to run a spreadsheet. You know how he is with that stuff."

"I want you to be careful what you say to him, Leigh. I don't feel right that you know before Jack does. And if Mom or Mema should find out, Lord… the whole town will know." She agitated the tank another five seconds and checked the timer. "I think I've given everyone enough cause for gossip for one year."

"I doubt I'll have to drop hints. You're so thin it won't be long before you start showing and everybody guesses. You'd better tell Jack as soon as possible."

"I will," she said, but with little conviction.

"Lucky, do it. Don't make things worse by having him find out some other way."

"I will, okay? Nagging me about it won't help. I'll tell him." And she would, but she dreaded it because she knew how Jack would react. He'd be thrilled. He'd want to move back in. But not for *her*. Not because he wanted to be with *her*. Only for the sake of the baby. And when that happened, she'd never be able to trust his feelings again.

She put her hand to her stomach. Her elation at becoming a mother was wrapped in resentment. A part of her wanted this baby very much. Another part of her didn't. Because she was certain, beyond a doubt, what the news of it would do. This pregnancy would destroy any hope she had of saving her marriage.

CHAPTER THREE

LEONA HARRISON stood before the security gate and stared at the house beyond. White shutters hung at the windows and wind chimes on the porch played random notes in the breeze. The yellow paint and the flowers bordering the walk gave the place a cheery look. The yard had jasmine; she could smell it even though she couldn't see it.

She'd learned, though, that facades, just like faces, could hide something different within. That was true of Horizon House, as well as the people of Potock. That was particularly true of the man Leona was about to visit.

Her husband had refused to come, and she guessed that was a good thing, considering how he felt. He hated Terrell. Everyone in town did. Because she was Terrell's aunt and only surviving blood relative, they hated her, too. Twenty-one years after the tragedy, some people still crossed the street to avoid having to talk to her.

No one ever said anything ugly to her face, but the seats next to her at church were always left empty and, although she'd shopped at Hanson's market for nearly thirty years, she'd long ago quit getting decent cuts of meat from the old man or even a polite hello from his son. The good people of the town had branded her guilty by association, just as they'd branded her nephew a killer without the benefit of a trial or a body.

Leona hesitated with her finger over the call box, wanting nothing more than to get in the car and drive home, but a promise to her dead sister, Margaret, to watch over Terrell made her go ahead and push the button. She gave her name and was let in. The residence manager came to the front door and ushered her inside.

The state had moved Terrell here five weeks ago in response to some court ruling Leona didn't really understand. Before that, since he was seventeen, he'd lived at an institution for autistic adults up in Huntsville, and she'd dutifully driven the 240-mile round trip once a month to see him.

This place was more convenient, but having him back in the community was causing problems. The anonymous hate mail had started again, and two nights ago someone had written *murderer* in red paint on her front door. Since Terrell's arrival, Horizon House had reported threatening calls.

Leona talked briefly to the manager, then made her way to the common room where Terrell spent his days staring at the aquarium or working on his drawings. Today he had out a pad and pens and an assortment of colored inks and was sitting alone at one of the round tables they used for activities.

The years had not been good to him, and he appeared much older, more used up, than he should at thirty-eight. Deep lines etched his face. He'd once been a handsome boy, but now he was nearly bald on top, and the sides and back of his hair had turned the color of new tin.

He didn't look up or acknowledge her presence,

only turned to a clean page of his art pad. As he started a new picture, he rocked from side to side, a mechanism he used to comfort himself.

"Hello, Terrell," she said, sitting across from him. "It's Aunt Leona. I hope you've been well."

She didn't expect a response and didn't get one. Terrell had never said a word, to her knowledge, but he could make sounds, and Margaret had told her he'd often cried all night as a child, as if life was simply too painful for him to bear.

She didn't think he cried anymore. A few tears, the attendants said, once when they'd transferred him here and the second time when they'd drained the fish tank to clean it, and he hadn't been able to watch the water.

The only problem they'd encountered was keeping him contained. Sometimes he scaled the wall and disappeared, not running *away* from the house but running *to* something, the irresistible something that drew him as strongly now as it had when he was a boy—the river. Years away hadn't diminished his fascination with it.

As long as no one interrupted his routine, moved his things or tried to touch him, he was fine—almost invisible and seemingly content. He stayed closed up in his silent world and didn't bother anyone.

He was a sweet boy, always had been. Never would she believe he had killed Eileen Olenick. Terrell didn't have it in him to hurt anyone.

But thanks to Matt Mathison's editorials in the *Register* at the time, Leona hadn't been able to convince anyone of her nephew's innocence. In truth, it was the Mathisons' youngest daughter—Lucky they called her—who had really been the one to seal Terrell's fate, and with only a few words. People had taken the unfounded fears of a child and accepted them as truth.

Leona removed her cross-stitch sampler from her purse and worked on the *S* of *Home Sweet Home* as she talked. Terrell continued to ignore her. He occasionally swapped colors. A couple of times he traded his pen for a brush and dipped it in an ink bottle or a small jar of water, swishing it lightly along the paper or painting with painstaking slowness.

Did he remember her house? she asked him. "Of course you do," she answered for him. "Your mama used to bring you over to see me and Uncle Edwin and you'd make so many pretty pictures. Even then you had talent."

Extraordinary talent, or so they'd discovered. He was a savant, Miss Olenick had said, because he could draw or paint anything and with the tiniest details, even things he'd only seen once.

Unfortunately, instead of being a gift that brought happiness, his art had been the catalyst for trouble. If only Miss Olenick hadn't taken an interest in him, his life might have turned out differently.

Well, no use thinking that way, Leona told herself. What was done was done. No one could change the past.

She stayed for her usual hour, then put her needlework back in her bag. Edwin would be wanting his lunch and she still had to stop for bread.

"I'll come back and see you again, Terrell," she told him, standing. "You be good and Aunt Leona will bring you a plate of gingerbread next time. I remember how much you love gingerbread with applesauce."

He removed the page he'd been working on and set it on the table, then packed his supplies into a plastic carrier and shuffled off in the direction of his room in that strange walk of his. He never looked back.

Leona came around the table and picked up the sheet, and her heart nearly stopped. He'd drawn a picture of Eileen Olenick as she had looked twenty-one years ago, a picture as vibrant and colorful as the woman herself had been, and so meticulously detailed it nearly resembled a photograph.

Leona might also have called it "lifelike" except for one thing. The body reclined in a pool of blood. He'd drawn her dead.

JACK CLOSED THE FOLDER on the Bagwell case and tossed it on the growing stack of files. For a town of its size, Potock had a fair share of accidents and crime. Burglaries and thefts, mostly. Husbands and wives trying to beat the crap out of each other. Every weekend some guy got drunk and showed what an idiot he was by urinating in public or pulling a knife and trying to cut one of his neighbors.

Right now they had open cases on sixteen burglaries, a weapons charge, the train death, two cases of vandalism, the bomb threat and a request for assistance from the feds on the sale of historical artifacts that might have been illegally obtained.

With only five investigators, including himself, and a jurisdiction of 24,000 residents, the workload was piling up. He needed more people, and the ones he had weren't sufficiently trained.

Back at his old bureau, not even a first-day rookie would have screwed up like Swain had done this morning. Jack would recommend he be busted back to patrol if he didn't need him so badly. Besides, Swain wasn't the only one around here who didn't know what he was doing. He, at least, had the excuse of inexperience.

Taggert and Domingo had more than fifteen years between them and were officers, yet sometimes acted as if they knew little more than Rogers and Whatley, who'd only recently passed their exams.

Sometimes Jack wondered what the hell he was doing in Potock. He'd once told Lucky that "Podunk" was a better name for it, given its backwoods atmosphere, but naturally she *liked* it for that very reason. The day he and Lucky ever agreed on anything, he'd probably fall over dead.

Taking his pen from his pocket, he circled a phone number on his legal pad. The call from Wes, his ex-boss in Major Crimes, had been a surprise. He'd decided to retire at the end of the year, and if Jack wanted to apply for the position, Wes would write him a recommendation. The commander and the assistant chief were also offering recommendations.

With Jack's training and experience and the endorsements from his former superiors, he'd have an excellent shot at the job he'd coveted since he'd gone into law enforcement.

Except he was no longer in a position to go after it.

His excitement had lasted all of ten seconds before he'd thought of Lucky and how this news would go over with her. If he couldn't get her to leave the cabin, he wouldn't have a chance in hell of getting her to move out of state. Things were so strained right now, he didn't dare bring it up. Talk about poor timing.

He tore off the page of notes, started to crumple it for the trash, then stopped. Wes wouldn't announce his retirement until October, and it was only June. The selection commission needed sufficient time to take applications, do assessments of the candidates and make recommendations for the job and for various down-the-line promotions the opening would create. Nothing would be decided until January—or conceivably even as late as February or March.

He folded the paper and put it in his wallet. Maybe if he explained how much of a raise in pay it would mean and what a great opportunity it was, Lucky would go for it.

And pigs might grow wings, Cahill.

Laughter interrupted his ruminating, and he looked out the glass partition to see Taggert, Whatley and some of the patrol personnel huddled around Lucky in the division room. He glanced at his watch. Four o'clock. Somehow he'd let the time get away from him, and his growling stomach reminded him he'd again missed lunch.

No doubt they were congratulating her on the dirty trick she'd pulled on him with the film. He chuckled under his breath. The little monkey. She'd really gotten him good.

She broke away from the officers and came to the door. "Hi," she said solemnly.

"Hi."

"I kept waiting for you to storm the office with the SWAT team or fire tear gas into the upper story of the newspaper building. When you didn't, I decided I'd better bring these and see how much trouble I'm in." She shook the large envelope she carried. "Contact sheets and prints. I also typed out a statement and put it in there.''

This was awkward, and he didn't know what he could say to repair the damage they'd done to each other this morning.

Apparently neither did she, because she didn't come farther, but waited in the doorway with a wary look, as though she'd turn and run if he made the wrong move. Seeing her so uncertain of him put a knot in his gut. Marriage wasn't supposed to be like this.

He picked up his own envelope from the desk. ''Negatives only. I didn't feel right wasting taxpayers' money printing photos of produce.''

''I figured that. Will you consider an even swap?''

The small group beyond her was watching, obviously speculating on what was being said. Jack rose. ''Come in,'' he suggested. ''We have an audience.''

She glanced over her shoulder, turned back and nodded. ''I guess they've been giving you a hard time.''

''You could say that.''

Taggert was still snickering, the asshole. He was probably the one responsible for the stupid cartoon making its way around the building.

''You know I wasn't trying to embarrass you by switching the film,'' Lucky said, ''but apparently I did. I was so mad I didn't stop to think of the consequences.''

''I'll live.''

He came around and closed the door behind her, and also drew the blinds for privacy. Picking up the phone, he punched in the secretary's extension and asked her to hold his calls for a few minutes.

He and Lucky exchanged envelopes. She declined the chair he offered her, saying she preferred to stand. She moved restlessly around the room and examined the certificates on the wall as if she'd never seen them before.

Finally she stopped pacing and turned, keeping several feet between them. "I've been thinking a lot about this morning, and I'm wondering how two people who claim to love each other can act the way we do."

"I've been wondering the same thing."

"Did we make a mistake getting married?"

His insides seemed to drop to his knees. "Do *you* think we made a mistake?"

"I don't know. Sometimes. When we fight, I do. When we aren't fighting, I can't imagine *not* being married to you. Lately, though, we fight more often than we don't."

"All couples fight."

"And half of them end up divorced."

Now it was his turn to feel restless, smothered by the topic she'd chosen. "That won't happen to us. I'm crazy about you. You know that."

"But it *is* happening to us. Don't you get that? With this separation we're already part of the way there. Our marriage is failing."

"No, it isn't. I admit we have problems, but we can fix them."

"How? How do we fix them?"

"I can think of a couple of things for starters." He moved toward her, intending to take her in his arms and apologize for having been such an ass earlier, but she scooted around the desk out of his reach.

"No, don't start this, Jack. Stay over there and promise you won't touch me."

"Why can't I touch you?"

"Because."

The answer made no sense, so he came forward again. They did a little dance back and forth. He went left. She went left. He went right. She went right. "This is crazy," he said, stopping. "I feel like I'm in first grade again, playing tag with Mary Louise McGillray. Why can't I touch you?"

"Because for once I'd like to have a conversation with you without ending up flat on my back with my underpants around my ankles."

"We're in my office. That's not going to happen."

"Of course it will. We played a game of Toad in the Hole not more than two weeks ago on this very desk, and we've been downright acrobatic in that chair several times."

He smothered his amusement at her euphemistic choice of words, knowing that if he laughed, he'd only make her mad.

She was deadly serious. Her expression told him that. And she had a point. They'd engaged in a little creative sex in his office before, and their arguments often *did* end with it.

But in his own defense…every time they'd made love here had been after hours and with the door locked. This was afternoon, and the building was full of people. He wasn't about to do anything. Holding her had been the only thing on his mind.

Well…probably.

He grumbled to himself. Okay, admittedly, when he held her he usually ended up kissing her. And when he kissed her, they both had a way of coming out of their clothes. But she was his wife, dammit, and he enjoyed making love to her. In resignation, he backed up and folded his arms across his chest. "All right, I'll stay over here. Let's talk this out. What do you think we should do?"

"I want us to go for marriage counseling."

"Ah, hell, no. You can forget about that."

"Jack, please. The least you can do is consider it. Don't be pigheaded."

"I'm not airing our problems in front of some stranger. I categorically refuse."

She swore under her breath. "Fine. Then *you* come up with something. You never go along with anything I suggest."

"If we'd dated longer or taken the time for a real engagement, we'd probably have worked out the things we're fighting about now. Do you agree with that?"

"Yes, I guess so."

"So is there any rule that says we can't start over again? That makes a hell of a lot more sense to me than going to some guy we don't know and whining about how we don't have anything in common."

"What exactly are you suggesting?"

"That we pretend we're not married and do it right this time. We go out. We try stuff we haven't tried before and take an interest in each other's hobbies. We get to know each other better."

He'd caught her interest. Her mouth had started a slight upward turn. "As in a real courtship?" she asked.

"Sure, if that's what you want to call it. Dates. Movies. Picnics. All the things couples do when they meet and start to fall in love, but that we *didn't* do the first time around.''

''We spent all our time together in bed.''

''I know, and it was a mistake. But to prove my sincerity, I'll even go fishing with you.''

''You're joking. You hate the thought of baiting a hook.''

''You can do that part for me. And in return, I'll teach you how to play golf.''

She wrinkled her nose in distaste, then faked a smile. ''Golf. Sounds…wonderful.''

''You don't have to like it or even pretend to like it, but you do have to try it. That'll be our new rule. We don't discount anything, even if it doesn't sound fun or it's not what we'd normally do. If the other person enjoys it, we give it a shot.''

''Would you still keep the apartment?''

''For the time being.''

''Oh.'' Her mouth fell a bit.

''That's the sensible thing to do. Where we live is the biggest problem between us, and we're not going to resolve it easily. We know that already. But we can make a commitment while we're *courting* and try to mutually work out a solution.''

''Without fighting, I hope.''

''Definitely without fighting. No fighting will be allowed.''

''We could even pretend to get engaged after a few months, couldn't we?''

''Absolutely. You could plan a *real* wedding this time.''

Her eyes lit up. ''With a long dress and a church ceremony and everything?''

"If that would make you happy. Invitations. Reception. Flowers. The works."

"Oh, Jack!"

"So what do you say?"

Her delight suddenly turned to obvious distress. Her whole body seemed to sag. "But we can't. Oh, God, it would've been perfect, but we can't do it. It's too late."

"No, it's not."

"Yes, it is!" Pain leaped into her eyes. "Why couldn't you have come up with this idea four months ago, instead of moving out and starting all your stupid games? Ooh, I could just kill you!"

"What the hell..." Why was she suddenly furious at him?

"We can't have a courtship now!"

"Why not?"

"Because, Mr. 'I forgot my basketball,' I'm going to have a baby!"

THE WORD *FLOORED* suddenly made sense to Lucky as she watched Jack sway and his knees buckle. "Oh, no!" She grabbed him, but he was too heavy for her to keep upright. Muscle and bone seemed to melt and slide downward. All she could do was hold on around his middle and guide him as he sat down hard on the carpet.

He prided himself on being tough, but at the moment he looked more like a vulnerable little boy who'd gotten the shock of his life. Her anger fizzled, or maybe her love for him was stronger than her anger. She was equally responsible for this little problem, and it hadn't been fair to put all the blame on him. And, too, this was supposed to be one of the happiest moments in a couple's life, and she had spoiled it for him, for both of them. She'd never forgive herself for that.

"I'm so sorry." She knelt and tried to help him regain his equilibrium. "I didn't plan to tell you like this. I was heartless to blurt it out in anger. Are you okay?"

"Yeah, it's just... I didn't expect... How did this happen? The pill's supposed to be nearly one-hundred percent effective."

"*Nearly* being the problem. My doctor said that in clinical trials, the type I was taking works ninety-nine point nine percent of the time, but in the real world, the failure rate is more like five to eight percent. Even missing one pill, or varying the time you take them each day, can cause disaster."

"Did you skip one by mistake?"

"No, I'm positive I didn't, but apparently certain other medications can also reduce their effectiveness."

"Sinus infection," he said, figuring it out.

"Uh-huh. I had that bad one in the spring. I received a shot and a prescription for antibiotics. If I'd known..."

"Hey, it doesn't matter. Whatever the cause, I'm glad. Hell, I'm thrilled." He grinned stupidly. "I'm going to be a father!"

"I've been trying to tell you for a while, but the right moment never came up." This definitely wasn't it, either. From the first day of their marriage he'd talked about having children. This news had to mean everything to him, and she'd hurled it at him like a stew pot.

"How long?" he asked. "I mean, when will it be here?"

"Early January. I'm a little over two months pregnant."

"Is the baby okay? Are you okay?"

"We're both fine. My blood pressure's a tad high, but the doctor says it's nothing to worry about as long as I try and stay relaxed. She actually wants me to gain a minimum of thirty pounds during the pregnancy because I'm too thin."

"Damn, Lucky, you scared me. For a minute I thought you were going to tell me you wanted to call our marriage quits."

"I can't pretend that I haven't seriously thought about it."

He stared at her, even more dumbstruck than before. "You're joking."

"No, I'm not. I love you. Don't ever doubt that. But we've had major problems from the beginning because we're so different. Now with a baby coming, those problems will only get worse."

"No, they won't."

"Yes, they will. You know they will."

He seemed to catch his breath, and was able to stand. Pulling her close, he slid his arms around her. "Sweetheart..." He rubbed her back with soothing motions. "This is exactly what we need. We'll be a family now. I can't think of anything better...."

"And I can't think of anything worse. Babies don't repair bad marriages. They kill them."

He pulled his head back so he could look at her, but still kept his hands loosely on her waist. "We don't have a bad marriage, only a temporary bad spell. There's a big difference."

"I hope you're right, and not only for the baby's sake but for ours. I refuse to allow this child to grow up listening to us constantly quarrel. I'd rather separate permanently than have that happen."

"That sounds like Leigh talking, not you."

"Leigh has nothing to do with this."

"Then why are you wanting to divorce me?"

"I don't want to divorce you. I'm only trying to be realistic about our problems and do what's best for our child."

"Well, divorce sure as hell isn't the answer."

"Then tell me what is."

"Being together." He rubbed his fingers lightly against her belly. "That little baby in there needs us to be a family, Lucky. I need it, too."

Her heart went out to him. "Oh, Jack…"

"Don't give up on us."

"I don't want to, but…" She sighed, feeling so uncertain, so confused. They fought over the same issues again and again, and emotionally she simply couldn't take it anymore. "I wish…we really *could* start over, like you suggested. Wiping the slate clean might have given us the second chance we needed."

"We can still do it."

She shook her head sadly. "It's a little late for romance, don't you think?"

"No, it's a great time. Perfect."

"Oh, sure. In a few months my belly button will stick out like it's deformed, and I probably won't be able to find my feet. You won't want to even *look* at me, much less touch me. Stretch marks and romance aren't a very good combination."

"You'll be beautiful with your sticking-out belly button. I can't wait to see that. And I'll *always* want to touch you, Lucky, stretch marks or not. Hell, I think about it all the time."

"I'm about to get very fat. You realize that, don't you?"

"Yeah, but you'll finally have some boobs."

His effort to produce a smile from her worked. She chuckled despite her gloom. "You're horrible." She moved in closer and played with the front of his shirt and the leather of his shoulder holster, enjoying the feel of his muscles beneath them. "I thought you liked my flat chest and skinny legs," she murmured.

"I love them. I love every part of you, from that spaced-out brain to those long, knobby toes." He slid his hands down and over her butt. "I especially love the lower parts."

"Oh, there you go again, trying to charm me out of my pants."

He grinned with devilment.

She really should scold him, but Lord, he was cute when he was playful like this. And that smile... Seeing it always made her fall in love with him all over again.

"Stop worrying so much," he suggested. "I promise you things will be better. I'll even give more thought to marriage counseling if that'll ease your mind. Okay?"

That lightened her mood considerably. "Okay."

"I'll do whatever it takes to make you happy. Now, I think what we both need more than anything is to celebrate our news. We could go out, but you look tired, so you head on home and I'll stop at the grocery store when I get off. You can put your feet up and I'll come over and cook."

"That sounds wonderful, but I can't. I'm not through working and I have an assignment tonight."

"Lucky, you were out before six o'clock this morning."

"And I've been up since four, but I'm committed to taking photos at the Lions' Club dinner. I won't be home until after ten. I plan to hit the mattress one minute later."

"You don't need to be working those kinds of hours."

"I agree and I'd rather spend tonight with you, but I promised Leigh and it's too late to back out. How about we celebrate tomorrow? I'm off the next two days and I told her I absolutely wouldn't work unless the town started to burn. Which, with the way my luck usually runs, is a possibility, so don't light any matches."

"I need to come in for a few hours in the morning and work on this Bagwell case—try to clear up some loose ends—but I should be through by lunch. We can do it after that."

"I thought the death was a simple accident."

"It probably is."

"Probably?" She cocked her head. "Did you find something suspicious?"

"No, nothing unusual."

"Then why do you still have loose ends? I figured this would be a down-and-dirty investigation."

He gave her that look, the one that said she knew better than to ask.

"Oh, come on, Jack. I found the guy."

"That doesn't mean he belongs to you."

"I know, but I feel somehow responsible for him. I want to follow through with this."

"That's *my* job. I don't want you sniffing around in any more of my cases. Understood? I worry enough about you as it is. Don't make things harder on me."

"But maybe I can help. I know people you don't. And his daughter, Carolyn, went to school with Shannon. I bet she'd talk to me."

"I've already talked to her."

"What did she tell you?"

"Nothing you need to know. About tomorrow... maybe we should make it a family celebration. Have you told your parents about the baby?"

Reluctantly she allowed him to change the subject. "Not yet."

"Then we'll get them and your grandmother out to your place and share the news. Ask Leigh to come, and call and see if Shannon and Bill are free. I'll get Cal to help me move my stuff, and then I'll grill hamburgers for everyone."

Lucky's heart sank. "You're moving back in?"

"Well...yeah, unless you want to reconsider moving to the apartment."

"I don't think so."

"Then I guess I'm moving back in."

"I'm not sure that's a good idea. We'd better keep things the way they are and not make any drastic changes. Let's ease back into living together."

"Wait a minute, what gives? Five minutes ago you *wanted* me to come home."

"And five minutes ago you said no because you weren't ready. Jack, I *do* want you home, more than anything on earth, but for the right reason. Let's not jump from one mistake into an even bigger one."

"I can't think of any better reason than having a baby."

"How about…you love your wife and want to be with her?"

"That, too."

"Please be sure. This is such a major decision."

"I *am* sure. Look…I can't pretend I'm thrilled about living in that cramped cabin again, but if that's what it takes to be with you during this pregnancy, then I'll manage until we can come up with a solution. I've lived in worse places."

"When you stayed with your cousin?"

"Who?"

"Your cousin. You said last night that you lived in the back of your cousin's store while you worked for him."

"Oh, yeah, I stayed there for a while after high school. It was pretty awful. No shower. No kitchen."

She frowned. Hadn't he said it'd been after his parents died? He'd been sixteen, not out of high school. And the way he'd told it before…he'd gone into the army right out of school.

An uneasiness settled over her, the same uneasiness she felt each time his past came up. Nothing he said about his early years ever seemed to mesh. But why?

CHAPTER FOUR

ON SATURDAY AFTERNOON, Lucky guided her small fishing boat into an isolated slough, turned off the motor and let it drift. Dusk was when she was most likely to see the panthers she'd been watching the past several weeks, but she hoped at least one would appear earlier.

She took a drink from her water bottle and wiped off the sweat that had formed under the brim of her Kiss A Bug cap. Jack and Cal were probably at the cabin by now, moving Jack's clothes. The rest of her family would arrive soon.

Looking back, she couldn't remember ever telling Jack he *could* move back in, but discussing it with him wasn't worth the stress that would undoubtedly create. Peace and calm were what she and the baby needed right now, and the river provided it. She always felt better after a few hours with her old friend.

Most people only saw the main body of the Black Warrior and its headwaters, the Locust, Mulberry and Sipsey rivers, but its heart lay in places like this, the hidden ones, where the water seemed bottomless and the adjoining land appeared virtually untouched since prehistoric times.

The area wasn't completely virgin, but she liked to think it was. Settlers, her ancestors among them, had planted cotton and corn in the low areas, harvested

trees from the forests and dug coal from the banks
and shoals. Before them, the Creek and Choctaw Indians inhabited these lands, and the river, or Apotaka
Hache as the Choctaw called it, had been a border
between the nations.

Before the modern Indians, the land was home to
mound-building people in whose culture women, fer-
tility and the river all played major roles. Lucky
sometimes dug up their flint points or pottery shards
when she planted her small garden.

She'd explored extensively the river and its forks,
but it would take several lifetimes to see everything.
The state, federal government and the University of
Alabama all owned thousands of acres of trees and
swampland she'd never walked. Probably few had in
modern times. A surveyor or two, perhaps, or an occasional logger or pulpwood harvester.

This was her home, but more than that, it was a
vital part of who she was. Take her outside the county
and nothing about her was special. But here, on the
river, she could name each insect, fish and bird. Here,
she felt connected to her past and the generations of
Mathisons who had come before her.

Her tie to the river was strong and unbreakable,
something Jack could never understand. Giving it up
wasn't an option. She'd wither if she had to live in
town again. And to leave Potock altogether, as he'd
suggested more than once during their arguments,
would surely kill her.

Maneuvering the boat closer to the bank into the
shade of the trees, she stretched out on her stomach
so she could watch the insects zigzagging across the
surface of the water and observe the acrobatic drag-
onflies. Birds rustled in the underbrush. The water

lapped gently against the side of the metal boat, almost lulling her to sleep.

Far off but coming closer, the heavy crunch of leaves intruded on the stillness. Something large was moving through the woods.

As quietly as she could, she sat up and brought the camera to her eye. She'd probably get only two or three shots of the panther before the sound of the autowinder scared him off. Each shot had to count. Except…this couldn't be an animal; it was making too much noise. Only a human thrashed around like that.

The land sloped to the water down a hill tangled with plant growth. On her way out of the cabin, Lucky had grabbed her old Canon with its zoom lens, and she used it to focus on the faintly discernible path made by the tread of deer.

A man emerged with his head down, unaware of her presence, and went straight to the water. He crouched as if to take a drink, but instead, sank his bare arms in the water to the elbows. He brought them up, then slapped the surface several times, letting out a squeal each time.

Lucky continued to watch, feeling a bit anxious at the peculiarity of it. He seemed to be almost… playing.

Suddenly he sensed her and jerked up his head. Her viewfinder framed a face that represented every nightmare she'd had since the age of nine.

Terrell Wade.

She sucked in a breath. Fear kept her frozen, unable to move. She'd known the autistic man was back in Potock. Leigh had written a story at the time of his relocation.

He wasn't supposed to be out unsupervised. The idea of him wandering around by the river and only a couple of miles from her cabin sent a chill running along Lucy's backbone.

No more than fifteen feet separated them. If he took a few steps to his right, he'd be close enough to the bow of her boat to get in.

She lowered her camera bit by bit so as not to startle him, until it hung heavily by the strap around her neck. If he made a move, she wanted to be able to grab something to defend herself. She *might* have time to get the motor cranked if he came at her, but maybe not.

For what seemed an eternity, he did nothing but stare back from his catlike position. That in itself was enough to unnerve her. She'd never seen his eyes before. She couldn't recall him ever holding his head high enough that anyone *could* see his eyes. He'd always kept his face down when you came near, as if ashamed or afraid.

Did he remember what she'd done to him?

Did he even recognize her as the child who had condemned him?

He cocked his head, then sprang upright. Lucky jumped just as quickly and lunged forward, but her sudden movement upset the boat and set it rocking. For a heartbeat she held on to the paddle *and* her balance, but then she lost both. The paddle flew out of her hand into the water and the lens of her camera bounced up and smacked her above the left eye, nearly knocking her out.

What people said about seeing stars was true. They sparkled for a second in front of her, then gave way to pain. Blood clouded her vision.

The boat drifted. She scrambled for the motor, pushed the primer button and pulled the cord, but it didn't crank. Desperately she hit the button again. A second and third pull of the cord produced no results.

Terrell moved, coming along the bank as she feared.

Ten feet away.

He had something in his hand.

Five feet away.

He stepped into the boat and reached out toward her.

Once, when Lucky was small, she'd picked up a pretty black-and-red-striped ant that had promptly stung her hand. She'd screamed so loud that her granddaddy had said she'd blistered his eardrums.

The scream she let out this time was louder.

WITH CAL'S HELP, Jack hauled over what personal items he needed for the next few days and set about replacing the old fan in the living room with something that actually stirred the air. He'd bought a second unit to install in the bedroom.

When he was growing up, he'd promised himself he'd never live in another dump, that when he had a house of his own, it would be a nice house, nothing too fancy, but sturdily built and roomy enough to raise kids the way they should be raised.

He never again wanted to wonder if the water was hot or the refrigerator had food. He'd had his fill of peeling paint, cast-off furniture and paper-thin walls.

He looked around and shook his head. Well, this dump, at least, was clean. No rats trying to take a bite out of him in the middle of the night. No bugs except the ones Lucky caught to photograph.

Snakes…now, that was something he'd have to talk
to her about. Snakes inside were unacceptable from
now on, along with any kind of animal, dead or alive,
except for her dog.

With some work, he could make the cabin more
livable. New plasterboard for the walls and fresh paint
would help. New tin for the roof and exterior would
go a long way toward making it look better.

He sincerely hoped they'd be gone before the cold
weather came. He could tolerate cold, and winters
here were mild compared to what he'd experienced
in Pittsburgh, but he'd found out the hard way that
the dampness penetrated everything on the river. The
few months he'd spent with Lucky in the cabin last
winter had been miserable for him.

The rent at his apartment was paid through the end
of next month, so he'd decided to keep most of his
clothes there and move the rest only when he had no
other choice.

The cabin had an attached storage room with a rack
for hangers, but Lucky had fishing poles, life jackets
and God knows what else crammed in there. She'd
have to clean out her junk again to make space for
him to put his good shirts and suits.

"This clunker's been here a lot of years," Cal said
from the stepladder. He loosened the last screw on
the fan and together they brought it down and set it
on the floor. "I was only a kid when Dad and my
granddaddy put it up."

"Did your dad grow up here?"

"Sure did. Him and my uncle Steve. My grandmother hated the place, but Granddaddy's people had
lived here for generations, so he wouldn't budge."

"Sounds familiar."

"Yeah," Cal said with a nod, "pretty much the same story as you and Lucky."

Jack stepped back and the dog let out a yelp. He knelt and petted her. "Sorry, Beanie, but you've got to stay out from under my feet." She looked up at him with big eyes that said he was forgiven, thumping her tail against the floor.

Her breed was indecipherable. She had the face of a hound, but her body seemed an amalgamation of hound and terrier. Black, shaggy hair covered all of her except her muzzle, which had turned gray with age.

Usually her hair drooped and covered her eyes, making him wonder how she could possibly see. Since today was a special occasion, he'd pinned it back with a pink bow-shaped barrette, an old one of Lucky's from when her hair was long.

The dog wasn't pretty, but she was the first pet he'd ever owned, and he liked the experience. Well, technically she belonged to Lucky, but Beanie didn't understand that.

"The more time that dog spends with you, the more worthless she becomes," Cal said. "Could she get any fatter?"

Beanie thumped her tail again, knowing they were talking about her. She seemed to smile.

"She doesn't like dog food," Jack explained.

"And why should she when you feed her junk all the time? Has Lucky seen her lately?"

"Not in a few weeks."

"Oh, man, you're going to be in *big* trouble."

Jack made the dog lie down in front of the couch out of the way, then unpacked the new fan. He rechecked to make sure the power was off, then Cal helped him position the new unit and secure it.

"Did your grandfather ever consider moving away from here?" he asked, continuing their earlier conversation.

"Papa Sam?" Cal snorted. "Imagine a male version of Lucky, and that's a pretty good description of my granddaddy. He thought the river was heaven. You couldn't pry him out of here with a crowbar, even after he started having heart problems. He dropped dead right out there by the water."

"I don't understand what's supposed to be so great about this place."

"Me, neither, to tell you the truth. Leigh, Shannon and I used to hate coming out to visit because there wasn't anything to do, but Lucky spent most of her time here. She would've lived with Papa Sam if our mom had let her. When he died, no one was surprised that he left the land and cabin to Lucky. She's the only one who ever really appreciated them. And Mema was thrilled to move in with Mom and Dad."

"I've tried to adjust, but there's no damned space, and she has all these weird things she's picked up and won't throw away."

Cal laughed heartily at that. "You should've seen it in here three or four years ago. She's given a lot to the museum over in Tuscaloosa, the stuff with value, anyway."

"It couldn't havé been much worse than this."

"Oh, brother, you wouldn't have believed it. You never saw the pine tree she had growing up through the house." He pointed to a corner where the plywood had been patched. "It pushed right through a rotten place in the floor and Lucky thought it was the coolest thing she'd ever seen. She wanted to leave it and open a hole in the roof for it to grow through.''

"You're kidding."

"I swear. It took us a couple months to convince her that a tree growing up through the living room wasn't such a good idea."

"There's no place to store anything and hardly room to sleep. I don't know what we'll do when—" He stopped himself, realizing what he was about to reveal.

But it didn't make any difference. Cal grinned. "When the baby comes?" he supplied.

"She told you?"

"No, but I'm not as stupid as she and Leigh think. Lucky's hardly ever sick and she's never squeamish, but suddenly she's puking every morning and you're moving back in. It wasn't too tough to figure out what was going on."

"So Leigh knows, too."

"I'm pretty sure she does. They've been whispering behind closed doors."

Leigh arrived a few minutes later with her daughter, Susan. The child went off to play in the yard with a warning from her mother to stay out of the water and off the pier.

Leigh walked to the kitchen table and set down a covered bowl and a bag of chips.

"Lucky's pregnant," Cal announced.

Leigh gasped. "Pregnant? You're kidding!"

Her performance was poor. Deliberately poor, Jack suspected. She wasn't surprised. And she wanted him to know that Lucky had confided in her.

"Drop the act, Leigh," he said. "How long have you known?"

"I only found out yesterday morning."

He gritted his teeth. Damn! Had *everyone* known?

"Before you get all bent out of shape, Jack, she didn't actually tell me. I guessed." She looked around, frowning. "Where is she, by the way?"

"She left a note saying she was taking the boat out for a couple of hours." He glanced at his watch. She should've been back by now.

"I noticed the change in Lucky," Leigh said, pulling two gallon jugs of iced tea from a sack, "because I'm with her every day. If you weren't around to see something was different, you have only yourself to blame."

Touché. Leigh always went for the jugular.

"I admit I've made some mistakes, Leigh, but I'm trying to fix them. I've moved back in."

"So I hear. Frankly, I think that's a mistake."

"Jeez," Cal said, "give the guy a break."

"Does he deserve one? Walking out on our sister was pretty low. If it was me, I'd think twice before giving him a chance to do it again."

Jack reined in his temper, determined not to let Leigh get to him. "But Lucky isn't you," he told her, "so I'd appreciate it if you wouldn't interfere. This is between us."

"I haven't interfered."

"Let's keep it that way. She looks up to you and respects what you say. The last thing I need is you convincing her she can raise this baby alone."

She reddened, telling him he'd guessed correctly. Leigh was the one feeding Lucky ideas of divorce.

"Look, Leigh," he continued. "I'm sorry for everything you and Susan have been through during the past few years. I really am. God knows you didn't deserve what Keith did to you. No woman should have to put up with that crap. But I'm not him. I didn't abandon Lucky, and I'd sure as hell never walk away from my child like Keith did. You can't punish me for what he did to you.''

Her expression turned hard. "I'm not trying to. Lucky's happiness is all that concerns me. I'll do whatever is within my power to ensure she isn't hurt.''

"So will I.''

Cal, forever the peacemaker, jumped in again. "Come on, guys, don't argue. Not today. You don't want to upset Lucky.''

Jack and Leigh stared at each for several seconds, then both acquiesced.

"He's right,'' Leigh said, but the hard edge remained in her voice. "This is silly. She doesn't need the added stress of us going at each other.''

"I agree.''

Leigh peered out the kitchen window to the side of the house. "Mom and Dad are here, anyway. Mom would skin us both if she caught us fighting.''

"Truce?'' Jack offered. Matt and Ruth had always been good to him. Even during the separation they'd continued to treat him like a son. He didn't want to upset them any more than he did Lucky.

Leigh nodded. "All right, I'll keep my mouth shut. For today.''

Jack welcomed his in-laws. They'd brought food, which they took into the kitchen while he helped Lucky's grandmother sit in a cool spot on the porch. At eighty-four she was still lovely. White hair. Striking blue eyes behind her glasses.

He'd never met his own grandparents. If any were still alive, he didn't know.

She kept his hand, patting it affectionately. "I'm so happy to see you and my granddaughter back together."

"I'm glad, too."

"Be patient with her. She's special."

"Yes, ma'am."

"When Sam and I married, we were very different from each other, and I worried that would be a hindrance to our happiness. I didn't share his love for this land and his river."

"That's what Cal told me. Did you ever come to love it?"

"Oh, not really. I like nice things, and Sam was happy in his overalls with a fishing pole in his hand. But as the years passed, I realized what made our marriage interesting was that we *weren't* alike. Every day was a new challenge. Variety is the spice of life, they say. You'd do well to remember that."

"I will."

Lucky's other sister, Shannon, and her husband, Bill, arrived a few minutes later with their daughters, ages two and five. Everyone was there but Lucky.

"I'm getting worried about her, Cal," Jack said, pulling him aside. "Her note said she'd be back by noon. It's nearly three."

He'd told Lucky a million times to take her cell phone wherever she went in case she had trouble, but he'd noticed it earlier on the kitchen counter.

"I'm sure she's okay," Cal said. "You know how she is when she gets interested in something. She loses all track of time."

"Yeah, I suppose."

But when another hour passed and Lucky still hadn't returned, even Cal expressed concern. "Come on. Joe Mueller down at the marina will lend us a boat."

They explained to the others where they were going, but before they could leave, Leigh waved at them to stop. "I see her coming," she said, rushing up to Cal's truck. "She's paddling. Looks like she had problems with the motor."

They waited for her on the pier. Lucky pulled up, threw a rope to Cal and asked him to tie the boat.

"What the hell happened?" Jack asked.

"I got in a hurry to crank the motor and flooded it."

"No, with your head, dammit! You've got a goose egg on it and blood all over your shirt."

"Good Lord," Leigh said. "It *is* blood."

"It's only a little bump. I had some trouble."

Jack took her camera bag and helped her out, then quickly examined the cut. It wasn't bad, but she'd have a hell of a bruise. "What kind of trouble? Are you injured anywhere else?"

"I'm okay."

"Do you need to go to the hospital emergency room?"

"Heavens, no! I'm just a little shaken up. I was taking photos in a slough near where Mosquito Creek comes in, and I ran into Terrell Wade."

Cal shouted, "Shit!"

"Oh, my heavens!" Leigh said.

Shannon walked onto the pier and wanted to know what was going on. When Leigh told her, she screamed, and that brought Ruth, Matt, Bill and the children running.

"Terrell Wade attacked Lucky," Leigh told her parents.

"No," Lucky said, "that's not—"

"We should call the police," Ruth said.

Leigh pointed out that Jack *was* the police.

"Then call for help and get some men out here."

They all started talking at once about what should be done, Ruth insisting that he not only call for backup, but notify the National Guard, as if they handled police complaints. Cal and Bill thought they should get guns and go after this Wade person.

The talk of guns and the shouting got Shannon's two-year-old crying, and that, in turn, set off the other little girls.

"Hold it!" Jack said. "Shut up for a minute. Nobody's getting guns and going after anybody." He turned back to Lucky. "Did this man touch you or hurt you?"

"No, I hurt myself. I banged my head with my camera."

"Who is Terrell Wade?"

Lucky's dad supplied the answer. Wade had murdered a local woman years ago, he said, but they'd never found the body or her missing car.

"*Suspected* of murdering, Dad," Lucky corrected him. "We don't know for sure that he's the one who did it."

"I'm sure," Matt said. "He'd been stalking her."

"She helped him with his paintings."

"He's mentally retarded," Matt told Jack. "And dangerous."

"No, he's *autistic*," Leigh corrected this time. "He's actually got above-average intelligence. But I agree he's dangerous."

The story sparked Jack's memory. Patrol officers had standing orders to pick up Wade whenever he was seen on the street and return him to Horizon House, a facility on Wilcox Avenue.

A US Supreme Court ruling had paved the way for the man to return to the town of his alleged crime. The justices said states could be required under the Americans with Disabilities Act to provide community-based services rather than institutional placements for people with disabilities.

"Shannon, calm the kids down," Jack ordered, "and go reassure your grandmother that everything's all right. She has to be worried. Bill, my police radio is lying on the front seat of my car. Go get it. Ruth, see what you can find to clean this cut, please."

Ruth took off ahead of him while Jack picked up Lucky and carried her against her protests into the cabin. He set her in a chair by the kitchen table and pulled up a second chair for himself. Ruth had found alcohol and cotton and she handed them to him.

"Now," he said, gently dabbing the wound, "tell me what happened."

Everyone crowded around, anxious to hear. She had a captive audience as she related her story.

"...and I screamed bloody murder because he was *right there,* not a foot from me, and the stupid motor wouldn't crank and I'd lost the paddle when I fell."

"Wait a minute, you fell?" Jack asked with concern. "How hard?"

"Only a little stumble onto my knees. I'm perfectly fine. Where was I? Oh...I thought about hitting him with my camera or going over the side and taking my chances in the water, but then I noticed what he had in his hand."

"What?" Leigh asked. "A knife? A gun?"

"No, it wasn't a weapon." A strange look came over her face. "He did the weirdest thing. I expected him to hit me or choke me or something, but instead, he…he… God, I still can't believe it."

"Well, for heaven's sake, tell us!" Leigh snapped in frustration. "What did he do?"

Lucky pulled a piece of white cloth from the pocket of her shorts and held it up for them to see. "He offered me his handkerchief."

CHAPTER FIVE

ONCE SHE'D CHANGED out of her bloody shirt and washed off, Lucky felt better. Jack had used his radio to tell the dispatcher to contact the sheriff's department, since the area where she'd seen Terrell was beyond police jurisdiction. A deputy spotted him shortly after, picked him up and returned him to the group home.

"I still think he should be in jail," Shannon said across the picnic table.

Jack and Cal had grilled the hamburgers, and everyone was finished eating except Lucky. Feeling a touch nauseated and fighting a headache, she picked at what was left on the paper plate. "What do you suggest they charge him with?" she asked Shannon. "Being too polite?"

"With escape or something."

"He's not a prisoner," Jack explained, pulling up a metal folding chair. He put it at the end of the table, near her parents and grandmother. Beyond him, the three children played, trying to coax a reluctant Beanie to fetch a stick. "He's under supervision for *his* protection, not the town's. And since Lucky caused her own injury, there's nothing I can have him charged with."

"But he could've murdered her!"

"I don't think he would've hurt me," Lucky said,

surprised to discover she believed those words. "He had the perfect opportunity, but he didn't use it. That end of the slough is so isolated he could have killed me and scuttled the boat. None of you would ever have known what happened."

"Just like Eileen Olenick," Leigh said.

"I guess, but...he was so incredibly gentle, almost like a little boy offering me a gift." That brought a scoff from her father. "No, Dad, listen. When I wouldn't take the handkerchief from him, do you know what he did? He put it down on the seat and backed away, like he understood how afraid I was."

"Don't be fooled, baby," her father warned. "He's very cunning. You shouldn't go out in that boat alone."

"She won't," Jack said pointedly.

Lucky frowned, but didn't respond. This wasn't the time to discuss it.

"Wonder what he was doing out this far in the first place," Cal said, and they all echoed similar curiosity.

Lucky shrugged. "I don't know for sure, but I'd guess...he wanted to play in the river." She told them about his strange behavior, how he'd delighted in slapping the water.

Cal shivered, as if suddenly hit by a blast of cold wind. "Yow! This story gets creepier by the second."

Jack, always the cop, wanted to know details about the murder and the victim. "Who was this woman?"

"Miss Eileen was the art teacher where Cal and I went to elementary school," Lucky said. "She was in her late thirties. A bit eccentric, but really, really nice. Extremely pretty." Everyone voiced agreement. "I always wondered why she hadn't married."

"Because she had a lover and he was already married," Lucky's mother told her. "You were too young to hear the gossip, but that's what we all believed."

"I was definitely in love with her," Cal said.

"You were twelve," Lucky pointed out.

"So? I was still in love with her."

Lucky elbowed him in the ribs for being silly, then continued, "This was the spring of 1980, right before my tenth birthday. Shannon was...fourteen or fifteen?"

"Fifteen," Shannon supplied.

"...and was at the high school with Leigh and Terrell, who were both seventeen. Terrell took special classes in the morning. I guess that must've been before they started putting kids with mental or physical disabilities in regular classes. I don't remember. Anyway, Miss Eileen heard he had talent and she took it upon herself to work with him privately. Mostly she gave him lessons at the school, but sometimes, on weekends or in the afternoon, she went to his house. She was the only person outside of his family who ever spent any time with him. Nobody else wanted to."

"Too weird," inserted Cal.

"He couldn't talk, and all the kids learned pretty quickly that he did strange things, so we stayed clear."

"What kind of things?" Jack asked.

Leigh fielded this question. "Like spinning, or crawling into closets or cabinets. In Sunday school he'd bang his head against the wall and upset the teacher. After he got to be six or seven, he was so difficult to control his mother stopped bringing him to church altogether."

"Did he seem dangerous?" Jack asked her.

"Not then. At least not dangerous to anyone other than himself."

Lucky took up the thread. "Looking back, I don't think any of us gave Terrell much thought, period. He was a ghost. A nonentity. He was in our neighborhood and our school, and at one time he'd been in our church, but he wasn't *really* a part of our world. We didn't *see* him."

Until a certain Sunday morning. Then everything changed....

First Baptist Church of Potock, May, 1980

LUCKY DECIDED she must have a touch of the supernatural. Her body had this weird way of twitchin' and slidin' about when she was bored, even when she told it not to.

It was twitchin' now. Her legs swung back and forth and her butt wriggled to find a more comfortable spot on the pew.

Under the stiff white collar of her best Sunday dress, her neck also itched something fierce from the heat. She took off her gloves and clawed at the prickly skin, wishing she could also get rid of her tights and the stupid shoes with bows on top, passed down to her by her sister Shannon.

For the third time that summer, the power was off. The church was old and the nearby river was about to take it after years and years of trying. The lines on the walls marked each flood: the bad one back in '38, which the old people still talked about, when the water reached all the way to the cemetery on the hill and brought up the coffins; the one in '45 that got the kitchen; the one in '69 that took the new piano and left the sanctuary full of mud and dead water moccasins.

Last year the pews had drifted away, most ending up a mile downstream in a hay field. For weeks afterward you couldn't walk down the road without finding hymnals in the trees.

Each time the water rose, another little piece of the building floated off down the river. Soon, Lucky predicted, they'd have to give up the church and all become Methodists.

She pulled at her neckline and made a noise of frustration. The temperature inside felt near two hundred degrees, and she was trussed up worse than a turkey at Christmas dinner.

Leaning down, her mama whispered, "Be still."

That was easier said than done. If a body could get 'lectrified, Lucky was sure that was what had happened to her. Like lightning had struck her and sent her skin to crawlin'. Like her skin maybe even wanted to jump right off her bones.

Accidentally her swinging foot touched the seat in front of her.

"Erin Renee, don't make me tell you again."

"Yes, ma'am."

On the other side of her, Lucky's daddy patted her leg, then winked. Beyond him, Cal sat with Leigh, Mema and Papa Sam. Cal leaned forward and snickered because she'd gotten in trouble. She gave him a look that said she'd get him later.

Most Sundays she liked church. Preacher Sutton had a nice face, a soft voice, and he didn't go on and on with the sermon or holler the way Preacher Hardesty had. And unlike Preacher Hardesty, he didn't think Lucky was going to hell, although he did say the Almighty might be a bit unhappy with her for slipping those catfish in the baptismal tank last Sunday. God, it seemed, did not have a sense of humor.

"...But God hath chosen the foolish things of the world to confound the wise," the preacher said, quotin' scripture. "And God hath chosen the weak things of the world to confound the things which are mighty."

No, Lucky couldn't blame the preacher or the sermon for her restlessness. She couldn't really even blame the heat. Miss Eileen Olenick was totally at fault, and Lucky planned to tell her so the very next minute she set eyes on her. For the first time Lucky could remember, Miss Eileen hadn't come to services. Without her, without her funny straw hat, a kid didn't have anything worthwhile to look at in church and so shouldn't be blamed if she got a little antsy.

Every Sunday until now, Miss Eileen and her hat could be counted on to make the sermon go down a whole lot easier. She always came in at the last minute, breezin' in the back door and down the center aisle to the front row, where she wasn't supposed to sit. Everybody knew the front pews were for rich people and those kin to rich people.

Lucky didn't think Miss Eileen was rich or kin to anybody important, but probably nobody had ever told her the rules about where to sit at church. Or maybe she just forgot them because she wanted to sit in the front row. Miss Eileen liked to be different.

Take that hat, for instance. It was an ordinary straw hat, like lots of ladies wore to church, but Miss Eileen dressed it up each week with some interestin' bit of decoration: a turtle shell found down by the river, a door hinge painted to look like a butterfly, magnolia leaves from that big tree in her front yard. Last week she'd stuck on some Indian symbols and feathers and had made some earrings out of pretty blue rocks.

Miss Eileen was a strange bird, all right, the most fun person in Potock. "A bit peculiar, but nice," Lucky's mama said. Goin' to her house was a treat. She had a bunch of paint and clay and other neat stuff that Lucky was allowed to play with just about whenever she wanted. That was worth looking past Miss Eileen's strangeness.

Color was Miss Eileen's big problem. She liked it more than a body should. Red, green, purple—it didn't matter to her if the colors shouldn't go together. She wore green shoes with red dresses, bright pink scarves with purple blouses, even wild stripes with checks and plaids. She was so bright that staring at her sometimes made you swimmy-headed. Even her car was two colors, a funny-shaped yellow-and white Metropolitan.

Lucky had looked up the word *metropolitan* once in the dictionary and found it meant "the major city." That didn't fit Miss Eileen at all. Like Lucky, she didn't know beans about big cities. She'd never been out of Alabama in her whole life.

And she never, ever missed church on Sunday morning.

A scream and a commotion at the back of the church made the preacher stop and everybody turn. More ladies started screaming. People jumped to their feet and pushed toward the aisle, blocking the way. Lucky tried to see what was happening, but she was too short. She only caught a quick glimpse of the boy who'd come through the open door, then somebody got in her way again.

Hurriedly she scrambled up on the seat, Cal doing the same. The boy who'd caused the screaming had fallen to his knees, and red dirt and big splotches of something covered his clothes. He crushed some object to his chest, but Lucky couldn't make out what it was.

Terrell Wade. She knew the boy. Truth be told, she didn't really *know* him. Nobody knew Terrell, except his poor family. She knew who he *was,* just like all the kids did who'd been warned by their mamas to stay away from him. At seventeen he was as big as any man in town. He was also dumber than dirt.

The screaming in the church had stopped, but unnatural noises were coming out of Terrell that robbed Lucky of breath. He rocked and rocked, holding that thing to his chest like a baby.

Preacher Sutton came forward. "Son, are you hurt? Do you need help?" Only then did Lucky recognize the dark stuff on his clothes.

Terrell wailed and stretched out his arm to the preacher, a crushed and blood-soaked hat in his fingers. The hat was straw. White ribbon and small tinkling bells decorated it. The whole church seemed to gasp in one big breath, but nobody moved. Even Lucky felt glued in place. She wanted to move, or scream, or…something, but couldn't.

In that awful moment she knew why Terrell Wade had blood all over him. And even worse, she knew what had happened to Miss Eileen Olenick. Finding her voice, she blurted out what was surely on the mind of everybody in that place, although nobody wanted to be the one to say it. "Gawd help us all! Terrell's done gone and murdered Miss Eileen!"

"THE AUTHORITIES SEARCHED for weeks, but they never found her body or even a crime scene," Lucky said. "This area is dotted with old mine shafts, caves, sinkholes and abandoned quarries, any one of which could've been used to dispose of her body and her car. And there's the river, of course. Drop something in the right place and you'll never see it again."

"Could he drive?" Jack asked.

"No one was ever sure, but he certainly had the physical strength to at least *push* her car a short distance. It was a tiny two-seater."

"Disposing of her body and car and then implicating himself by turning up bloody, clutching with her hat, doesn't make a whole lot of sense."

"No, but like Leigh said, he did weird things. His brain circuits were all screwy. We figured he killed Miss Eileen in a frenzy of lust, panicked and hid the car somewhere. Maybe he got confused about the hat. Who knows what went on in his mind that day?"

"Did they prosecute?"

"The district attorney felt that, without a body and no witness, it wouldn't do much good, but Dad wrote editorials urging the town council to petition the state to have him put away."

"Wade holds your father responsible for his commitment?"

Lucky cleared the lump in her throat. "No, not exactly. There was a hearing—the mental-health people, the DA, Terrell's widowed mother, a handful of witnesses. At first the judge seemed to lean toward no action. He said he saw nothing to suggest Terrell was a danger to the community, even though the case-worker testified that he'd been extremely agitated and unmanageable since the morning he showed up at church. He'd gotten so out of control his mother had been forced to remove him from school.''

"Does she still live here?"

"His mother? No, she died several years ago. Her sister, Leona Harrison, is his only remaining relative."

"Was he present at the hearing?"

"Yes, but he wouldn't—or I guess, couldn't—communicate and never tried to explain or defend himself. The judge said he deserved the benefit of the doubt about Miss Eileen's disappearance, though. He pointed out that even if it came to pass that Miss Eileen *was* the victim of foul play, Terrell could simply have found her hat."

"That's possible, isn't it?"

Her chest tightened. She'd asked herself the same question a million times.

"I suppose it is." She swallowed hard. "But then a witness testified that she'd seen Terrell following Miss Eileen a few days before her death and that he peeped in her windows."

"You," Jack guessed.

She nodded. "What I told the judge that day changed his mind. Terrell went to a state hospital for an evaluation and ended up staying twenty-one years."

THAT NIGHT after everyone had gone home, Jack cleaned the kitchen and washed the few dishes they had used.

"I can get those," Lucky called from the couch.

"No, take it easy. I can handle it. Read your newspaper."

When he finished, he came and sat with her. Beanie, who'd been at his feet by the sink, followed like a shadow, plopping down with an audible thud on the hard floor between his legs. She laid her head across his foot. It seemed she wasn't happy unless she was touching him. He understood completely. That was how he felt about Lucky.

He took his wife's hand in his lap, nesting his fingers between hers, thankful to have her to himself. *My wife.* He'd always liked the way that sounded. Pretty soon he'd also be able to say *my son* or *my daughter.* Nothing could be better than that. He inadvertently let out a sigh, but Lucky misinterpreted his noise of contentment.

"Tiring day," she said. "One more crisis and I'm down for the count. I can't believe everything that's happened in the past eight hours."

"Me, neither."

After lunch, when everyone had finally begun to stop talking about Terrell Wade, Shannon and Bill's oldest child had accidentally locked her baby sister in the bathroom, sending her parents and grandparents into another fit. Shannon had wailed louder than her daughter.

"I'll fix that door this week so the kids can't mess with it again," Jack said.

"I didn't know that old lock still worked. Being here by myself so many years, I've never had any reason to use it."

"A slide bolt farther up that only adults can reach would be better. I'll take care of it."

"I didn't realize you were so handy. The new fans.

The neat trick you did with the paper clip. You had the door open before I could even find the key. How'd you do that?''

"Old cop trick."

"You'd make a first-class burglar."

"I'll consider that when I retire." The newspaper was folded to one of the inside pages that showed some of her extra photographs from the train death, and he motioned to them. "Great photos, by the way. Where were you standing to get the big one Leigh printed on the front?"

"Uh...on top of the fire truck."

He guessed from the elevation that had to be what she'd done. "How'd you get up there?"

"I was very, very careful," she said, patronizing him. "It has some little fold-out steps and I held on really tight. I didn't put the baby in any danger. I promise."

"Did you climb the bank to get up to the track or walk in from the road by the barricade?"

"Climbed the bank."

"With that steep an incline? Must have been a tough climb."

"Deaton helped me. He pulled me part of the way up."

"Could you have made it by yourself?"

"I don't know. Maybe. Maybe not." She eyed him curiously, then turned to the photograph to take a second look at it. "Why are you asking me about that bank? What's so important about it?"

"I didn't say anything was important about it. I was wondering how you got up and down, that's all."

"I've just been sneakily interrogated, haven't I."

"Man, you have a suspicious mind."

"Comes from being married to a cop."

"I worry about you, Lucky. I don't want you falling."

"Uh-huh. But that's not the only reason you're quizzing me, is it."

"Mm," he answered noncommittally.

"When do you get the autopsy report on Mr. Bagwell?"

"A few days for the preliminary, but the final one will take a while. They're backed up in Birmingham, so it could take months for all the results to filter in."

"Expecting anything out of the ordinary?"

"No reason to. How's the head?"

She growled in frustration and slapped him with the paper, making Beanie lift her head to see what was going on. "Ooh, I hate it when you change the subject like that. Drives me nuts. My head's fine, thank you very much. Tender, but okay."

"Headache gone?"

"Finally. You were great this afternoon, taking charge like that and keeping my family sane. Thank you."

"All in a day's work."

"I can't believe I was stupid enough to nearly knock myself out. It's a good thing Terrell wasn't really trying to hurt me."

Worry lines appeared on her forehead. He sensed there was more she wanted to say. And he had a good idea what.

"Don't let what he did get under your skin and make you second-guess your actions, Lucky."

"What do you mean?"

"Just because he was nice today doesn't mean you were wrong about him twenty-one years ago."

"I know, but...I've never told anyone this before, not even my sisters or Cal, but I've worried my whole life that I did something bad when I testified against Terrell. That inability to trust my judgment—a lack of confidence, if you want to call it that—has undermined my choices ever since. I've been fearful to step beyond the comfort of my small world."

"That's understandable."

"Maybe, but I've never gotten past it. And today, when he was so polite, it brought back all those old doubts. What if he didn't kill Miss Eileen, but was only a witness to her death?"

"Sweetheart, any scumbag can be polite. Doesn't mean he's not a scumbag. In some of the worst cases I've worked, the perpetrators have been people whose neighbors swore they were saints. Meanwhile, they were chopping up their wives or putting rat poison in their husband's food."

"Were you ever wrong about any of them? Have you ever helped convict someone you later found out was innocent?"

"Not that I'm aware of. Most of these creeps got off with less punishment than they deserved. Throw that—" he pointed to the rectangle of white cloth she'd folded and put on the coffee table "—in the trash and forget about Wade. Save yourself grief."

"You're probably right," she said with a sigh, but she remained pensive and he knew it continued to bother her.

Before they went to bed, he showed her a few self-defense moves to use if anyone ever attacked her for real. "Use your fingernails in his eyes or poke him with your thumbs. Hit him in the nose with your fists as hard as you can. That'll put a man out quicker than anything.''

''I shouldn't try to kick him...down there?''

''If you can knee him hard, yes, but if you don't disable him, he'll come back and be twice as mad. You're better off going for the nose.''

After the session, he gave her something more pleasant to dream about. ''Your parents seemed happy when everything settled down and we finally got a chance to tell them about the baby.''

''Oh, especially Dad. Did you hear him? He put in an order for a boy.'' She imitated her father's authoritative voice. '''Enough girls in this family already.'''

He chuckled. ''That's word-for-word what Cal told me before he left. He said he's tired of being surrounded by females.''

''Well, that stinker. What did you tell him?''

''That we don't care about the baby's sex. We don't, do we?''

''Doesn't matter to me.''

''Me, neither. A boy and a girl would be nice, but I don't care what order they come in.'' Her expression didn't change, but he felt a subtle shift in her emotions. ''What's the matter?''

''You're getting ahead of yourself. This reconciliation isn't even a day old and you're talking about more children.''

''Nothing wrong with being optimistic.''

''No, there's not, and I like it that you have so much confidence in us. But personally, I'm having a hard time right now seeing that far ahead. I guess what I'm saying is I need to go slow, take each day as it comes. Can you understand that?''

He couldn't blame her for her hesitancy. She was wary of him, uncertain about their future, and he'd have to regain her trust. "All right. Whatever you say."

"An open and honest relationship. I realize you can't always share your work, but in our personal lives—no secrets."

"No secrets. Got it."

"We do our best to give each other space."

"I'll go along with that."

"And respect each other's differences," she added. "Agreed?"

"Agreed." When she didn't say any more, he asked, "That it?"

"I guess." Thinking a second, she added, "Oh, I do have one question." A hint of a smile touched her lips, but she tried to hide it. She leaned over and studied Beanie asleep on the floor as if she'd only just noticed her. Looking back over her shoulder, she asked with feigned outrage, "What in heaven's name have you done to my dog?"

CHAPTER SIX

Jessup, Maryland

FOUR MONTHS of wearing the ankle device had given Ray Webster a rash, but he couldn't complain. House detention was better than prison any day.

"That's it, Ray," the corrections officer said, cutting the heavy plastic band that held the electronic monitor in place. "You're a free man."

Free. Now that he could no longer enjoy freedom.

When he added up all the times he'd been in jail or prison, Ray figured he'd spent nearly a third of his sixty-four years in the joint, and the other two-thirds either on probation or plotting some crime that was going to get him in trouble.

Maybe when he was eight he'd been free. Or not. Come to think of it, even as a kid he'd been stealing cigarettes from the drugstore on the corner and money from his mother's purse.

Ray didn't know what it felt like to really let go of the past and start fresh. Only once, when he'd married Grace and the kids were little, had he straightened himself out and lived clean for more than a few months, but the only job he'd been able to get was selling cars for four hundred dollars a month plus commissions. That hadn't exactly been the golden egg he was searching for.

If he'd possessed an honest face, he might have made a success of it, but people said he had a look of the devil about him, and, for sure, he'd always had a bit of the devil *in* him. Ray had realized quickly that he could make more money stealing cars than selling them.

So he'd done both for a while, and other things— burglary, fencing stolen goods, a little bait and switch. The money rolled in. Life was good.

Grace hadn't known of course. She'd thought he was better than he really was, and he'd liked that. He'd come home every payday with his pockets full of cash and pretend he was the best salesman the Ford dealership had ever had.

But the past always caught up with you. If he hadn't learned anything else, Ray had learned that.

One night, while he was doing a little after-hours "shopping" at an electronics store, the cops had shown up two minutes after he got inside. From that point on, pretense didn't do any good. Grace saw what he was, what he would always be, and had given up on him. When you were born useless, you stayed useless.

"All your papers are signed," the officer said, handing Ray an envelope, "and I've put my card in here with a letter to your new parole officer. Check in when you get settled."

"I will."

"You understand this is irregular?"

"Yes, sir, and I appreciate the consideration."

Parolees weren't allowed to move out of state without permission, a decent place to live and a job. Ray had the first two, but not the last. Only because he received a small monthly disability check because of a supposedly bum arm had the state agreed to let him relocate.

He gotten the "injury" from an overeager cop who'd twisted the arm while arresting him for walking away from a work-release program. Best deal Ray had ever had—free money from the government for doing nothing.

The ten years they'd tacked on to his existing sentence for escape hadn't been a thrill, but along with the good you had to accept the bad. He hadn't had to serve most of the time, anyway.

"You didn't earn early release, Ray. You got lucky."

He knew that. Overcrowding, nothing else, had set him free.

"Don't think they won't put you back in. You've been given another chance, and you'd be a fool to screw it up."

"I won't screw it up."

And he wouldn't, but not because of the lecture, which he'd heard a hundred times before, and not because he'd suddenly gotten right with the law after all these years, but because he was getting old. And old meant slow. He could no longer pick a lock or fleece a mark without worry. The scams he'd once run so easily took too much out of him now.

He was an old con without a game, and nothing much to look back on but bad memories and regrets.

His wife was dead, and his daughter had run off when she was just a kid, burying herself so deep that no one had heard even a whisper of her whereabouts in years. She might be dead like Grace, for all he knew.

The boy was still alive, though, and living in Alabama. Ray had kept up with him through associates. "Cahill" he was calling himself these days, which made Ray chuckle every time he thought about the name.

Patting the envelope in his shirt pocket, he said goodbye to the officer and left. He'd stashed enough money to buy a used car, and what he'd borrowed from his friend Vinny would help him get set up.

Ray whistled as he descended the steps. He'd heard Alabama was a nice place. A nice place indeed.

AFTER THE INCIDENT with Terrell, Jack was adamant about Lucky not going out on the river alone, but she thought he was being his usual controlling self. Terrell hadn't really done anything except frighten her, she argued. And being able to putt around in her little boat was one of her reasons for living on the river.

"Please don't take that away from me, Jack."

He offered a compromise: she could go, but had to carry her phone and stay on the main part of the river. "No sloughs or out-of-the-way places," he insisted. "And you have to let me know where you are when work takes you someplace isolated or unfamiliar. Especially after dark."

After several days of discussion, she agreed. It was the best deal she was likely to get.

But the telephone check-in was a pain. Nearly always she got his voice mail because he was too busy to answer his private cell phone. When he returned the call, more often than not she had her hands in chemicals or happened to be somewhere she couldn't talk.

Most days they played telephone tag and never spoke directly. She called him and left a message. He called her and left a message. She called him…and on and on and on. Pain. Pain. Pain.

The ritual took an unexpected twist one hot afternoon when her patience wore thin. She'd been going nonstop since lunch and was tired and sweaty. Somehow her dang jeans had gotten too small overnight. How was that possible?

Letting Jack know her whereabouts seemed an unnecessary chore on top of everything else.

"I know this is for your peace of mind," she recorded, "but it seems silly if you can't ever talk to me. I'll be at the fairgrounds for an hour, then I'm headed home." She raised herself a bit and unfastened the snap on her pants, then unzipped them with a moan of relief. A bit of mischief struck her. "Hear that? I'm getting naked. Aren't you sorry you didn't answer the phone?"

He called her back ten minutes later as she parked and didn't bother with a preamble. "Naked? I've got one hell of a fantasy going right now."

She chuckled to herself. Now she knew what it took to talk to him. "Mmm, I'd like to hear about this fantasy. Tell me every explicit detail."

"First I do this…"

The erotic description that followed made her temperature shoot up for a different reason than the sun.

"Next I do this…"

"Wow! I'm not sure my legs can even bend like that."

"We'll test them tonight."

"Wish I didn't have to wait that long."

"Drive over and I'll give you a preview."

"I would, but I have three steers anxiously awaiting my presence, and I can't disappoint them."

"Sounds exciting."

"Yeah, I lead such a glamorous life." She opened the console to get her mileage logbook and noticed something she hadn't seen earlier. "What the…?" The little box had a white ribbon around it, and she quickly undid it. Inside was a tiny porcelain music box. Her gasp made him ask what was wrong.

"My secret admirer left me another present. I just found it."

"Did he?"

She smiled, enjoying their game. It had begun when she'd stepped into her shoes one morning and found wrapped chocolate "kisses" inside. Later a pot of violets—her favorite flower—had appeared on her desk while she was out for lunch. After that a photography book she'd casually mentioned had found its way under her pillow.

Several gifts had mysteriously appeared over the past several days. Funny windup toys. A little whistle in the shape of a boat. Bubble bath.

Jack always pretended innocence.

"Sounds like somebody's courting you," he said now.

"He's doing an excellent job. And he has very good taste. This is beautiful." She turned the small metal crank and the theme from *Love Story* began to play. "How sweet."

"I'm sure he'd be happy to know you like it. He was probably a little unsure if you went for that kind of thing."

"Oh, I do! Is it an early anniversary present, do you suppose?"

"I imagine he simply wanted you to know how much he loves you, and the anniversary present will come later."

"Too bad I can't call him up and tell him how much I love him back. I also have this very, very naughty fantasy I'd like to describe to him."

"Oh? Tell me, instead."

When she did, he coughed a few times in disbelief. "You're serious?"

"Mmm-hmm. I think that would be delicious."

At six she drove up the dirt road to the cabin. Jack's car was already parked next to the house, which was unusual. He rarely left work before six-thirty or seven and almost never beat her home.

Anticipation raced through her body. She was suddenly more aroused than she'd ever been in her life.

Would he?

He would. He met her at the door wearing nothing but his shoulder holster.

"LORD HAVE MERCY!" Lucky collapsed onto his chest. "That was wonderful, but next time let's try to make it all the way to the couch."

The hard floor was hurting her knees, and the dog kept trying to insinuate herself between them. She scolded Beanie gently and pushed her away. After her heart had stabilized, Lucky struggled to her feet with a groan.

Jack sat up and groaned even more loudly. "I'll have a fondness for this floor from now on, but I think I broke my back."

Lucky snorted and gave him a hand up. "Maybe you're getting too old to be having wild sex."

"I hope I'm never too old for that. But you're right, next time we find a softer place to do it. I've got splinters in my ass."

They took a bath together and washed each other's hair. It reminded her of when they first married; lately it seemed as though he never got enough of her, and they made love again, leisurely this time.

"Are you starting to show?" he asked as they dressed, watching her struggle with her zipper. His obvious delight at the idea made her want to punch him.

"It's only a little water weight. Don't get excited." If he had his way, she'd already be wearing those awful maternity clothes and walking around resembling a blimp. That was coming soon enough, and she wasn't looking forward to it. At least, thank goodness, the morning sickness had gone away. She didn't need to deal with that on top of being fat.

He put on cotton briefs and a clean pair of jeans, then stepped to the mirror to comb his wet hair. Lucky gave up on her own jeans and slipped on a T-shirt and a pair of loose-fitting shorts with an elastic waist.

"We should decide on some names," he suggested.

"Don't you think it's a bit early for that?"

"Won't hurt to at least think about it. Besides, it'll be fun."

She grumbled under her breath. "Okay. A family name. If it's a boy maybe Samuel or Matthew. How about we name him after you and call him Junior?"

He frowned at her in the mirror. "I don't think so."

"Well, what was your father's name?"

Horror seemed to cross his face, but it vanished so quickly she decided she'd imagined it. "Raymond. But I hate that name. We're not naming a baby that."

"Okay, forget Raymond." She wasn't crazy about it, either. "What do you like?"

"What about Andrew? Benjamin? Clay?"

"Andrew is nice, but I'm not too keen on kids calling him Andy. Benjamin will probably end up being Bennie. Clay...I'm not sure how I feel about that one."

"Bennie. Beanie. Forget it. Sounds too much like the dog. No offense, girl," he said, bending over to scratch her under the chin.

"What if it's a girl? Any names you like?"

"Grace. I want one of her names to be Grace, after my mother."

"What was her middle name?"

"Ellen."

"Grace Ellen Cahill." She repeated it several times. "I like Grace, but not the Ellen part. Cal's last girlfriend was named Ellen. The image that name brings to mind is downright scary."

"Is she the woman who burned up the engine in her car because she didn't know she had to put oil in it?"

"That's her. Leigh named her 'Miss IQ.'"

"Leave it to Leigh..."

"Leigh liked 'Miss IQ' better than 'Miss Halloween Hairdo,' but she couldn't tolerate 'Miss Silicone Implant.'"

"What's her nickname for me? 'That Bastard from Pennsylvania'?"

"Close. Until lately it was 'The Yankee with the

Fast Feet.' Now it's 'That Yankee You're Living With.'"

He chuckled. "Joke's on her, then. I was born in Mississippi."

"Mississippi?" Lucky's shock turned to hilarity, and she laughed so hard she had to sit down on the side of the bathtub. "Oh, that's priceless. She'll die when she finds out. Where in Mississippi?"

"Biloxi. We lived there until I was three."

"Is that when your family moved to Pennsylvania?"

"No, we lived in a lot of different places first— Texas, South Carolina, Ohio, Michigan. My dad was a salesman for a chemical company and they relocated him several times."

"No wonder you don't seem to have a definable accent. Tell me about your mom. Did she work?"

"Sometimes. But only to keep busy. She liked to be there when I got out of school."

"She sounds like a good mom."

"The best. They didn't come any better."

"You know, this is the most you've ever volunteered about yourself. I was beginning to worry I'd married into the Addams family."

"I'm secretly Vlad the Impaler. I'll show you later how I impale my victims."

"I think you've done enough impaling for one day, Vlad."

He shooed the dog out of his way. They took their conversation to the kitchen, where Jack poked through the refrigerator for a snack while she picked up the clothes she'd discarded by the door.

Her jeans pocket had loose change in it. She dug it out and opened her purse. Terrell's handkerchief was right there, visible in the clear plastic sandwich bag she'd stuck it in, so she quickly stuffed the bag in a zippered pocket. Her secret admirer might decide to hide a gift in here, and he wouldn't understand why she was still keeping her memento.

Not that she understood herself. Twice she'd actually put it in the trash can, then gone back and retrieved it. She'd even washed it at the self-service laundry, then run an iron over the wrinkles.

"If it's a girl," Jack called out, "what about naming her Ruth after *your* mother?"

"Too Biblical, and it doesn't go well with Grace. But you're right about deciding on something pretty quick. I don't feel right calling the little booger 'It.'"

"Booger. There you go. Booger Cahill. Works for either a girl or a boy."

That made her smile. He could be so silly sometimes.

His clothes lay tossed over the back of the couch. "By the way," she said, "you forgot to leave me the receipt for your shirts this morning like you said you would. I got halfway to the cleaners and then remembered I didn't have it."

"Get it now while you're thinking about it. I think it's in my wallet." She heard him close the refrigerator door. "Do we have chips?"

"Look in the bread box."

She emptied his pockets onto the lamp table and put his pants and dress shirt in a bag for the cleaners. The socks and underwear went into the laundry basket in the hall closet. Coming back to the living room, she opened his wallet and searched. He had a million pieces of paper stuck in it.

"Don't feed Beanie any," she warned without

turning around, knowing that for every chip he put in his mouth, Beanie also got one.

"I'm not."

"Yes, you are. I can hear her chomping. Remember what the vet said about her weight."

"Ah, hell, what does he know?"

She continued her search for the cleaning receipt. A name and number scribbled across the outside of a folded slip of paper caught her attention. "Hey, what was the name of your old boss? Wes Campbell, wasn't it?"

"Yeah, why?"

"Have you talked to him lately? I see you have his number here."

He came up behind her. "A couple of weeks ago. He, ah, called and offered me a job. How about that?"

She faced him. "A job? What kind of job?"

"His job."

"I don't understand. Why would he call and offer you *his* job?"

"He's retiring at the end of the year. He said he'd put in a recommendation for me if I wanted it."

The air suddenly felt too thick to breathe. "Do you?"

"Nah. I only listened to him to be polite."

But she could see through the thin paper. Had he written those notes to be polite, too? "So you've already turned it down?"

He faltered slightly. "Not yet, but I will."

"Is it a good job?"

"I suppose." He shrugged as if he didn't care, but she felt he was restraining himself. "The benefits are fair."

She decided to see for herself. Unfolding the paper,

she scanned the figures. The salary was twice what he was making here and came with reasonable premiums for family medical coverage. The health insurance included a dental plan, something they didn't have now.

"More than fair," she said. "Why haven't you mentioned this?"

"I thought about it, but c'mon, Lucky, what good would it have done? You'd never have agreed to move to Pittsburgh."

"I like where we are, and I want to be near my family. Is that so wrong?"

"No, and I never said it was wrong, only that it's how I knew you already felt. So when I found out about the baby, I put the idea of moving out of my mind, because it was never going to happen."

"But you want the job, don't you?"

"I did...maybe for a few seconds, but I haven't even thought about it since Wes called. Honest."

"I ruined it for you."

"Hey, listen to me. You didn't ruin anything." He took her gently by the upper arms and looked deeply into her eyes. "I'm here because it's where I want to be. Yes, I'd love to have that job. If circumstances were different, I'd ask you to think about a move. But I know this is your home, and I'm not going to take you away from the people you love. Besides, nothing can match being with you and Booger."

"You've given up so much."

"Ah, but, sweetheart, look at what I've gained."

THE PRELIMINARY REPORT on the Bagwell case came in four days later. Jack called Deaton Swain into his office to go over the findings and assess where they were on the train death.

"His BAC was point-one-two," Swain read, referring to the victim's blood-alcohol content.

Point-zero-eight was considered legally intoxicated, but as Jack knew, that didn't mean the guy couldn't function with a level above that. Give three shots to a frequent drinker, and you might not be able to see a perceptible difference. Give three shots to a nondrinker, and it could put him under the table.

"The bartender served him five or six drinks," Swain continued, referring to his case notes and witness statements. "He didn't recall anything out of the ordinary. Bagwell kept to himself as always. He watched a little TV. He didn't bother anyone and no one bothered him."

"So he was a regular customer?"

"Two or three nights a week. He'd overindulged at least a couple of times in the past six months and had to bum a ride home because he was too drunk to drive. The bartender knew that, so he didn't think anything about it when he closed up at two-forty-five and Bagwell's car was still in the parking lot."

"He didn't notice the flat tire?"

"No."

"What about the injuries to the body?"

"They say here 'Injuries appear consistent with reported cause of death.'"

"Anything come out of your interviews with his family or friends that would lead you to believe he might have purposely lain down on the tracks?"

"Nothing. His logging crew said he'd been depressed since his wife died a few years ago. His drinking got a little worse after that, but I don't find that unusual. Do you?''

"No."

"He had a nice house. A profitable business. A new grandchild, Doesn't sound like a suicide to me.''

"Anybody have reason not to want him around?''

"Not that I could find. He got into a yelling match a few weeks back with the dad of one of the kids he coached in baseball, but they patched things up. I think we're looking at an accident. The guy has too much to drink, finds his car has a flat tire and picks the wrong path to walk home. He passes out. We've had two or three deaths like it over the years on that same stretch of track.''

"Anything turn up yet on the break-in reported at his house after his death?''

"Nothing so far, but I've alerted area pawnshops to call if anybody tries to sell the electronics and silver. Had to be one cold son of a bitch to steal from a dead man.''

"Burglary's a crime of opportunity. A smart thief takes any advantage he can and hits the easiest target—families on vacation, people who live alone. He checks the obituaries like the want ads, because there's no better victim than a dead one.''

Jack asked him the estimated date and time of the break-in. "The daughter discovered it around two Saturday afternoon when she drove up from Mobile, which is about seven hours south of here.''

"Then in this case, we're probably looking at a friend of the family, an employee of the victim or a neighbor.''

"How so?''

"Bagwell died early Friday morning. Prior to that, he hadn't reported a burglary, had he?"

"There's no record of a report."

"Did you see any evidence of theft on Friday morning when I sent you over there after the accident?"

"No, the house was locked up tight and nobody came to the door. I also checked the shop and office out back and didn't see anybody."

"We didn't release his name to the media until Saturday afternoon, *after* somebody broke in. That suggests a couple of possibilities."

"I see what you're getting at. The burglary was either a coincidence or somebody found out by word of mouth that he'd died, knew the daughter lived out of town and decided to clean him out before she arrived."

"I'd bet on number two."

"So would I."

Jack tapped his pen on the desk, thinking. Certain things about this death had bothered him from the start. The first was why the victim had chosen to walk on the dark track. The road was well lit, the shoulder flat. Even the bottom of the grade, on the grassy strip between the track and the highway, would have been easier going for him than the railroad.

How he'd climbed the bank remained a puzzle, too. Doing it in daylight, sober, was hard enough. How had he done it at two in the morning with that much whiskey in him?

As much as Jack wished it could, no forensics report would ever answer those questions.

They had an overload of work, so he told Swain to pull off the death until they got more information from DFS, but to keep working on the burglary. He needed to turn his attention to the most pressing of his pending cases. If anything came up in the more detailed reports, they could follow up.

"Leave this with me and I'll sign off on it. Call the daughter and let her know they'll be transporting the body to the funeral home later today."

"I'll call right away." Swain jotted down the number before handing over the file.

"Let's do what we can to clear up some of these other burglaries. Ask Rogers for a hand. She's finished with court."

"Thanks, I could use the help."

"Anything turn up on that assist the feds asked for?"

Swain shook his head. "Nothing so far, and I don't hold out much hope."

"What's the problem?"

"I've worked these cases before, and we hardly ever get a break. The information is always vague. This time it came from a wildlife-enforcement officer working undercover who bought some old pots off a guy through an Internet auction. The guy told him he bought them from another guy who 'might have' dug 'em up on federal lands in our county. We don't have a specific location, and I haven't been able to trace the digger."

"Okay," Jack told him. "Keep on it, but the burglaries need to take priority."

"Roger, that."

Dismissed, Swain walked to the door, but he hesitated and turned back "Something else?" Jack asked him.

"My mother and Lucky's are in the garden club together. They, you know, gossip, and, uh..."

Jack didn't encourage familiarity with his officers, and usually they respected his wishes. But Swain clearly had something personal to say.

"Spit it out, Deaton. I'm growing old here."

"I heard about the baby and about you and Lucky being back together, and wanted to say that I'm glad. I've known her since...hell...forever. You got a good one when you got her."

"She thinks a lot of you, too."

"Tell her congratulations for me, will you?"

"I will."

"Oh, and congratulations to you, too, Captain."

"Thanks."

When he left, Jack shook his head with a chuckle, then went back to work on his own cases, but Bagwell's death kept intruding on his ability to concentrate. Something about it wasn't right. His gut warned him.

He reread everything in the file, then studied the different sets of photos, not sure what he was looking for. When he found it in one of the black-and-whites Lucky had taken, he picked up the phone and dialed DFS. He asked them to run one last test before releasing the body.

CHAPTER SEVEN

THE BAGWELL VISITATION was Thursday night at the Riverlawn Funeral Home, a colonial-style building next door to the city's largest cemetery. Lucky felt she should go, and Jack said he'd accompany her. Going in, they met Shannon.

"Is Bill keeping the girls?" Lucky asked her sister.

"Yes, but I promised I'd be back before seven-thirty so he can finish grading papers. Plus, he has a hard time putting them to bed alone when they get rowdy, which lately is all the time."

"Those angels?"

"Yes, those angels. You two wait. You'll find out what it's like. Enjoy the peace while you can."

Carolyn Bagwell, now Carolyn Carter, headed a line of family members greeting visitors. She wasn't a thin woman, but the strain of her father's death made her seem gaunt. Her pale face had a sunken look. Dark circles marred the skin under her eyes.

A man Lucky guessed was her husband sat in a chair behind her, with an infant in a carrier in the chair next to him. A boy, five or so, bounced restlessly on the other side.

Shannon hugged her and said how sorry she was. "Do you remember my sister Lucky? She was a few grades below us."

"Yes, of course. The little daredevil. One of your

former partners in crime is investigating Dad's accident.'' Her owlish eyes widened behind her glasses as she remembered something else. "You were the one who found Daddy, weren't you? Or did I misunderstand that?''

Lucky confirmed that yes, she'd been the one.

"You probably also know her husband, Jack Cahill, from the police department,'' Shannon said.

"Yes, Captain. It's good to meet you in person.'' She shook his hand. "I didn't realize when we spoke on the phone that you were Shannon's brother-in-law.'' She turned back to Lucky. "Your husband's been wonderful through this horrible time. So supportive.''

"We're both very sorry, Carolyn. If there's anything we can do to help, please call me.''

"I will. Thank you.''

After meeting her husband, Lucky and Jack followed Shannon through the receiving line and spoke to others in the family. Carolyn was an only child, but Charlie Bagwell had two sisters, who had come in from out of town.

Jack leaned close. "Daredevil?'' he asked Lucky in a low voice. "Partner in crime?''

"In my younger years I was a little wild.''

"How so?''

"The only kids in the neighborhood my age were boys, and they became my best friends—Larry, Bomber, Ari and Deaton.''

"Bomber?''

"He liked to blow things up,'' she explained.

"I thought you spent most of your time at the cabin with your grandparents.''

"I did on weekends and in the summer, but during

the week I was stuck at Mom and Dad's, where Cal had his own buddies and Shannon and Leigh thought they were too cool to have anything to do with me.''

"We *were* too cool," Shannon threw over her shoulder.

"These boys were all fearless, so I pretended I was, too. All they had to do was accuse me of acting like a girl and I'd do any stupid thing. It's a wonder we didn't kill ourselves."

"Or end up in jail," Shannon said. Having gone through the receiving line, they moved to the corner, out of the way. "We were certain that Deaton, at the very least, would someday be named to the FBI's Most Wanted list, although Lucky was almost as bad. He was the instigator of the pranks. Lucky was the fool who usually carried them out."

"Carolyn was at the house visiting one day when Deaton dared me to climb out on the roof and hang a pair of Shannon's underpants from the TV antennae."

"That's a three-story drop," Jack said.

"You're telling me. I was scared to death, but I knew if I chickened out, there'd be hell to pay. Of course, when my mother caught me and blistered my backside in front of everyone, that was *worse* than hell. I never did forgive Deaton for goading me into it."

"What happened to the other boys? Where are they now?"

Lucky told him they still lived in town except for Ari, who'd become a concert violinist. "Larry sells insurance and Bomber, believe it or not, became a Methodist minister."

The casket sat closed at the end of the parlor. The

room was small and quickly filled up with people who'd come to pay their respects. Jack spotted the police chief and raised his hand in greeting. "I should go over. I've been avoiding him all week."

"How come?" Lucky asked.

"He's been bugging me about joining some kind of community-service project we're involved in. We're supposed to go out and pick up litter off the streets."

"Adopt-a-Mile," Shannon said. "You adopt a mile of highway and keep it clean. Bill's school does it."

"I'm sure it's worthwhile, but with Lucky pregnant and all the repairs that need doing at the cabin, I don't want to commit to something that's going to eat up my time."

"Oh, you should do it. I think it's only one Saturday morning a month, and it makes a huge difference to how the town looks."

"I'll think about it." He wandered over to speak to the chief, leaving them alone.

"Are you two planning to stay at the cabin after the baby's born?" Shannon asked. "Jack hasn't insisted you move?"

"Why should we move? He's beginning to like living in the country."

"Oh, Lucky, you can't believe that. The place is a disaster area."

"No, it's not. Jack's been working on it in his spare time."

"But surely that's only because he wants to make it more livable *temporarily*—until you can buy a house."

"Uh-uh," she told her with confidence, then frowned as the words planted a seed of doubt. She and Jack hadn't talked about the cabin since he'd returned. The repairs he'd done—she'd seen them as his acceptance that they were staying put. Maybe that wasn't the case.

"Oh, look, the Wyatt sisters." Shannon smiled and wiggled her fingers at them, but under her breath commented on how old they were both looking.

She had Leigh's instinct for information, and gossip had always been her favorite pastime. She made a circuit of the room and got the scoop on the people Lucky didn't know.

"Those men over there are part of Mr. Bagwell's logging crews," she said, indicating a group of eight or so men.

"So many?"

"He had four trucks. I imagine it takes several people to cut the wood and load it, plus someone to drive."

"I recognize several of them, but not the two men on the right. Who are they?"

"The balding man with the glasses is Paul Hightower. He's a timber manager or contractor or something for the park service. The guy he's talking to is Carl Brown from the paper company."

"Probably business associates."

Shannon looked toward the door. "Well, I'm surprised to see *him* here."

"Who is that? He seems familiar."

"Joe Tagliotti. You know him. He owns the dry cleaners in that block below the *Register*. He married Harriet Lynn."

Of course. She'd seen Tagliotti only yesterday when she'd picked up Jack's shirts. Usually there was a woman at the counter during lunch hours, so Lucky had never talked to Tagliotti, but she'd sometimes seen him working in the back of the store.

"His ten-year-old is on the baseball team that Mr. Bagwell helped coach," Shannon said. "He's a real hothead. Rumor has it that he and Carolyn's father got into it pretty hard last month because he yells at the kids when they mess up. The other parents have complained about him to the league."

"Did they actually come to blows?"

"I'm not sure, but Bill heard that Tagliotti got so abusive Mr. Bagwell had him thrown out of the park."

That was interesting. She wondered if Jack knew that or if it was important.

Leigh had quoted the district attorney in the paper as saying Charlie Bagwell's death appeared to be accidental and unavoidable. All deaths routinely went before a grand jury, but the DA said charges against the train's operators were unlikely.

Despite that, she knew Jack was still working on the case. He'd brought files home several times and read through them at his desk in the makeshift office he'd set up along one wall of the storage room. When she'd asked him why he hadn't closed the case, he'd said he was only being thorough.

Shannon stayed another twenty minutes, then had to go. Lucky looked for Jack, deciding they should head out, too, but first she signed the guest book, something she'd neglected to do on the way in.

"Leaving?" a voice asked. Lucky turned to find Carolyn.

"Yes, but we'll be at the funeral in the morning."

"I wonder if I might ask a favor of you. Could you come by Dad's house sometime tomorrow afternoon?

Say, maybe three o'clock, if that's convenient? My aunts should be gone home by then.''

"Yes, I can do that. Is there something you need help with? Jack can—''

"No, please, come alone. And...I'd appreciate it if you didn't mention the visit to your husband.''

That piqued Lucky's curiosity, but she didn't like going behind Jack's back. "Is something wrong, Carolyn?''

"I'm sorry, I don't mean to sound so mysterious. I feel a bit foolish even asking, especially since we don't know each very well, but I have to talk to someone, and it occurred to me tonight that you'd be the perfect person.'' She squeezed Lucky's arm. "Please, I'll explain tomorrow. Will you come?''

AT FIVE MINUTES past three the following afternoon, Lucky arrived at the late Charlie Bagwell's house and parked in the driveway behind a silver Ford.

Leigh had reported that thieves had broken in the day of the man's death, and it was easy to see how the crime had gone unnoticed for nearly twenty-four hours. This was an old subdivision of country estates. The lots were two or three acres, and all were heavily wooded to offer privacy.

Carolyn came to the door with her three-month-old baby in her arms and ushered Lucky into a marble foyer. The house was huge, and even more beautiful inside than out.

"Thank you for coming. I've asked my husband to run errands with my other son so we won't be bothered. The baby's still breastfeeding, otherwise I'd have sent him along. He won't be a problem, though.'' Rubbing his head, she talked to him in that special voice a mother reserves for her child. "You're a very good boy, aren't you? Yes, you are." He smiled and waved a chubby arm in response.

"He's adorable, and I love his red hair. I think he favors you more than your older boy." Lucky followed her to the spacious kitchen.

"We're hoping it stays red. Do you have children?"

"No." Lucky shook her head. "Oh, one on the way. I suppose that counts."

"How wonderful! When's your due date?"

"January seventh."

"The time will fly." She motioned her toward the table. "Would you like some coffee or juice?"

"No, thank you."

Carolyn sat down and put the infant in a carrier in front of her, gently rocking him as she talked. "The first baby is a lot of fun. I loved picking out the crib, decorating the room, deciding all the important things like whether to have natural childbirth. Pregnancy was such a special time for me."

She went on about breastfeeding versus bottle-feeding, the importance of having a good doctor and other issues that Lucky hadn't considered yet.

"I'm sorry," she said after several minutes. "Here I am rambling on about babies, and I'm sure you're wondering why I asked you here." She sobered. "How well did you know my father?"

"Not well. We'd speak on the street. That was about it."

"He was a good man, Lucky. I want you to know that first off. Very generous. Thoughtful. He had a poor upbringing, but he worked hard."

"I'm sure he did."

"I know every daughter believes her father's the greatest on earth, but mine truly was. I never lacked for his time or for anything material as a child, and although he once had an affair, it was many years ago, and he and Mother got past it and stayed together. He was a terrific grandfather. He doted on Adam, my oldest. As soon as Adam was born, Daddy created a trust fund so we won't have to worry about sending him to college when the time comes. And he told me he planned to do the same for Kyle. He never neglected the boys. He called to talk to Adam every couple of days."

"Must've been hard on him with you living so far away."

"Oh, it was, especially after Mother died, but he was a strong man, and I never would've left him alone if I hadn't believed he'd be okay. And he *was* okay. Sad, naturally, but he quickly jumped back into work and coaching baseball."

The baby was falling asleep. She rose to get a lightweight blanket from the diaper bag on the counter to cover him.

"A couple of months ago," she continued, sitting down again, "I noticed a change in Dad."

"How so?"

"He stopped calling as often, and when he did, I suspected he'd been drinking. He seemed worried about something. If I brought it up, he'd get defensive, so I stopped. Then, when I was here last month, he got a call from someone one night and they argued horribly. He locked himself in his office in the shed out back, but I could hear him yelling even from here. I assumed this person was doing something wrong, because Dad told him more than once 'It has to stop.' ''

''What has to stop?''

''I don't know. I could only understand bits and pieces of the conversation.''

''Did he ever mention a man named Joe Tagliotti?'' Lucky related what Shannon had told her about the argument at the ballpark.

''I don't think so, but then again, he never called the man by name. This person could've been a woman, for that matter. I got no indication of whether it was a friend or someone he worked with. All I know is that afterward, out of the blue, he started talking about giving up the business, selling his house and moving to Mobile, which was really strange because we'd suggested that numerous times and he'd always fought the idea.''

''People change when they get older. They get lonely and want to be around their families.''

''It was more than that, Lucky. I found out… He was about to be audited. I found the notice on his desk. The IRS has requested his bank and company records.''

''An audit is enough to put anyone on edge.''

Her body slumped. ''I can't believe my dad would ever do anything wrong, but… We had a break-in the day he died. Did you know about that?''

''Yes, I understand some things were taken from the house and from a storage shed.''

''The shed is next to the workshop behind the house, and they cleaned it out. I don't know what was in there because Dad always kept it locked, but in here they stole my mother's silver, the television and the VCR. I thought originally they'd taken my mother's jewelry. I couldn't find it in the house, or the box at the bank, but then I remembered something from when I was a child. I saw Dad putting papers behind a board in the closet of his bedroom. He had a secret place where he kept things. My mother didn't know, I'm certain of it."

"Carolyn, are you sure you want to tell me this?"

"Yes, because this concerns you in a way."

"Me? How?"

"You'll understand in a minute. First let me tell you about this 'cubbyhole,' as Dad called it. When he caught me watching, he made me promise never to open it. For thirty years I kept that promise. Yesterday morning I broke it. I looked inside. I found the jewelry, but I also found deeds for property I never knew he owned, certificates for gold he'd purchased and stored in a depository in Florida and nearly $150,000 in cash."

Shocked, Lucky didn't know what to say. She squirmed in her chair, uncomfortable about being privy to this information. It wasn't what she'd expected when she'd agreed to come here.

"Apparently," Carolyn added, "he's taken a few expensive vacations over the years. I didn't know anything about them, either. I found the receipts. Hawaii. Mexico. The Caribbean. He didn't miss a call to me or the children, but he also never revealed he was out of the country. The last one was back in November. Aruba for two weeks. He let me believe he was in Georgia cutting timber on a contract."

The crazy shirt with the flamingos now made sense to Lucky.

"Carolyn, I really think you should be talking to someone who can give you legal advice."

"I've debated that all night. I've also considered calling your husband or Officer Swain, because I'm not sure if this has any bearing on what happened to Dad. I don't know *what* to do. I haven't even told my husband. I'm afraid…" She broke into tears. "I'm afraid that everything I've always believed about my father may be a lie. Daddy made a good living, Lucky, but not *that* good. What if he was doing something illegal?"

"All the more reason to talk to an attorney."

"I suppose you're right—I should. But I wanted to tell you first."

"Why, Carolyn? I still don't see how I fit into this."

"Because of your past and something else I found in the cubbyhole. This—" she picked up an envelope from the table and opened it "—scares me more than the money." Withdrawing a stack of newspaper clippings, she handed them over. "These are from the *Register.*"

Lucky scanned the headlines of the first few articles. Her confusion deepened. She flipped through the stack of yellowing newsprint. "These are all about Eileen Olenick and Terrell Wade. And…and my testimony at his hearing. They're more than twenty years old."

"Except one." She pointed it out and Lucky picked it up—the piece Leigh had written two and a half months ago on Terrell. "Daddy's behavior changed about the time Terrell Wade returned to Potock. And look at his notation."

Underlined in pen was a sentence that said Terrell was suspected in the 1980 disappearance of Jackson

Elementary School teacher Eileen Olenick, but that
no charges had been filed.

In the margin beside it was one word printed in
bold letters: INNOCENT.

JACK HAMMERED another nail into place and tested
the steps he'd spent the past few hours replacing in
front of the cabin. This was his first full day off in
ten, and aside from the funeral that morning, he'd
spent all of it working in the yard. He'd cleaned out
brush around the foundation and secured places where
the tin had come loose, as well as fixed the steps.

Lucky pulled in shortly after five. Pale and silent,
she walked by without a word and went inside.

Jack looked at Beanie. "Well, what do you think?
Should we go see what's wrong, or are we better off
leaving her alone?" The dog wagged her tail and
sneezed. "That's what I think, too. Let's not press
our luck."

He scratched at an itchy place on his arm and returned to work. At seven-thirty Lucky came out,
sleepy-eyed but looking better. She wore her bathing
suit bottom, but with her bra.

"Hey," she said, approaching with hesitation.

"Hey."

"I was tired. I took a nap."

"Beanie and I figured as much, so we let you
sleep."

"I wasn't nice before. I'm really sorry."

"Already forgiven."

She rubbed the dog's ears then put her arms around
Jack's neck, burying her face in his T-shirt. "How do
you stand me?"

"It's not easy," he teased. "You're so ugly and

foul-tempered.'' Normally that would have made her laugh, but it didn't this time. Something *was* wrong, and it went beyond being tired. ''Want to tell me what the problem is?''

''Yes, but right now I'd rather take a quick swim before it gets dark.''

''I'd change first.''

''I just did.''

''You're wearing your bra. Not your bathing-suit top.''

''I am?'' She looked down and frowned. ''Oh. It was the spider's fault.''

''You had a spider in your bathing suit?''

''No, in the window, silly. That's why I'm still wearing my bra.''

There was logic in there somewhere, he supposed. Lucky's kind of logic.

''Let me guess. You started to change clothes, but then you saw the spider and something about it fascinated you, so you stopped to watch it or take its photograph, and you forgot you hadn't finished putting on your bathing suit.''

''Well, isn't that what I just got through saying?'' She rolled her eyes, as if she couldn't believe he was so thickheaded. ''Guess I'll skip the swim and watch the sunset, instead.''

She settled in the big canvas hammock on the porch. When he'd washed off, he dabbed himself liberally with insect repellent, since he was starting to itch all over, and joined her, pulling her slight body close to his side. She put her head on his bare chest. Beanie lay down beneath them.

Everything had gone still and the few boaters

who'd been out that afternoon were gone, their racing motors replaced by night sounds.

"What are those?" he asked. "Tree frogs?"

"Mostly. They're singing for mates."

"What do suppose they're saying? 'Hey, baby'?"

"More like 'hey, baby...hey, baby...hey, baby.'"

"I'll have to try that with you." He put his lips against her temple and murmured, "Hey, baby." She still didn't laugh, and usually she did so easily.

"I don't think you and I have any trouble mating," she said. "The other ninety percent of the time is what we have to watch out for."

"Things are better, aren't they? You've been happy since I moved back?"

"Yes, I've been very happy."

So it was something else that had her brooding. She'd tell him eventually.

They watched as the trees turned to silhouettes and the water became a ribbon of winding light. Darkness swallowed up the pinks and oranges of sunset, and the sky filled with stars.

"Nice," he said. "As a kid, I used to climb onto the roof wherever we were living and watch the stars for hours. I thought I was really seeing them, but now I realize I wasn't."

"There's less pollution and fewer city lights out here to interfere. Makes it perfect for watching meteors and eclipses."

He had to admit that, at times like this, when he wasn't having to worry about finding a coffee cup without rust stains in it or putting his foot through a hole in the floor, he almost understood why she liked this place. Good view. No neighbors to bother them. Stars.

"Are the windows on your car rolled up?" she asked. "It's going to rain."

"Lucky, it's a beautiful night. Not a cloud in the sky." Nor had he heard anything on the radio about bad weather.

"Still…it's going to rain. I smell it and feel it on my skin. Better check your windows."

"Mm."

She fell asleep while they talked. One minute she was telling him about a comet she'd once photographed, and the next she was dead to the world.

He could easily stay like this all night, holding her, listening to the light snoring sounds she made when she slept on her back, but the bug repellent didn't seem to be working any longer, and the last thing he wanted to be was a feast for mosquitoes.

He eased up and to his feet with a minimum of disruption to the hammock. "Come on, Beanie, let's put Mama to bed."

Gently he picked up Lucky, carried her to the bedroom and tucked her in. She stirred but didn't wake. He decided that he, too, would turn in early, but his eyes hadn't been closed a minute before a rumble made him open them.

Thunder. He got up and pulled on his pants. One of these days, maybe he'd learn to listen to her.

"STOP SCRATCHING! You're going to spread it." Lucky dabbed cortisone cream on Jack's arms and hands. She'd never seen a worse case of poison ivy in her life, or one that had come up so quickly. His arms were covered. Lines of it had risen on his chest and neck. Bumps were appearing on his face. What had he done? Rolled in it?

He clawed at his skin. "Shit! I can't stand this. I'm going nuts."

They stood in the bathroom, Lucky still in the bra and bathing suit bottom she'd worn to bed. Jack had showered and was dressing for work, but had gotten no further than a pair of briefs.

"Three leaves. Don't touch. Remember?"

"This had seven leaves. I thought it was safe."

"Were they paired and pointed with one on the top?"

"That sounds right."

"Poison sumac, then. There was a patch near the chimney."

"Well, why the hell didn't you get rid of it?"

"Because I like the look of the greenish-white berries it sometimes puts out. They're pretty. Besides, I didn't know you'd be digging around out there."

"Normal people don't let that kind of crap grow, Lucky. They have grass and shrubs. Your yard's a death trap of brambles and poison."

Normal people. *Your* yard. The words hurt.

"I'm sorry. I didn't think to cut it down. I'm not allergic to it."

"Well, I am," he snapped. "Look at me! It's everywhere." He pulled down his shorts in front, and sure enough, it was *everywhere*. She bit her lip. "Don't you dare laugh!"

"I'm not." She squeezed out more cream. "Call the doctor as soon as he opens and see if he'll let you run by for a shot and a prescription. In a few hours you'll feel fine."

"Yeah, right. I'm not going to work like this. Hell, I'm long overdue to take a sick day."

"No! You can't do that!"

He peered at her. "And why can't I?"

"Because Carolyn Carter is coming by to see you. I was going to tell you last night, but I didn't plan on falling asleep. She found some strange things at her dad's house, and I convinced her she should talk to you about them."

He paused in his scratching. "Strange things?"

She told him about her visit and what Carolyn had found. "So you've *got* to go to work. You have to follow up on this."

"Why did she confide in you?"

She explained about the newspaper clippings. "I can't blame her for being afraid of what they suggest. Do you think there's a connection between Miss Eileen's disappearance and this extra wealth Mr. Bagwell accumulated?"

"I doubt it. Probably half the people in this town clipped articles about that case when it happened."

"But how many do you think hid them from their wives in a cubbyhole in the closet?"

"Still not proof that he knew anything about the case." He had her smear cream on every spot that even thought about being a bump, then pulled on his undershirt and socks. "I'll look into it. Find that doctor's number for me, would you?"

After she wrote down the number and placed it next to his cell phone, she followed as he went to the storage room and put on a clean shirt. She'd cleaned out the room so Jack could keep his clothes and belongings there.

"What if Miss Eileen was the woman he had the affair with? If they were lovers and she threatened to tell his wife, he could have killed her to shut her up. That doesn't explain where he got all that money, though." She tapped her teeth with her fingernail, thinking. "Maybe it's blackmail money. He was a witness to the murder and he'd been blackmailing the killer."

"For twenty-one years? Not likely."

"Okay, that was stupid, but here's something interesting...." She passed along what Shannon had told her about the man at the cleaners. "The two of them had a shouting match."

"I know about it." He finished dressing. At the front door he stuck his comb, change and billfold into his pants pockets and put on his shoes. He grabbed his raincoat from the stand behind the door. "Have breakfast before you leave, please. Neither one of us ate last night."

Eating was the last thing on her mind. "Was his death *really* accidental? I know what the DA is saying publicly, but you've been working a lot of extra hours on the case. What do you think?"

"I think...that I need to get going."

Damn him. Why couldn't he, for once, be a husband first and a cop second? He'd let her do all the talking and hadn't given her one useful bit of information.

"Jack, what if—?"

"Lucky, don't fret over this. I said I'd look into it and I will. All you need to worry about is taking care of yourself and the baby. Don't nibble. Eat a real breakfast. And don't forget your vitamins."

"I could be with you when you talk to Carolyn. She feels comfortable with me, and my schedule's pretty loose this morning. What do you think?"

"No way. I don't want you talking to Carolyn or anyone else. And you can't tell what you know. Not

to Leigh. Not to Shannon. Not to anyone. Understand?''

The request put her in an awkward spot with Leigh,
but Carolyn's trust and privacy also had to be considered, so she promised him she'd keep her mouth
shut. "I don't suppose you'll tell me what you find
out...will you?''

"Baby, you know I don't like discussing the details
of an investigation with you. Your imagination starts
running wild.''

"That's not fair! I helped put Terrell away for most
of his adult life because I believed he murdered Miss
Eileen. If it turns out he didn't, I have the right to
know. And frankly, this town needs to know. Everyone was so quick to condemn him.''

"This probably doesn't have anything to do with
that woman's disappearance or Terrell Wade. You're
making another one of your leaps in logic.''

"Okay, I'm brainless. I admit it. But that doesn't
mean I'm wrong.''

"Lucky, you're not brainless. You have one of the
most creative minds of anyone I've ever met.''

That was nice. He'd never complimented her mind
before. "You really think that? Honest?''

"Honest. You're inquisitive, open-minded, in tune
with your environment. You see things most other
people never even notice. I wish I had half your intuition.''

"That's so sweet.''

"I mean every word. Now I have to run.''

She walked out with him to the porch door. Beyond
it, rain poured down. The river had become a muddy,
churning mass.

"Bad," he said, looking at it. "Is it likely to get worse?"

"Oh, pooh, that's nothing. It'll be down by tomorrow." She waved away his concerns, her mind on something more important. "I'll bet you're going to find out that Mr. Bagwell was seeing Miss Eileen on the sly. You heard what my mother said about gossip at the time—that she had a married lover." Something else occurred to her. "Oh, but I didn't ask if Charlie Bagwell's affair happened around the same time as Miss Eileen's death. They could've been years apart. Dang it!"

Jack chuckled and kissed her on the forehead. "Goodbye, Sherlock Holmes. See you later."

CHAPTER EIGHT

JACK DID INTERVIEW Carolyn Carter about the cash, deeds and gold certificates she'd found at her father's house. Deciding this area of the case would best be handled by the IRS, he advised her to notify them. That had been a few weeks ago.

He'd heard since from Carolyn that the audit of Charlie Bagwell's logging business would extend back just three years, a relief for her. She'd owe tax and penalties on unreported income from that time period only. Further action was unlikely since Bagwell was dead.

Jack continued to concentrate on the criminal aspects of the death and Bagwell's possible connection to the theft of Indian artifacts on federal lands.

On a Saturday afternoon, seven weeks after the train had killed the man, additional reports came in from DFS. As far as Jack could see, nothing in the lab work shed new light on the case.

Bagwell was alive when the train hit him, which ruled out the possibility that he'd been murdered first and then dumped on the tracks. Jack scanned the pages. No evidence of trauma, other than the obvious. No suspicious findings in the blood, serum or tissues so far.

He rubbed his forehead, disappointed that there weren't any results on a pair of small circular marks on Bagwell's neck. Simple bruises? Or something more sinister?

He'd noticed the marks in one of the photographs. If Bagwell was incapacitated that night by a stun gun, which was Jack's guess, the jolt of electricity from the prongs would have caused changes in the tissue at the cellular level.

The guns were readily available for sale in most states and on the Internet, but the marks they left— burns, bruises or scratches—could easily be dismissed during a forensic examination as the result of normal trauma.

He'd asked DFS to run further tests. That report might not be available for months, though. Sighing, Jack flipped the page.

The tool-mark analysis on the car tire showed the puncture was from a nail. No surprise there. But this was curious...*nail head clipped and point achieved by filing*, he read to himself. A nail with points on both ends. What the hell would that be used for?

His watch said four-forty, and he'd told Lucky he'd try to make it home by four. He put everything in the file and returned it to the top tray on Deaton's desk. This case was going nowhere. If the screwup by his people on the scene had destroyed evidence, he might never solve it. That possibility stuck in his craw.

He tried to call Lucky as he walked through the division room, but his cell phone was dead again. He banged it with the heel of his hand and cursed, then banged it a few more times.

"Problems, Captain?" Detective Rogers asked, looking up from her desk.

"This piece of crap keeps going dead on me."

She smiled. "I don't think hitting it charges the battery, sir."

"No, but it makes me feel better."

"If you say so."

He saw she was working on end-of-the-month burglary reports. "What's the tally going to be?"

"The statements from the two men that patrol caught out on Sweetbriar Street helped clear four more. That makes eleven altogether."

"Excellent. Have you and Detective Swain come up with anything on the Bagwell burglary?"

"No, not yet. Evidence is pretty thin. No fingerprints. No unfamiliar vehicles seen in the area. Without serial numbers on the electronics, I don't see how we'll have much luck recovering them. And we can't look for what was taken from the storage shed, because nobody knows what he had in there. We're pretty much at a dead end with that."

Whatever Bagwell had been keeping in that shed was probably connected to his unexplained wealth. Too bad they didn't know the contents. Jack had a feeling that if they did, it would explain a lot of things, including what had happened the night Bagwell died.

"Keep on it," he told Rogers. "I'll be in the chief's office for a minute, then I'm gone for the day. If anything comes up and I'm needed, go through the radio dispatcher."

"Oh, sir? Before you leave..." She pulled a folder from her stack. "You asked me to keep you posted on the investigation of the bomb threat we had out at the box factory. Something has me puzzled."

Jack perched on the corner of her desk. "What's the problem?"

"The call came in from a public phone downtown. The caller was probably male. He attempted to disguise his voice, as you'd expect, but it sounded to me like it had been more than simply muffled. So I sent a copy of the 911 tape to an expert down at the university, and I was right. The voice was electronically altered and the message most likely taped in advance and played into the receiver."

"Somebody wanted to make extra-sure he wasn't recognized."

"That's what I don't understand. Is it usual to go to such lengths? I mean, I figured we were dealing with an employee who decided at the last minute he didn't want to go to work, or some teenager with too much time on his hands, but this took forethought."

"If there really had been a bomb that morning, I'd say, yes, you should have expected it. But you're right, for a crank call that's going overboard. Can your expert clean up the tape?"

"He's tried, but so far, no luck. The perp knew what he was doing. Should I keep working on this?"

"If something presents itself, follow up, but we have bigger cases that need our attention. I'll leave it to your judgment."

"Yes, sir. Thank you." Jack rose. "Have a good weekend," she told him.

"Same to you, Rogers."

Earlier, on a trip to the records room, he'd passed by the chief's office and noticed his light on. He wanted to have a word with him before he left. The secretary didn't work Saturdays, so Jack went straight through to the inner door.

"Hey, Jack, have a seat. Sorry we didn't have you

out on the road with us this morning picking up trash.''

Rolly Akers was a civic-minded man who got along well with everyone and whose good ol' boy personality hid a keen intelligence. He'd probably been a hell of an investigator before moving into administration. With more than thirty years' experience to his credit, he was eligible to retire, but nobody thought he'd do it anytime soon.

"Jolly Rolly" some people called him. Lucky and her sisters referred to him as "Officer Rolly," as did most people who'd attended his safety programs as children. He still visited the schools a couple of times a month.

"I'm sorry, sir. I've been playing catch-up all month with these burglaries."

"I understand. What can I help you with?"

Jack told him about the autopsy results and outlined the suggested connection between Bagwell and the missing Olenick woman. "I'm told you worked her case."

"I did."

"I know it's unlikely Bagwell killed her, but from what I've been able to piece together from talking to his daughter, this affair her father had coincides time-wise with the disappearance of the victim. Bagwell and Olenick knew each other. They were members of the same church. If they were involved, that suggests a possible motive for her death."

"Most people know each other round here. I went to that church myself before the river destroyed the building. My ancestors were among those who settled out that way. The Akers, the Mathisons, the Bagwells, the Olenicks...''

"He had opportunity. My in-laws don't remember seeing him in church that morning."

"They won't remember seeing me, either. Had a toothache and stayed home."

"Was Bagwell a suspect at any time?"

"Not that I remember, and my memory's pretty good. That autistic boy, Terrell Wade, was our primary suspect, and I focused my investigation on him. 'Course he's not a boy anymore."

That was procedure—to pursue the obvious—but Jack wondered if, in this case, it had resulted in the wrong man being accused.

"I've looked for the files and the evidence, but nobody seems to know what's happened to them. They aren't in the locker where they ought to be."

"An old case like that…we've probably discarded them."

Jack let out an incredulous breath. "We toss evidence?"

"We're a small town, son. We do the best we can with what we have, but our best isn't always good enough. You see how space is at a premium here."

"I understand that, but I'm surprised we can't find room to store evidence on an unsolved murder case, regardless of how much time has passed."

"We should, and it might be back there somewhere, but it might also have been thrown away. Much as I'd like a new building, I felt it was more important to put what money the city budgets us into manpower, equipment and vehicles rather than facilities."

"Sorry, sir. I didn't mean to sound critical."

"Don't apologize. You're young and bright and you're used to a professional environment. That's why I hired you. You'll help us modernize. You've already made major leaps in your division.''

''Thank you.''

''Now about this case… What are you looking for?''

''Do you recall any details of the investigation?''

''Oh, vividly. Most frustrating case I've ever had. She simply vanished.'' The chief spent several minutes telling Jack about the search for the body, how the only evidence was Wade's appearance at the church and the bloody hat he carried. Wade had gone missing that morning from his house. He often disappeared, Akers said. His mother called two or three times a week asking if patrol could look out for him and bring him home.

''You never found the crime scene?''

''Not the first clue. The murder, if she was murdered, didn't happen at her house. We did determine that. I think she drove out to the woods or the river that morning to pick a bit of decoration for her hat for church. She ran into Wade. Or maybe he was in the car with her already. He tried to sexually assault her, she fought, and he killed her. He may not even have meant to do it.''

Plausible but weak. ''Did you know her personally?''

He nodded. ''I visited her school quite a bit and got to know her. She was a nice lady. Sweet. Friendly.''

''Attractive? I can't tell from the newspaper clippings.''

''Very.''

''Attractive enough to inspire a married man to be foolish?''

"Yes," Akers said, his expression changing, "she was that attractive. A real beauty. Men liked her."

"And did she like men?"

He paused before answering. "I'd say she did. Her flirting caused problems in more than one marriage."

The tone of his voice made Jack wonder if the chief's marriage had been among them. "At the time of her death, who was she seeing?"

"Someone special, according to her friends. Someone she was in love with. Married, but they didn't know his name. I think you're barking up the wrong tree with Charlie, if you want my opinion. I never found anything that pointed to him as being her lover."

"Are you convinced Terrell Wade killed her?"

"I am."

The telephone rang and he asked Jack to excuse him for a moment, but not to step out. Jack was about finished, though, so he stood.

Guessing from the end of the conversation Jack could hear, the caller was the chief's wife. "...yes, he's...uh-huh. Oh, no, sugar, I don't mind a bit." He chuckled, looked up at Jack and winked. "You tell me what you want. Uh-huh. The hot ones?" He started writing on the pad in front of him. "And what else? Oh, boy. You planning on putting those together, are you?" He grimaced and chuckled at the same time. "That it? I sure will. You take care." He hung up. "Pregnant women. They're a hoot, aren't they?"

"Your...wife's pregnant?" Jack tried to ask delicately, but the man had to be in his late fifties or early sixties, and Jack's surprise was stronger than his tact.

The chief roared with laughter. "Oh, hell, no, son.

Your wife. She's cute as a button. I always did like that girl.''

"That was Lucky?"

"Couldn't get you, so they switched her up here. Told her I'd give you the message to quit dawdling.''

"I'm sorry she bothered you. We're supposed to celebrate our first anniversary tonight, and I guess she's wondering where I am.''

"Well, you go on. Don't keep that sweet angel waiting any longer.'' He tore off the note and handed it to him. "And stop by the store. She's craving a little treat.''

Jack looked at the list. Sardines in chili sauce. Rocky Road ice cream. He groaned with embarrassment. "I'm sorry.''

"Ah, now, don't you be mad at her. Talking to her was the highlight of this old man's day.''

Jack thanked him for his help, walked to the door and then turned. "If you think of anything else, I'd appreciate hearing about it.''

"Are you reopening the Olenick case?"

"I don't know that there's reason to officially. I'm trying to satisfy my own curiosity more than anything…and Lucky's. She's been upset ever since Wade came home.''

"I can understand that.''

"There's more.'' He told him about the encounter she'd had with Wade in the slough, and how Lucky was now questioning whether or not he was a killer. "I'd like to ease her mind about what she did as a child and to know, for my own peace of mind, whether or not she's in any danger from him. I want the truth.''

"I understand. Do what you feel is necessary.''

Akers cleared his throat. "There's something you should know, though, if you plan to be digging around and asking questions. Talk to Matt. Ask him about his relationship with Eileen."

His father-in-law? Oh, hell. Dread eased up his spine. "Am I going to like what he tells me?"

"Probably not, son, but the truth isn't always pleasant."

LUCKY HAD SPENT most of the day in the water floating on an inner tube, but late that afternoon she'd showered and changed into shorts. On her way in, she saw a huge snapping turtle sunning himself on the crown of a submerged log thirty feet out from the end of the pier. She came out with one of her cameras, thrilled to capture him on film.

Several shots later Beanie let out a howl and looked toward the house, indicating that Jack was coming down the dirt road. The dog was too fat to move quickly. She waited in wriggling anticipation as he parked and went inside the cabin to deposit his grocery sack.

When he walked to the pier, the dog was all over him. Jack tried to keep her off his good pants, but it was hopeless. He gave up and returned the affection.

"I want some of that," Lucky said, tucking her camera under one arm and reaching out with the other. Jack obliged by grabbing her around the waist and pulling her close. As they kissed, she was nearly jerked off her feet. A jealous Beanie had grabbed her rubber flip-flop by the heel and was pulling it.

"She's jealous you're getting my attention," Jack said.

Lucky wrestled away her shoe. "She'll have to learn to share it."

In the house she dove into the sack he'd brought and pulled out the tin of sardines. Normally she could take or leave the things, but all afternoon she'd been thinking about a sardine and onion sandwich with ice cream as a chaser.

"Uh-huh," Jack said, taking them away. "Wait until I'm not here. Just the *idea* of you eating them makes me sick. The smell will kill me."

"But I'm hungry." She took out the carton of ice cream. A dang pint. "Is this all you got? That bitty ol' thing won't feed a flea."

To her frustration, he took that away, too, and stuck it in the freezer. "Save it for later. We have dinner reservations at seven."

The new dress she'd bought for the occasion was blue silk but without a waistline, since hers had started to expand. A little cantaloupe now inhabited the place where her flat stomach used to be. The neckline dipped to show off her newly acquired cleavage.

Dressing up in something this fancy felt odd, but Jack had insisted.

"Nice," he said. He ran his finger along one breast and into the V. "Those must've come with the dress. I don't recall seeing them before."

She chuckled and slapped away his hand. "And you won't see them again if you don't quit teasing me."

The restaurant he took her to was lovely. She had to admit she'd been wrong to suggest they stay home tonight. The atmosphere was romantic, the food excellent.

He seemed nervous all through dinner. After dessert he took a jewelry box from his pocket. She'd hinted for a pair of nice earrings, and he'd let her believe that was what she'd be getting, so when he pulled a diamond ring from the box, she was stunned.

"I don't remember the exact moment I fell in love with you," he said, taking her left hand, "but I remember the exact moment I realized I was in love. You'd flown up for the weekend and we'd spent most of the night doing what we always did when we were together. I woke up before you did the next morning. You were snoring in my ear."

Lucky blushed, embarrassed. "Oh, how horrible."

"No, it was sweet. And that's when I realized I must love you, because I wanted to wake up the same way every morning."

Ignoring where they were, he came around and got down on one knee beside her chair. The other diners turned to watch. And smile. "Oh, Jack...you don't have to."

"Yes, I do. I messed up the first time. No ring. No engagement. I didn't make you happy. But I promise, this time will be different if you'll give me the chance. Erin Renee Mathison, will you marry me?"

EVEN IN MOONLIGHT the ring sparkled. Lucky held out her hand for the thousandth time and twisted it one way and then the other, enjoying the flash of light.

Jack stood above her looking through the telescope she'd bought him as an anniversary present. When they'd gotten home, they'd changed clothes and set it up on a flat spot in the front yard. He was fascinated by what he saw through the lens and hardly remembered she was there.

Finally he left it and sat down beside her on the blanket she'd spread. "You checked for poisonous plants before putting this down, I hope. If I never go through that misery again, it'll be too soon."

"Free and clear of poison, milord. I chased off the snakes, too."

"Not funny. You know how I feel about those things."

"I don't understand how somebody with a third-degree black belt in tae kwon do can be afraid of a snake."

"Easily. They have fangs and they can kill you."

"Don't worry, I'll protect you." She kissed him softly on the cheek. "I love my ring."

"I'm glad. I was worried you might not accept it, but we've been *courting* two months and it's time to take the next step."

"Two months isn't very long."

"I never claimed to be a patient man."

"No, no one could accuse you of that."

"We're making this work, aren't we? We're not fighting. You told me you've been happy."

"Yes, but that's because we haven't really addressed the major problems we were fighting about before. Like my continuing to work at the *Register*. Like…the cabin. It's easy for me to be happy when you're giving me everything I want."

"We'll work those things out."

"Kind of hard to work them out when we never talk about them."

His silence was revealing.

"Jack, don't close up on me."

He lay down with his hands behind his head. "I've

been afraid to talk,'' he admitted. "I don't want to mess up what we have.''

"I know. I keep telling myself that, given time, everything will resolve itself, but we don't have the luxury of time, at least about the cabin. Pretty soon we'll have to buy a crib and start fixing up a room for this baby, and I don't want to fight with you over where that's going to be.''

"I don't want to fight with you, either.''

"When you started making repairs around the cabin I thought…he's come to like it here and wants to stay, but I know I was fooling myself. You'd move tomorrow if I said the word, wouldn't you?'' He didn't respond, but he didn't have to. "I thought so. You hate it here.''

"I don't hate it, Lucky. It's just not what I imagined for myself when I got married and had a child.''

"What did you imagine?''

"A nice house, nothing extravagant. A bedroom for us. A couple of bedrooms for kids. A family room of some kind. Maybe some actual grass in the yard.''

"In town, I suppose.''

"Not necessarily. I'd settle for land on the river as long as the house is good, we can connect to city services and we don't have to worry about getting flooded out. I'm not asking you to sell this place. We could keep it to pass down to one of our children. I know how much it means to you.''

No, he could never know how much. Not in a million years. Her earliest memory was sitting in a baby swing on this very spot, wearing a diaper and a little sun hat. She couldn't have been more than eighteen months old, but she remembered the beautiful water, the sun glinting off its surface, the graceful trees all around her that seemed to be waving hello in the wind....

She loved this land.

But she loved this man more.

"Okay. I'll agree to look for a house and we'll move. But it has to be on the river."

He sat up abruptly. "Say that again."

"Find us a house. I'll move if that's what will make you happy. As long as I can keep this place and stay here now and then."

"You're serious!"

"I am. You've committed to this marriage. I guess it's time I did, too."

JACK WAS SO EXCITED he couldn't stop talking about the house. He'd had a picture of it in his head for years—the yard, the rooms, the den where his children would lie on the carpet watching TV. Even after they settled into bed, he got a notebook and sketched out a floor plan. He showed it to Lucky and told her he'd call a real-estate agent on Monday to start the search.

She promptly burst into tears.

"Oh, hell, what did I say?" He held her and tried to comfort her. "We don't have to start looking right away."

"No, it's not that." She couldn't stop sobbing. "The baby. I just felt it."

"What?" Delighted, he put his hand on her stomach. "What does it feel like?"

"Feathers tickling me on the inside. Oh! There it goes again." She cried harder. "I'm really pregnant."

He held her, not understanding. "Of course you're

pregnant, sweetheart. Did you think you swallowed a watermelon?''

"Don't make me laugh. I don't want to laugh."

"Tell me why you're crying."

"Because I'm *really* going to have a baby."

"I thought you understood that weeks ago. The little sperm wiggled its way into the egg and—"

"Oh, sometimes you're such a *man*. I hate it."

She fled to the bathroom and locked the door. From the other side, he could hear her crying, and it confounded him.

"Lucky, come on. Whatever I said or did, I'm sorry."

She wouldn't answer. He threw up his hands and left her alone. Beanie, confused by all the commotion, had come in from her pallet in the kitchen. She rested her chin on the bed and looked at him as if to ask, "What's going on?"

"Don't ask me. I'm a man and therefore clueless." He sent the dog back to the kitchen.

After a while he heard the water running, and a minute later Lucky slipped into bed. Turning, she put her arm across his chest. He pulled her close.

"Better?"

"Yes," she said, but she still sniffled. "I'm sorry. That was silly."

"Don't worry about it. The booklet from the doctor said you'd get irritable and weepy these next few months."

"Don't start being a man again, or I'm going to have to hit you."

"Sorry. Did I do something to make you cry?"

"No. Go to sleep. We're both tired."

"I'd rather hear what got you so upset."

"You'll think I'm terrible if I tell you."

"No, I won't. I love you too much to ever think you're terrible."

"Promise?"

"I promise."

She sat up, so Jack raised himself on his elbow. "When I found out I was pregnant, I was afraid this baby would end our marriage. I resented it a little bit. At first I thought you only came home because of it and not me."

"You know that's not true."

"I do now, but I didn't then."

"I'd already pretty much decided to move back in. Another week of sleeping alone would've done it."

"Really?"

"No doubt about it. I was running out of things to pretend I'd left behind." She wiped her eyes with her hand and chuckled, letting him know the crisis was about over. "So what made you cry tonight?" he whispered. "Can you tell me?"

"I guess its because all these weeks I haven't wanted to care about the baby or accept that it truly exists. I've been scared."

"Of what?"

"Of our situation. Of failing. Maybe even scared of the responsibility—being someone's mother. But when I felt the baby move tonight, it hit me. This is real. A living little person. Our child. I realized that, despite my fear, I'd come to want him or her very much."

"Come here." He pulled her down and rubbed her back, intending to hold her and let her fall asleep. "At the risk of being a man, can I tell you something?"

"Yes."

"I think it has to be normal to be scared. Hell, I'm scared. I worry every day about what kind of father I'll be."

"You don't think I'm terrible for resenting the pregnancy at first?"

"No, and I think you're going to be a terrific mother."

"Mmm. You always make me feel better." She slid her hand across his chest, then moved it downward to stroke him through the cotton boxers he liked to wear to bed. She slipped it in through the flap. "Nifty little thing, that hole in the front."

"I thought you were tired."

Her thumb lightly grazed him, but it was enough to make him leap in response. "I was, but I just remembered that your being a man has definite advantages."

CHAPTER NINE

RAY LIKED the boardinghouse he'd moved into in Potock. The food was good, the other tenants didn't disturb him, and the owner was a nice-looking widow named Carla who called him "handsome" all the time, as if it was his name.

She cooked pot roast twice a week because he'd mentioned it was his favorite dish, and winked at him a lot. He didn't mind. He winked back. One of these nights he might do more than wink if she gave him the signal.

He'd told her right off he was an ex-con and a thief and that sometimes the itch to steal was pretty powerful. Instead of showing him the door, she'd showed him around.

"If you see anything you want, take it now as a gift," she'd said. "But if you live here, I won't put up with you stealing from me. Are we clear?"

"Yes, ma'am. We're clear." He respected a woman who said what she meant. He'd moved in right away. And not once in all these weeks had he taken anything or wanted to.

The sheets smelled clean, but not like the ones from the prison laundry that reeked of starch. These had a sweet kind of scent from being dried outside on the clothesline, and that made it nice to lie between them at night.

The best part about the place was the quiet. Prison was never quiet, never dark. He'd had a hard time sleeping here in the beginning because he was used to the drone of voices always running as an undercurrent in his sleep. The only noise at night now was the occasional car passing outside.

He wasn't too keen on his job at the car wash, but it gave him something to do and kept his parole officer off his back.

He'd been good. The clean life grated a bit on his nerves, but for once he thought he could hack going straight.

Still, he hadn't yet faced J.T., hadn't told him he was out of prison and in town. His son wouldn't be happy to hear the news. But then, nothing between them had ever been easy.

SUNDAY AFTERNOON the Mathison clan gathered, as they often did, in the backyard at Lucky's parents' house. After lunch her mother took her grandmother to the hospital to visit a friend who'd broken her hip.

Lucky, Leigh and Shannon stretched out in loungers to watch the men play basketball, while the children played with their dolls nearby. Cal had brought a female friend, whom Leigh had quickly dubbed "the Prom Queen," because she looked eighteen. She'd left a while ago, though, to go to work. Now only the three sisters were left.

Lucky's engagement ring had gotten nods of appreciation from everyone in the family but Leigh. "So what does this ring mean, exactly?" she asked. "Does the Yankee intend to stay this time?"

"Leigh, for goodness' sake," Shannon admonished.

"It's okay, Shannon. Yes, Leigh, he intends to stay. I want him to. And he's not a Yankee, for your information. He was born in Biloxi, Mississippi."

She thought that would shut her sister up, but it didn't. "You've been married to this man for a year and you're just now finding out he was born in the next state? Don't you think that's a bit strange?"

"Not at all. He went through a terrible time when his parents died and he doesn't like to talk about the past."

"But Lucky—"

"Don't, Leigh, please. You're my sister and I love you, but sometimes you don't know when to quit."

"Hear, hear," Shannon said.

That did it. Leigh sulked quietly, nursing her glass of tea.

The men shed their shirts with the rising temperature. Despite his pale body, Jack looked delicious in only shorts and tennis shoes—muscular and fit. Those stomach crunches he did every morning really paid off.

Shannon nodded toward him. "You need to put that man back in the oven and brown him up a bit."

"I'm taking him fishing later. Maybe I can toast him on both sides."

"He does have a spectacular body, though. Mmm."

Even Leigh begrudgingly admitted he was well put together. "Nice rear."

"I'll bet the other side's pretty good, too," Shannon added, giggling.

"You two are terrible," Lucky told them.

"Bill used to have a six-pack like that, but all the

Little Debbie cakes he eats have given him a no-pack.''

That got them all giggling.

"WHAT DO YOU SUPPOSE women talk about when they're alone?'' Bill asked the other men, nodding at his wife and her sisters. "They sure are having a good time.''

Jack took his shot from the foul line and tossed the ball to Cal to take it out. "Babies probably.''

"Shopping and stuff,'' Cal said.

Lucky's dad chortled at that. "You boys sure have a lot to learn, that's all I've got to say.''

After three games Matt begged off, saying he was getting too old for so much activity and was going back to the house for a drink.

"That's it for me, too,'' Jack said, suggesting Cal and Bill go head-to-head. He put on his shirt and followed his father-in-law inside to the kitchen.

"Water or tea?'' Matt asked, filling two glasses with ice.

"Water.'' Jack wiped the sweat from his face and neck with the hem of his shirt. They both chugged their drinks and got a refill. "Matt, I need to talk to you about something while we're alone. Can we go to your study? I don't want anyone walking in on us.''

"Something wrong with Lucky or the baby?''

"No, nothing like that. A case I'm working on.''

"Come with me.'' In the study Matt sat behind his desk, leaving Jack to pull up a chair in front. "I don't do investigating anymore, but if you need help looking into something, maybe Leigh can—''

"No, she can't.'' Jack cut right to the chase. "I

wish I didn't have to be so blunt, because you've always treated me fairly, but there's no way around this. Were you having an affair with Eileen Olenick at the time of her death?''

Matt stopped drinking and set down his glass. Jack had stunned him; that was clear. "What's this question got to do with a case?''

"I'm looking into the possibility that Charlie Bagwell may have had something to do with her death. Rolly Akers seems to think you have firsthand knowledge that Charlie wasn't her lover.''

Matt grunted. "Rolly. Now there's a fine one to be pointing fingers at other people.''

"Rolly was involved with her?''

"I don't think physically, but certainly emotionally.''

Hell, this was getting more complicated by the minute.

"And were *you?*'' Jack asked him again.

He stood and walked to the window to look out across the backyard. "Sometimes even smart men do foolish things.''

"I understand that.''

He turned. "I'm talking about regrets. You've hardly lived long enough to have them.''

"Believe me, Matt, I have more than my share.''

"My biggest regret walked into the *Register* twenty-one years ago to ask me to write an editorial about the importance of art in the schools. I was a middle-aged man with four children and this lovely young woman acted as if I'd hung the moon. I was flattered by her attention, I guess, and I became her lover.''

"How long was the affair?''

"A few weeks. Didn't take me long to realize that what I had at home was worth more than the few hours of pleasure Eileen could give me, but the damage was already done."

"Ruth never suspected?"

"No, and it would kill her if she ever found out."

"She won't hear it from me. I promise you."

"Thank you. I ask for your silence not for my sake, but for hers. I wouldn't want her hurt by something that meant so little."

Jack nodded. His respect for Matt was stronger than his distress at the man's one indiscretion. And it would hurt Lucky, too, if she ever found out. Jack had no doubt about that.

"Do you know how Charlie Bagwell might have fit into Eileen Olenick's life?" he asked.

"I don't know that Charlie did. I never heard her mention him, but I wouldn't be surprised to learn she was sleeping with him, too. I discovered quickly that there were other men."

"Anyone in particular?"

"I can't be certain. Paul Hightower possibly."

"Hightower." Jack had to think to place the name. "We interviewed him on another case. Indian artifacts that might've been dug up on federal lands. He's a forest ranger out there?"

"Land Management Forester, I think, is the correct term, but yes, he's the head ranger. He's managed all the federally owned lands in this area for a lot of years."

"Would he have known Charlie Bagwell?"

"Oh, of course. Paul recommends the logging contracts and Charlie had some of them."

So Hightower knew Olenick, knew Bagwell and

also managed land where artifacts might have been illegally obtained. Jack sorted through the pieces of the puzzle, not liking the picture that was starting to form.

"Artifact theft," he said. "Is that something you've written stories about?"

"Plenty over the years. From what I understand, it's a major problem and big business. There's a thriving underground market of buyers and sellers."

"What kind of money are we talking about?"

"Hundreds of dollars for a simple pot. Thousands for items that are particularly rare, like human remains."

"Could somebody make a hundred thousand a year selling them?"

"I wouldn't think so around here unless he found a big site that hadn't yet been discovered and protected. To dig out enough for that kind of money would take a lot of time and effort." He said he'd kept clip files on all his stories and Jack could borrow them.

"I'd appreciate that."

"Is there a connection here? You've asked about Charlie and Eileen and now about artifact theft. Is Charlie's death somehow tied up in all of this?"

"Will what I tell you remain in this room?"

"Son, I just got through admitting the biggest secret in my life, so believe me when I say you can trust me to keep quiet. But if you don't feel comfortable…"

"Actually, Matt, it might help me to lay this out for someone I trust who knows all the players. Tell me if I'm crazy." He described the inconsistencies at the scene of Bagwell's death, the extra wealth Bagwell had socked away and the empty storage shed. "There seems to be more here than what's obvious on the surface."

"Do you think Charlie was murdered?"

"I have no hard evidence of that."

"What are your instincts telling you?"

"That someone had to help him up that railroad bank. Now, why anyone would kill him, I don't know. And whether or not there's a connection to the Olenick case, I don't know that, either. The more questions I ask, the more confusing things get."

"I have photographs from when Eileen disappeared if you want to see them. They're faded after all this time, but we kept negatives. Leigh had Lucky make a print or two off them for that article she wrote in the spring when they moved Terrell Wade to Horizon House."

"They'd be a great help. The police files and evidence are missing. Rolly says they were probably thrown away to make room for new files."

"I wouldn't rule out that he *made* them disappear."

"I'm not ruling anything out."

Matt looked at his watch. "I'll run down to the office now while nobody's there and get everything. I can be back in thirty minutes."

"Should I come?"

"No, that'll arouse suspicion. You stay here, and if any of my daughters ask, tell them I went to buy tobacco for my pipe."

"Who's an expert on Indian artifacts? I need to educate myself quickly."

"Down at the university in Tuscaloosa I'm sure you'll find any number of people, but there's someone local who knows as much as or more than anyone and probably has photographs to boot.''

"Who's that?"

"You're living with her."

"YOU'LL DO MUCH BETTER with a worm." Lucky wiggled one at Jack and smiled. He was sitting in the other end of the boat trying, with little success, to get a raw chicken liver to stay on his hook.

"I'll stick with this, thank you," he grumbled. He was obviously not thrilled about her dragging him out here this afternoon.

"They aren't snakes, you know. You don't have to be afraid of them."

He narrowed his eyes at her. "I knew I'd regret ever telling you that."

"Snakes have a bad rap. They're really very sweet, and unless they're threatened, they're much more likely to retreat than attack. They aren't slimy like people think. I'll catch one and show you if you want."

"That's okay. I'll take your word for it."

"Touching one might help you get over your fear."

"Nothing short of being held at gunpoint will ever make me touch a snake. I found one in my closet when I was a kid, and I couldn't sleep for a month worrying if he had a family."

"In the house? Wow, that's pretty strange. I've heard of it happening in really run-down places, but rarely in nice houses. How'd it get in there?"

"Crawled in through a vent, I guess. I don't know."

"That *would* spook a kid." She cast out her line

and reeled it forward a couple of turns. "I can't believe you've never been fishing before. How come your dad never took you?"

"Too busy."

"That's sad. Every kid should learn to fish. I believe it's one of life's little pleasures."

"I can see that," he said sarcastically. He accidentally caught his thumb with the hook and stuck the thumb in his mouth before remembering it tasted like bloody chicken liver. Immediately he made a "blah" sound and started wiping his tongue on his shirt.

Lucky sighed. This trip had been a disaster. He loathed fishing, just as she had loathed golf when he'd tried to teach her how to play.

They were total opposites. She was a morning person. He was a night person. She liked life to be casual and rustic. He planned his day to the hour and was happier in a suit than jeans.

"You'd better cover up," she told him. "You're getting pink." God knows she didn't want him to blister on top of everything else.

He pulled his shirt on over his head and adjusted his baseball cap to shade his nose. "How long does this usually take?"

"Depends on the weather, the water temperature, if the fish are hungry or not..."

"We've been out here for over an hour and I haven't caught anything. They're eating all my bait."

"That's how it goes. Sometimes you can stay out all day and not even get a bite."

He didn't respond but made a low growl in his throat that said he'd rather pick up snakes than fish all day.

After another hour had passed, he was definitely

getting antsy, shifting on the boat cushion, making unnecessary noise. When he stuck himself with the hook for the third time, she knew it was time to quit. Some things weren't meant to be.

She put her hand on her spine and stretched. "Ow, my back's starting to get stiff. I think I'm going to have to call it a day. Is that okay with you?"

"Yeah, that's fine," he said, perking up. He quickly brought in his rod.

"Before we go to the house, I want to show you something."

She brought in her own rod and closed her tackle box. Cranking the motor, she zoomed out and headed downriver, with Jack facing her on the front seat.

The Forks were only a few miles away, but she doubted Jack had ever seen where the Mulberry, the branch of the Black Warrior they lived on, flowed into the main river. You needed to be in a boat to really see it.

They met a string of barges three abreast. When Lucky passed the towboat at the rear, she waved and the pilot blew his big horn in response. "Hold on," she yelled over the wind, and angled the boat into the waves. They bounced hard a couple of times and water splashed up.

Jack mouthed an expletive, but Lucky loved getting sprayed.

When they reached their destination, she slowed, pulled to one side and cut the engine. The main channel of the river stretched out ahead of them.

"What do you think of my river? Isn't he wonderful?"

Jack grunted something noncommittal.

"He's bold and courageous like his namesake,

Chief Tuscaloosa," she went on. "Tuscaloosa defeated DeSoto when the Spaniards explored the southern part of the U.S. in 1540, but the soldiers later killed him."

"Did that battle happen around here?"

"No, much farther south. That's a whole different group of Indians than the ones we had in this area, but that's where we get our latest name for the river. *Taska* means warrior and *luce* means black. Taskaluse, or Tuscaloosa as it's spelled today, translates into 'black warrior.' The river's had ten or more names over the centuries."

"Do people find many Indian artifacts hereabouts?"

"A good many. Flint points. Ax and grinding stones. I've run across everything over the years, and people sometimes call me to look at artifacts they've found in their fields, since I know a bit about them. I uncovered a strange little effigy pot shaped like a woman when I dug a hole for that azalea bush out on the other side of the drive."

"What did you do with it?"

"Gave it to the university for the museum. I pass along anything like that, anything major I find. It's not illegal to keep artifacts if you find them on private land, but it doesn't seem right to hang on to them. At least when they're at the museum, other people get to see and enjoy them. And they can't be studied if they're sitting in a glass case in someone's living room."

"Ever think about selling what you find?"

"Selling history? Never. People do it, but I think it's wrong."

"No argument from me."

"Both the early and the modern Indians used the river extensively, so there are mounds and remnants of villages along it. Down the river in the central part of the state is a place called Moundville, where they've excavated a three-hundred-acre settlement from the Mississippian culture, which reaches back to A.D. 1000. It has something like forty mounds."

"Sounds interesting."

"Oh, it is. I'd like to show it to you sometime."

"Any mounds around here?"

"A few small ones, but nothing on that scale. Most of the things that turn up are from later tribes, the Creek and the Choctaw. Some people believe there was a town here at the forks that both those nations inhabited at different times, but others place it elsewhere."

"You're really up on all this stuff."

"I'm fascinated by it, so I've read a lot. Holding a pot or a flint point that was made hundreds of years ago—I can't describe how that feels. I guess that's why people want to own them."

"Got any books I could read?"

"You'd like to know more?"

"Yeah, I would."

Pleased, Lucky told him she had books, photographs and articles back at the cabin and she'd dig them out when they got home. "This is great! Whew! I have to tell you I'm relieved."

"Relieved?"

"Because we finally found something we both like. I was beginning to think we were hopelessly mismatched. We *never* like the same things, not even the same food. But now you don't have to suffer through fishing anymore, and I don't have to try and hit that stupid golf ball. Jeez, I detest golf. We can explore our common interest in Indian culture together.'' She smiled widely.

He didn't smile back. "Well, hell," he said, blowing out a breath.

"What's wrong?"

He hemmed and hawed for a minute before admitting the truth. Personal interest wasn't his reason for asking. He needed the information for a theft case Deaton was working on. "I should've told you that up front. Sorry."

"No, that's okay. I'm the one who jumped to conclusions."

"So you really detest golf?"

She winced. "*Detest* is such a strong word. I'm sure there are parts of the game I haven't caught on to yet, and when I do, I'll probably…uh…" He was already amused at her bullshit. He was grinning, and she could barely keep a straight face.

"You'll probably what?" he asked, laughing.

"*Really, really* detest it," she admitted, bursting into laughter.

"Don't feel bad, because I *really, really* hate fishing."

"I bet I hate golf more than you hate fishing."

"No way in hell."

They teased each other about it all the way home. Helping her out of the boat at the pier, he commented that their good-natured bickering proved they obviously agreed on one thing.

"What one thing is that?" Lucky asked. "I'd sure like to know."

"That we're always going to disagree."

JACK HAD TO ADMIT that what Lucky showed him that night was pretty interesting. She had a wealth of knowledge. But he was enjoying the teacher much more than the lesson.

"And here are some of the things people find," she said, leaning over to point to a photograph. He was at the desk he'd set up in the storage room. Lucky sat on the corner, her bare legs dangling.

He tried to keep his gaze on the book in front of him rather than the gaping neckline of the loose, short nightgown, but it was impossible.

She flipped the page. "See here? They worked shell and bone into tools and ornaments. You can tell a lot about the age by how they were decorated."

"Ah."

"A coiled rope used to press a design suggests one era. Shape is a clue, too. Remember how the bowls I showed you before looked more like cylinders? Here they have flared— Are you paying attention?"

"Uh-huh."

"No, you're not." She straightened and put her hands on her hips. "You're looking at my chest again."

"I can't help it. I'm not used to you having so much up top. It's distracting."

"You're turning into a pervert. I can't talk to you without you touching me or looking down my shirt."

"So satisfy my perversion and let me play with them." He glanced to the floor on either side of him. "Where's Beanie?"

"Still outside."

"Perfect. She wouldn't like it if she saw what I'm about to do to you."

"Something naughty, no doubt."

"Something very naughty."

He pushed back his chair, pulled her forward to her feet and made her straddle his lap. She didn't resist and rested her arms on his shoulders. "I thought you wanted to learn about pots and things."

"I do." The nightgown came only to her knees, allowing him to run his hands up her shapely thighs to her bottom. No panties. Arousal flooded him. He gathered the gown and pulled it over her head, then put a hand on each breast. "Mmm, these little babies sure have gotten big."

"Why are you working this case if it's supposed to be Deaton's?"

"It's not really even Deaton's."

Her nipples had grown larger from the pregnancy, and he rubbed one tip and then the other, smiling as they hardened.

"Who's is it?"

"Conservation is doing most of the legwork. We're assisting only, looking out for anything that might help. I thought I'd lend a hand."

He punctuated his remark by giving her left breast a gentle squeeze. Her hands had started to move over him, caressing his shoulders, stroking his hair and neck. She kissed his forehead, then down his cheek to his lips. She'd eaten a banana Popsicle a little while ago, and the pleasant taste of it lingered on her breath.

"Deaton should talk to Paul Hightower, the head ranger," she suggested. "If people are digging on federal land, he might know something."

"Deaton talked to Hightower weeks ago. He claims not to have any knowledge of people digging out there."

"I'm sure that's possible. The area is huge.

Thousands of acres. Only a few logging roads have been cut through it.''

Bending down, he angled one breast toward his mouth and lightly sucked. She arched to give him better access, burying her hands in his hair.

"Do you know Hightower?'' he asked, then gently sucked the other breast. Their ongoing discussion made this the strangest foreplay he'd ever engaged in.

"Never met...mmm, that feels good. I didn't know who he was until recently. Shannon pointed him out to me at Mr. Bagwell's visitation, and he was at the funeral.'' She gasped. "Oh, jeez, could Mr. Bagwell have had anything to do with the artifact thefts? Maybe stolen pots are what he had in his shed!''

Jack held a similar suspicion, but he had no evidence. "That's something I'm looking into.''

She took his hand and guided it between her legs. "Oh, yeah,'' she moaned. "Touch me right there.''

"Yes, ma'am. Whatever you say.''

"If Mr. Bagwell was digging artifacts on federal land, maybe Hightower was in on it and they had a falling-out. They argued on the phone and that's the conversation Carolyn overheard. Hightower could've gotten mad and thrown Mr. Bagwell in front of the train.''

"A good theory, but Hightower and his wife were in Atlanta visiting his mother when Bagwell died, and at least fifteen people at the nursing home and at the motel will vouch for his whereabouts. He didn't kill Charlie Bagwell.''

"Well, shoot, I thought I'd solved the case.''

"Bagwell wasn't *thrown* in front of the train, either.''

"But you suspect somebody killed him, don't you?

That's why you asked me those questions about the railroad grade.''

"Mm, maybe.''

"And you destroyed my pork roast the other night with stun guns because you think one was used on Mr. Bagwell.''

"Possibly.'' Frustrated by the delay in the report from DFS, Jack had bought several of the guns himself to test the width of the prongs and the marks they left on skin. The raw pork roast had provided the perfect "victim.''

Holding Lucky with one arm around the waist, he eased up and pulled down his boxers, slipping inside her as he brought her bottom back down to his lap. She was wet and tight, and enveloped him to the hilt. When she gripped him with her muscles, he had to concentrate hard to keep control.

"Oh, baby, don't do that.''

She grinned. "I have you at my mercy.''

"Absolutely.''

"Then tell me how this ties in to the death of Miss Eileen. Was he her lover?''

Bagwell, she meant. "I don't know if any of it ties in, and no, I don't think he was her lover.''

"Who was?'' When he hesitated, she squeezed him a little tighter. "Tell me!''

"I'm going to lose it if you don't quit that.''

"Then tell me. And what's that mysterious box you got from Dad? I saw it in the back of the Blazer.''

He figured she had. They'd taken her truck to her parents', and without a trunk it was difficult to conceal anything.

"The box has files in it. Since your dad's written stories about both the Olenick case and artifact theft,

I thought his clippings might help me. Nothing mysterious about it.''

Careful of her stomach, he put his hands on her waist and they rocked forward and back, forward and back, in a nice, easy rhythm, but being on top put her in control.

"That feels incredible." Her voice softened until it was nearly a purr. She nipped at his earlobe with her teeth, sending desire rippling out through every nerve ending. "So if Mr. Bagwell wasn't having an affair with Miss Eileen, do you still think Terrell was her killer? His aunt, Leona Harrison, has always insisted that he *witnessed* the murder, not committed it."

"It's probably going to turn out like most of the town believes, that he came upon her in the woods that morning while she was looking for something to stick on her hat for church, got too friendly and either purposely or accidentally killed her."

"No, that's wrong. She'd already decorated her hat."

He barely heard her answer. The pressure inside him was building, reaching an explosive level. He gripped a little harder, and she increased their rhythm.

The chair skidded a couple of inches across the floor. "Whoa, Trigger," she said with a giggle.

"Want to move to the bed?"

"No, I love this. I feel so powerful."

She used that power to bring him close to climax more than once, easing back each time. When he finally tumbled over the edge, she went spiraling with him.

Afterward she collapsed on his shoulder and groaned. "My heart feels like it's going to explode. Am I heavy?"

"Feels like I have a ton of bricks sitting in my lap." She bit him on the shoulder. "Ouch! No, seriously, the cane bottom of this chair is killing me. I've got to get up."

Lucky laughed when they reached the bathroom and she looked at his skin. "You're branded. You've got perfect little circles and X's all over your butt."

She ran a bath in the old clawfoot tub and he climbed in facing her. He bent forward and let her wet his hair and work shampoo into it. "What were you saying before about Eileen Olenick's hat already being decorated?"

"At church, the Sunday before, it was covered in petroglyphs, but *that* Sunday, the day she disappeared, she'd decorated it all in white—lace, ribbons and wedding bells pinned to the side. I remember looking at the photograph of the hat in the newspaper when they took Terrell in for questioning and wondering why she'd picked a wedding theme."

"What are petroglyphs?"

"Aboriginal art. We have a lot of it on caves and rocks. I've seen some on the bluff on the other side of the river. The indigenous people used symbols that had meaning to them, like on a few of the pots I showed you—concentric circles, spirals, crosses, birds. On the rocks they also put handprints and footprints. Your buddy the snake was very popular, too."

Indians again. He frowned, wondering if this was another piece of the ever-widening puzzle or simple coincidence. Could a disappearance that took place twenty-one years ago have anything to do with the events of the past two months?

"Is this important?" Lucky asked. "You're concentrating so hard your forehead looks like a plowed field. Tell me what you're thinking.''

He put a blob of shampoo on the end of her nose. ''You've been a big help to me tonight. I appreciate it.''

''I hear a *but* coming.''

''But...that's all you're getting out of me. I don't want you involved in this. If Terrell *did* kill Eileen Olenick, he's dangerous. I want you as far away from him as possible.''

''But what if he didn't, Jack? That's what worries me.''

''It worries me, too, because if he didn't, the problem's even worse. Somebody got away with murder. And he's still out there.''

CHAPTER TEN

THE HOT DAYS of summer passed, and the trees along the river began to dress themselves in the reds and yellows of autumn. From time to time Lucky asked Jack if there were any new developments in Mr. Bagwell's case, but he remained tight-lipped. All he would say was that *officially* he'd closed his investigation.

Unofficially she hoped he continued to search for answers, because the suspicious part of her brain was hard at work. She found herself looking at everyone around her in a different way.

Who had reason to kill Miss Eileen if it wasn't Terrell Wade? That nice Mr. Turner down at the drugstore? The man at the produce stand who always picked out the best tomatoes for her?

She started feeling she was being watched. Crazy. Still, she couldn't shake the sensation. Not that she ever really *saw* anyone. Well, once she thought she had while shopping at the mall, a reflection in a window that was there one minute, but gone by the time she turned around.

One night, while she and Jack were sitting on the porch, she'd felt a prickling at the back of her neck. The hair had risen on her arms. She'd stood, opened the screen door on the side by the driveway and stared into the dark woods, certain someone was out there.

"What's wrong?" Jack had asked.

When she'd told him, he'd gotten a flashlight and he and Beanie had looked around, but hadn't found anything. A few minutes later she'd thought she heard a car engine crank in the distance, but the more she ruminated about it, the more unsure she felt.

"I guess I'm spooking myself," she'd said, apologizing. "Once you reminded me that Miss Eileen's killer might still be around, I started worrying it was somebody I pass every day on the street—or even somebody I know. He might even work at the *Register.*"

"Damn, I should know better than to talk to you about my cases. Your imagination starts working overtime."

The uneasiness stayed with her. For the first time she regretted the isolation of the cabin. She began locking the door the minute she came in, something she'd never done before. At work she jumped when people spoke. Cal commented on it one day.

"What's wrong with you? Lately you're like a rabbit in a pen full of beagles."

She had negatives on the light box in the darkroom, and she leaned down to peer at them through her magnifying eyepiece. "Nothing's wrong. Can I help you?"

"No, I just thought I'd check and see how the new guy's working out."

"He's been a godsend."

Leigh had hired someone to assist with the processing and photography assignments. The arrangement was good for Lucky, because he was a college student who preferred to work nights so he could attend class in the mornings at Birmingham-Southern College in nearby Birmingham.

"Leigh was worried you might fight it."

"Not me. I'm too pooped to fight anybody these days. I'm thankful to go home at a reasonable hour." Now in her seventh month, she'd gained nearly twenty-five pounds, and her back bothered her all the time. Booger was probably going to be a soccer player, too, as hard as he kicked. Or she.

"Leigh was looking for you earlier, by the way."

"I've been in here all morning. Did she say what she wanted?"

"I didn't ask. How's the house-hunting going?"

"Slowly." She explained that they'd looked at houses nearly every Sunday afternoon for weeks, but she hadn't seen any she really liked. "Jack hasn't said anything, but I get the feeling he doesn't think I'm trying hard enough."

"Are you?"

"I think I am. I *want* to find a place and make him happy, but it's also a major decision, and if I settle for a house I don't like, that won't be a step forward. Has he said anything to you?"

"I've hardly seen him, he's been working so much. Although we did play a quick nine holes last week on his day off. I miss not having him come over to watch baseball."

"He's really been putting in the hours. He brings work home, too."

"Maybe you should *build* a house. Buy land and have an architect design exactly what you want. That would take more time, but in the long run you'll probably be happier."

"Not a bad idea, big brother. I'll suggest it. I don't

think I'm up to moving anyway, until after the baby's born. I can hardly get around now, and I've got eight weeks left." She put her hand on her aching back and straightened.

"Back hurting again?" Cal asked.

"A little. If I go for a walk at midmorning, it seems to help, but I didn't have a chance today. Last night I got down to do my exercises, and Jack had to hoist me up. I couldn't get off the floor."

He laughed. "He's really getting excited about your delivery. When we played golf, it was all he talked about."

"Don't remind me. He's driving my doctor nuts. I finally told him he couldn't come to any more of my checkups. He asks a thousand questions and gets mad if I have to wait more than ten minutes. He bullies the nurses."

"Better than him *not* being excited, isn't it?"

"Of course, but he's really going overboard. I feel like I'm living with a prison guard. He doesn't like me to eat any sweets, even though the doctor said it was okay within reason. He watches me exercise and writes down how many pelvic tilts I do, making me increase them every few days. Did he tell you he's bought this elaborate video camera to record the delivery?"

"He mentioned it a couple thousand times."

"The last thing I want when I'm in labor is him with a camera. He's already showed that grainy black-and-white ultrasound photo of the baby all over town, even to people he hardly knows. Imagine what fun he'd have with a video of the birth."

Cal got a good chuckle out of that.

She stretched again and winced.

"How about we walk down to Turner's and get a lemonade?" he suggested. "We haven't done that in a long time, and it might help your back."

"That sounds wonderful. And I can pick up Jack's shirts on the way." She clipped the negatives she wanted the new guy to process that night and slung her camera over her shoulder.

"Do you need that?"

"Where I go, it goes."

TURNER'S DRUGSTORE had been on the corner as long as Lucky could remember and still looked much as it had when she was a kid. Mr. Turner still filled prescriptions in the pharmacy. Mr. Byrd, who liked to be called simply "Byrd," still hand-squeezed the lemonade and made the sandwiches and homemade soups at the lunch counter.

Cal ordered two lemonades, a piece of pecan pie to share with Lucky and a second piece wrapped to take back for Leigh. They'd stopped by her office to invite her, but she hadn't been there. Lucky found them a booth next to the window.

"Don't you dare tell Jack I ate this," she said, sticking her fork in the pie for a bite.

"I don't need to be eating it, either. Pretty soon my waistline is going to look as bad as yours. No offense."

"None taken." She looked around. "This old place never seems to change. Do you think Byrd will ever retire?"

"Probably not. He'll die squeezing lemonade. Remember how we used to beg to visit Dad at the paper after school, but it was really because we wanted to sneak off down here and talk to Byrd?"

Lucky smiled. "I remember you also wanted to peek at the men's magazines, until Mr. Turner got wise and put them behind the counter."

"How else was I supposed to learn about women?"

Sometimes she wondered if he ever *had* learned about women. He had such horrible taste in them. As attractive and intelligent as he was, surely he could find some nice woman his own age to date. Someone with class. The last two or three had dressed and talked like hookers.

But that was Cal's business, and she'd always tried not to meddle in it.

They spent a pleasant and relaxing thirty minutes eating pie and talking about the fun they'd had at the drugstore as teenagers. "You're right—we haven't done this in a long time," Lucky told him, gazing out the window at the people passing on the street. "Maybe we should do it more often."

"Things have been pretty hectic for both of us."

"That's true." A man she'd noticed earlier as they came out of the *Register* was now across the street, smoking a cigarette. His red plaid shirt had caught her attention. Out of habit, she looked through the viewfinder at him, but she had her standard lens on and he was too far away. She stood and pressed the lens to the window to reduce the glare and took a couple of shots.

"What are you doing?"

"Messing around." She sat down again and put the camera aside. "You've really done a great job getting the paper back on its feet, Cal. Leigh says the money we saved on overtime from computerizing production has already paid for the equipment. I don't know what we'd do without you.''

"I enjoy it, and I like seeing us make a profit for a change. How about you? Do you think you'll come back to work after the baby's born?''

"Of course I will. I love taking photos. You know that.''

"Sure, but I also know Jack's been bugging you about setting up your own business so he won't have to worry about you.''

"He's only mentioned it once since he moved back in. Besides, I've stayed out of trouble lately. I haven't found a body in months.'' Superstitious, she knocked on the wooden sill.

"What about that ruckus at the convenience store a few weeks ago? You don't call *that* trouble?''

"I went in to buy a pack of gum.''

"Yeah, and ended up in the middle of a robbery.''

"*And* getting photographs of the robber. That's why I always carry this little sweetie.'' She patted her camera. "You never know what's going to happen.''

"Jack worries. I worry. You do seem to get yourself in bad situations. Hell, Lucky, you *chased* the guy. That was pretty stupid.''

She glanced across the street. The man smoking the cigarette had moved off, so she relaxed.

"I was in no danger. I promise you. He had a tiny little penknife and didn't weigh one-twenty. He was scared to death. The whole thing was funny more than anything. I ran after him and he was sprawled on the pavement, out cold. Must've slipped and hit his head.''

"But he could just as easily have been a two-hundred-pound thug with a gun who turned around and shot you. Have you thought about that?''

"Now you're sounding like Jack. He thinks a studio will keep me safe.''

"Actually it's not a bad idea from a financial, as well as a safety, standpoint. Local people have nowhere to go to get portraits taken except when that guy comes to the mall a couple of times a year. You could make some really good money.''

"Taking photographs of babies all day? No, thank you. I like getting outside. I like being in the middle of what's going on—not robberies. And the *Register* needs me. Don't you?''

"Sure we do. But I've come up with an idea, a way to help you out, bring something new to the community and also make a profit for the newspaper.''

"How?''

He outlined his plan. Renovate the upstairs area in the *Register* they weren't using and turn it into a portrait studio. Expand the darkroom to better handle color processing and let Lucky manage the complex.

"You could hire another photographer or two to take the portraits if you don't want to fool with those, and we could contract with your business to provide photos for the paper. You'd be doing some of what you do now.''

"Then what's the advantage of your plan?''

"You'd have a staff. You could give them the late-night assignments and stop chasing ambulances and fire trucks. You'd be in charge.''

"Could I still do assignments?''

"If it makes you happy. But I'd suggest you take the feature work and give the rough stuff to someone else.''

"A man, you mean. Shame on you, Cal."

"Sis, you know I'm not sexist. I think that creatively you're as talented as anyone out there, man or woman. But like I said, sometimes you put yourself in places and situations that are inherently more dangerous for a woman. You can be a great photographer without risking injury, can't you?"

"I'm careful."

"I know you *think* you are. All I'm saying is this could be a good option for you and for us."

"I still don't see what the advantage is to the *Register*."

"We'd be utilizing that space, bringing in new revenue and sharing staff. I'm thinking we might also create a day care for our employees and extend it to the children of people who work downtown. We could include it as part of the complex."

"I love that idea, but what about an entrance? You couldn't expect people to go in the front door of the *Register* and up those stairs, especially older people and the handicapped."

"We could open up the entrance on the side that's closed off and have a lobby area on the main floor." He drew a sketch on his napkin. "We can put the service elevator back into use and locate the day care right here in this big space on the main floor. We'd add a separate door so parents can pull up off the street and load and unload."

"You'd need a kitchen."

"True, but we already have bathrooms, so that eliminates one major expense. And we have plumbing on the other side of this wall—" he pointed to it on his sketch "—so putting in a kitchen won't take much."

"What about a play area? Kids need swings and sunshine and a safe place to run around."

"We'll buy that empty lot across the back alley. I've already done a little digging, and we can get it at a fair price. It's plenty big enough, and with fencing and grass, it'll be ideal. The kids can walk right out the back door into the playground."

"You've given this a lot of thought."

"I've been working on the plan ever since you told me you were pregnant."

She sat back in the booth. "Cal, I have to admit I like the idea the way you've presented it, but I wouldn't want you doing this only for me. You're talking about a huge commitment of company money."

"Sis, it's not only for you. The space has been sitting empty for years and should be rented, but renting to an outsider opens up problems I'd rather not deal with. Sure, it's a big investment of cash, but the return would be good. I've researched the market and run the numbers. The profit's right there, ready to be plucked. You've got the know-how to run the studio and the darkroom, and we can hire an experienced manager for the day care. Will you consider it?"

"Yes, I will."

They talked about it more as they crossed the street and walked to the cleaners in the middle of the next block. "You haven't discussed any of this with Jack, have you?"

"No."

"Good, because I want to think about it without him pressuring me."

"I understand. This will stay between us, although

I've outlined the idea to Leigh, so you'd better tell her not to spill the beans.''

"How does she feel about it?''

"She was hesitant at first because of the expense, but after I showed her the figures and a rendering of what it could look like, she really went for the idea.''

"I'd like to see that rendering.''

"I'll show it to you when we get back.''

At the cleaners both the female clerk and Joe Tagliotti were at the counter. Lucky took advantage of the opportunity. She handed the woman her ticket, but it was to Tagliotti she spoke. "Hello, Mr. Tagliotti. Good to see you again.''

He nodded and smiled, but clearly didn't know her.

"Wasn't it a tragic thing about Mr. Bagwell?''

"Yes,'' he said, his eyes narrowing. He spoke with a thick accent. Italian. Greek maybe. She couldn't tell. "Tragic. I'm sorry, your name is…?''

"Oh, Lucky Cahill. I'm the one who found Mr. Bagwell.''

"Yes, from the newspaper. I read the story.''

"This is my brother, Cal Mathison. He also works for the paper. You and I don't know each other, but I saw you at the funeral and wondered if you and Mr. Bagwell were friends.''

"Acquaintances is all. He coached my son.''

"I see. He seemed like a very nice man.''

"Yes, I'm sure he was.'' Joe Tagliotti didn't sound as though he really thought so.

"There were rumors you and he got into an altercation. I wondered if there were any hard feelings resulting from that.''

He stiffened. "Are you asking this for some kind of article?''

"No, just curiosity."

"Then excuse me. I've already been questioned by the police and I don't have time for silly gossip." Turning, he strode to the back of the store.

"Well, that was absolutely no help," she said under her breath, feeling foolish.

"What the hell was that all about?" Cal asked. "I've never known you to be so rude."

"I was trying to extract information. Sometimes you have to be blunt."

"Information for what?"

"Don't ask."

The woman returned and Lucky paid her bill. When she stepped out the door, she saw the same man who'd been at the drugstore now loitering across the street. He tossed down his cigarette and started to walk away.

"He *is* following us," she said to Cal, and then shouted to the man, "Hey, you!"

By the time she'd waddled across the street, he had turned the corner and vanished. She looked in through several storefront windows, thinking he might have ducked inside. She saw no sign of him. Maybe he'd cut down the alley.

Cal had arrived and he grabbed her arm. "What are you *doing?*"

"Did you see the man in the plaid shirt? He's been following me."

"I didn't see anybody. Why would anybody be following you?"

"Because…" She couldn't think of a single reason. "I don't know why, but he is. At least, I think he is. I saw him outside the paper and then the drugstore, and he was watching us while we were in the cleaners."

They started back toward the office, Lucky peering in every doorway and window.

"You've lost it, little sister. There wasn't any man."

"He was there. I saw him. And I can prove it." She smiled and pointed at her camera. "I got his picture."

BACK AT THE OFFICE Lucky developed her film, but was disappointed it didn't show more. There *was* a man, but even after she'd blown up the negative as much as she could, his features remained indistinguishable. The print was grainy. Shooting through the window without a filter hadn't helped the clarity, either.

She put the print on the dryer, anyway. If nothing else, it was proof that she'd seen someone.

Leigh was in her office when she went downstairs to show it to Cal, and she popped in there a minute first. "Cal said you were looking for me earlier. What's up?"

"Close the door."

Lucky closed it and sat down. Leigh wasn't smiling, but with Leigh that was pretty normal. "Am I in trouble?"

"I have something you need to see." She pulled an envelope from her desk drawer and handed it to her. "I called a friend from college who works for a newspaper in Mississippi. As a professional courtesy, he looked this up for me. No John Thomas Cahill was born in Biloxi on March 10, 1967."

Lucky stiffened. "Then your friend made a mistake. He didn't look in the right place."

"No, Lucky, it's not a mistake. He checked two years before and two years after that date and still found nothing. No John Thomas Cahill was born in Biloxi, period. Jack's lying to you."

Lucky took the printout from the envelope and read it. Listed was a John Thomas Parsons born on that date, the son of Ella and Walter Parsons, and a John Thomas Webster, son of Raymond and Grace Webster.

"I must've misunderstood him when he said he was born in Biloxi."

"Biloxi isn't a name you'd misunderstand. Go to him and confront him. Ask him why he lied. Ask him why his past is such a mystery."

Overwhelmed with hurt and anger, she shook her head. "And have him know what you've done? Why *did* you do this, Leigh?"

"Because I love you."

"Love me?" She stood, but her legs felt weak, and it was all she could do not to burst into tears. "You don't love me. You're so eaten up with anger about Keith's deception that you don't want anyone else to be happy, even your own sister."

"That's not true."

"My God, I can't believe you could be so uncaring. When I think of all those nights I sat with you after Keith left, when I cried with you… Is *this* how you pay me back? Well, I've had it with all your caustic remarks and whispered suspicions. I will *not* allow you to undermine my relationship with my husband."

"Lucky, I didn't do this to hurt you. Look at the paper. The truth is right there in black—"

"Don't." She hit the desk with her fist. "No more. I don't want to hear it. And I swear if you say anything about this to Jack—or anyone else—you and I are finished. I'll never, ever speak to you again."

LUCKY WANTED to leave work, but she had too much to do and she didn't want to give Leigh the satisfaction of knowing how much she'd upset her. She hid in the darkroom, crying. Jack showed up at three, beating on the locked door, wanting to know if she was okay.

"Cal called and told me. Let me in."

She opened the door. "Cal told you?"

"Yeah, he said you went nuts chasing some guy you thought was following you."

"Oh." Thank goodness. For a moment she was afraid Cal had overheard her fight with Leigh. "I'm okay now."

"Then why are you in here crying?"

"I guess it scared me a little bit."

He held her. "Sweetheart, you've got to curb your imagination. You're not helping yourself or the baby."

"But there *was* a man." She showed him the photograph. "It's not very good, but see?"

He looked at it and frowned. "So some man was standing on the sidewalk. That doesn't mean he was following you."

Obviously, like her brother, he thought she was a hysterical pregnant female.

"I'm sorry Cal bothered you about this."

"No, I'm glad he did. I needed to know." He tilted

her chin up and smiled tentatively. "Hey, call my cell phone if you suspect anyone's following you, no matter how silly you think you're being. Okay?"

"You'll answer?"

"I promise that whenever that phone rings, no matter what I'm doing, I'll pick it up. Will you call me?" She nodded, feeling better. "That's my girl. Now, I've got to get back to work. Are you going to be okay?"

"Yes. Don't worry about me."

He kissed her on the forehead. "I love you."

"I love you, too."

He started to walk out. "Jack…a lady came in today to buy some copies of a photo I took of her grandson, and she'd just moved here from Mississippi. I was telling her I'd married a man from Mississippi. Um…where did you say you were born?"

"Biloxi."

"That's what I thought."

CHAPTER ELEVEN

"YOU'RE THE ONE who suggested this," Jack said to Lucky, helping her back into the Blazer. "If it's not what you want to do, we won't do it, but the architect can't start on plans for the house until you make up your mind about the land."

He came around and got in the driver's side. They'd checked out at least ten pieces of property over the past two weeks, any one of which would have been fine, but she'd found fault with all of them, as she'd found fault with every house they'd looked at.

"I'm sorry, but it isn't right. Too hilly."

"Baby, it *has* to be high not to flood."

"I realize that, but I don't want to have to be a mountain climber to get to the house from the river."

"This piece has no more slope to it than your property."

"Then why buy it? We may as well stay where we are."

"Because it doesn't run solely along the water like your place does. We can build up here by the road and stay dry."

"And have to hike when I want to fish? No, thank you."

"You're being unreasonable."

"I am not. I'm being practical."

"I like this place. I want to call the agent back and tell her we'll take it."

"Jack, you promised me we'd make this decision together, and here you are up to your old tricks again, trying to dictate what we're going to do. You go right ahead and call the agent if you want to, but you can live here alone."

He sighed and started the engine. "All right, we'll find something else." He was beginning to wonder if she'd ever see anything she liked. He'd prepared himself for a long search, but not this long. Thanksgiving was around the corner, the baby was due in six weeks, and they were still quibbling over where to live.

"I'm cold," she said, so he punched up the heater. "My back's hurting, too. Can we just go home?"

"Sure." He tried to keep the disappointment out of his voice. Two other pieces of land were listed that he'd hoped to look at this afternoon. Now it would be next weekend before they could see them.

Back at the cabin, her mother had left a message on the answering machine. She wanted to know if they'd changed their minds about not coming for Thanksgiving dinner.

He let Beanie out, then asked Lucky what she wanted to do.

"I'd like to stay here." She went to the sink and took a couple of Tylenol. The doctor had said acetaminophen was safe after her first trimester, but she only took it when nothing else would ease her back pain.

"You want to stay here or you don't want to go over there?"

"It's the same thing."

"No, it's not. Are you feuding with Leigh over

something? Is that why you don't want to go to your parents' for the holiday? Cal says you two hardly speak at work.''

"Cal should learn to mind his own damn business. I'm getting tired of him running and tattling to you all the time.''

The outburst was uncharacteristic. She adored Cal.

"He didn't *tattle*, Lucky. He casually mentioned it. *Are* you fighting with Leigh about something?''

"No, she hardly crosses my mind.''

Well, that told him what he wanted to know. No wonder she'd been in such a foul mood lately.

He offered to heat some soup for her, but she said she wasn't hungry. Even hot chocolate didn't tempt her, which wasn't normal. Given permission by the doctor to overeat, she usually did.

She went to the bathroom for what had to be the fiftieth time since sunrise. How any human could pee that often in one day, he couldn't comprehend.

She came out grumbling, holding her back again.

"Want a back rub?''

"Would you? I'll give you a million dollars.''

"I'll rather have a smile.''

She gave him a joyless one. "I've been a grump today, haven't I.''

"Not too bad.''

"I'm sorry. I'm fat and ugly and ill-tempered.''

"You're not ugly.''

"Oh, just fat and ill-tempered?''

"Well...yeah.''

She hadn't expected that and she smiled for real this time. "I ought to punch you.''

"Never hit your masseur. Come on. Lie down.'' He helped her sit on the couch, then sat himself, easing her down to rest her head on his thigh. "How's that? Comfortable?"

"Pretty good. I'm sorry for what I said about you being dictatorial."

"No, you were right. I was. I'm anxious to get started on the house."

"I know you are, and I'm sorry to be so picky, but I'm determined to find the perfect place for us, somewhere that gives us both what we want. Can you understand that?"

"Yeah, I can." He pulled up her sweatshirt and rubbed the muscles of her lower back. "We're running out of time, though."

"I know. But we can manage here for a few more months, can't we?"

"I guess we'll have to. Do you want me to put the crib up tonight or wait until you're feeling better so you can supervise?"

They planned to turn their bedroom into a nursery, the only viable option. A bassinet and their bed wouldn't both fit in there, and they wanted the baby close by them at night.

They'd stored their bed at a rented locker in town and were sleeping on the extra one in the living room. The crib would go in the now-empty room for use when the baby was old enough to be separated from them at night.

"Go ahead and put up the crib," Lucky told him. "I'll never feel better."

"I doubt that's true."

"Easy for you to say. You don't have someone kicking your spine and bladder twenty-four hours a day."

"Booger's moving around because he's healthy."

"Yes, thank God for that." She gave her stomach a loving pat. "But Booger's a *she*. I have a feeling."

"Should I change the yellow paint to pink?"

Before she could answer, the phone rang. He started to reach for it, but Lucky said to let the machine pick up because she was too comfortable to move. Her mother left another message to call.

"You need to get back to her tonight. She sounds upset."

"I'll call her before I go to bed."

"Are you sure you don't want to have Thanksgiving dinner there? You've always gone. We had a good time last year."

"I'd rather we celebrated here, alone, just us. We have to start some traditions for *this* family, don't we?"

"Sure, but it doesn't mean we have to exclude the one you already have. If Leigh said something to hurt your feelings, I'd hate to have it ruin everybody else's holiday. Ignore her."

"She can be so hateful sometimes."

"Want to tell me what you fought about?"

"No. Just be thankful you never had any sisters."

"Yeah, I am," he said, but the words held no conviction.

That night, after he'd assembled the crib and Lucky had gone to sleep, he sat for a while at his desk, but couldn't keep his mind on work. He opened a carton containing his books and dug to the bottom for the cigar box containing the only mementoes he'd saved from his childhood.

He pulled out two crinkled photographs. The first was of his mother, and he rubbed his fingers across her face, wishing he could touch it in reality. As he'd told Lucky, she'd been a good woman, but she'd died broken and unhappy.

The other photograph made his eyes tear up. His big sister had been twelve, all legs and teeth with a promise of beauty to come.

"What happened to you, Emma?" he whispered to the image.

He prayed to God that one day he'd know.

LUCKY'S SITUATION with Leigh remained tense. They spoke for business reasons only and avoided each other whenever they could. If Leigh was sorry, she never expressed it, and Lucky couldn't forgive her for what she'd done.

On Wednesday afternoon the next week, Lucky had her doctor's appointment after lunch and took the rest of the afternoon off. Her checkup went well. She felt energetic for a change. After washing two loads of clothes at the downtown laundry, she walked to the produce market on the next block.

While picking out a few fresh apples, she felt the hair rise on her arms.

She leaned over the display and pretended to choose, but glanced covertly in the security mirror, instead. The man she'd chased outside the cleaners was watching her from behind a table of pumpkins.

Ambling along, she added a winter squash to the basket she carried and headed over to see if there were any bananas. The man hung back, and as she rounded a tall produce case, she used the few seconds he couldn't see her to grab her phone. Jack's number was on speed dial. He picked up immediately.

"I'm at the produce market and being followed by a man in a navy windbreaker and dark gray pants."

"Where are you parked?" She told him. "Here's what I want you to do…"

Lucky continued to shop, leisurely, giving Jack enough time to get into position. She bought the apples and squash, as well as a small bouquet of flowers, then walked back in the direction of her car, stopping now and then to window-shop.

The alley where Jack had said he'd be waiting was next to the greeting-card shop, but Lucky didn't glance in as she passed. Only when she heard the scuffle did she turn. Jack had the man pinned to the wall of the building, his face pressed to the brick and his right arm behind him. Lucky hurried back.

"See?" she said. "I wasn't crazy. He's the same one who followed me and Cal."

"I'm Captain Cahill of the Potock Police Department." Jack ordered him to put his left hand behind him and to spread his legs. He cuffed him. "Do you have any needles or sharp objects in your pockets?"

"No," the man said.

Jack carefully patted him down. "Why are you following this woman?" When he didn't respond, Jack took out the man's wallet and flipped it open. Abruptly it fell from his hands to the pavement. He grabbed the man and whirled him around. "My God!"

"Hello, J.T."

Lucky stepped closer. The man was sixty or so with graying hair, attractive despite the rugged, dangerous look of his face. She was certain he wasn't anyone she knew, yet something about him nagged at her brain. The shape of the jaw, the coffee-colored eyes…

Confusion turned to dreaded realization. She was staring at an older version of Jack, what he would look like in thirty years or so. She sucked in a ragged breath. *Jack's father.* The father he'd supposedly lost in a car accident at sixteen.

Her stomach plummeted to her knees.

"Well, Mr. Webster," she said, knowing without a doubt the name was right, "you look pretty darn good for a dead man."

SOMEWHERE IN THE BACK of his mind, Jack had known this day would come. He'd changed his name, changed where he lived and tried to change who he was, but he was tainted by his past, and the stain of it lingered no matter how hard he labored to scrub it away.

Disgusted even by the feel of the man's jacket beneath his fingers, Jack released him—his father, though he'd never called him that. Father. Dad. Daddy. Pop. None of those had ever seemed appropriate. The son of a bitch didn't know how to be a father. Growing up, Jack and Emma had both called him by his given name: Ray. "When did you get out of prison?"

"A few months back. I'm living here now. Got me a nice room at the boardinghouse over on Sixth Street and a job at the car wash three mornings a week. I'm a good boy. Don't cause trouble, and I report to my parole officer once a month."

"Why are you here?"

"To see you, J.T."

"I don't use that name anymore."

"So I heard."

"How in God's name did you find me?"

"Didn't have to find you. Knew where you were all along."

Jack swore. "Vinnie?"

"Asked him to keep an eye out for you. Pretty ironic, son, you being a cop. I guess you turned into Marshal Cahill, after all."

"I'm not your son."

"Whatever you say." He grinned and looked past Jack's shoulder. "Aren't you going to introduce me to my daughter-in-law?"

Jack momentarily closed his eyes, drawing strength. In the heat of his anger, he'd forgotten Lucky was even there. Her words haunted him. She'd called Ray "Mr. Webster." Somehow she'd known.

He turned to look at her, and what he saw in her eyes cut him to the bone—pain, distrust, disillusionment. All the blood had left her face. "Take the handcuffs off him," she said softly.

He glanced around; they'd drawn a crowd. The store employees had come out to gawk, and people on the street stood watching. "Police business. Move along," he barked, making them scatter. He released Ray from the cuffs. "I want you gone from this town by the end of the day. There's nothing for you here."

"And violate my parole?"

"You never gave a damn about it before."

"That's true, but I think I'll stick around now that I'm going to be a granddaddy. My family's here."

"You have no family, old man. No wife, no son, no daughter. You killed us all, you good-for-nothing son of a bitch—or at least, you made us *wish* we were dead."

"Daughter?" Lucky's sack and the flowers she held fell to the pavement.

"Where *is* Emma?" Ray asked.

"I don't know, and if I did, I wouldn't tell you. She hates you as much as I do."

Lucky turned and walked off.

"Lucky, wait!" Jack called, but she didn't stop. Forced to choose between following her and staying with Ray, the choice was easy. Jack swore and took off after her. "Wait, please," he begged, grabbing her arm. "We have to talk about this."

"Who *are* you?"

"I can explain everything."

"Explain? My God, how? I thought I was married to a man named Cahill who lost both his parents in a tragic accident. Now I find out the name is a lie, your father isn't dead and you have a sister you never bothered to tell me about. What about your mother? Is she really dead or can I expect her to pop out one day and yell, 'Surprise'?"

"My mother's dead. That part's true. Look, I don't want to have this conversation out here on the street." He thought about where they could go. Not the station. Not the newspaper. "I'll take you home."

"No. I don't want you taking me anywhere."

He swallowed a lump the size of a baseball. "Please don't push me away." She seemed so lifeless and pale it scared him.

"Leigh tried to warn me something was wrong about you, but I wouldn't listen." Tears sprang to her eyes. "She checked records in Mississippi and there wasn't a John Thomas Cahill with your birthdate born in Biloxi, but there was a John Thomas Webster with parents Raymond and Grace. Even when she showed me the proof, I defended you."

So that was how she'd known about Ray. "I *was*

born John Thomas Webster. I changed my name legally.''

"I told Leigh you'd never lie to me."

Her pain became his. "I'm sorry."

"You're sorry? That's all you have to say?"

"I didn't tell you because I was ashamed of my past, ashamed of my father and what he was and what he turned me into.''

"What do you mean?"

"He's a thief, Lucky. And he made me one, too.''

LUCKY SAID SHE FELT sick to her stomach, so he followed her in his car to her parents' house two blocks away, leaving Ray on the street. Jack planned to deal with him later.

He explained to Ruth and Matt that Lucky was okay physically, but had suffered an emotional shock.

"What happened?" her mother asked. She clutched her chest. "The baby?"

"No, it was my fault," Jack told her. "I did something that upset her. Can we have a few minutes alone?''

"Lucky?" Ruth asked, expressing concern about how chalky her skin looked. "Are you all right? Do you want to be alone with Jack?" She pulled a tissue from her pocket and handed it to her daughter.

Lucky debated, then nodded. She gave her a weak smile. "Let us have a few minutes, please."

Her father offered them his study. Lucky went in ahead and sat down.

"I don't know what you've done," Matt said in a low voice to Jack, "but whatever it is, make it right. Whatever she says, you agree. Whatever she wants, you give it to her. She doesn't need to be upset just now.''

"I don't know if I can make this one right, Matt. I screwed up royally.''

His father-in-law gave him a reassuring pat on the shoulder and closed the door. The man had been more of a father to him than Ray ever had. But when Matt found out the truth, Jack feared he'd lose his respect, along with Lucky's.

She had curled up at one end of the couch, and she watched him warily as he approached. He dragged a chair in front of her, sat down and rested his forearms on his thighs. "I'm sorry. I should've told you the truth the minute things got serious between us.''

"Why didn't you?''

"I was afraid, embarrassed. Ray's been a thorn in my side most of my life. I got used to pretending he was dead. I haven't seen him since before my mother died. That's been…more than eighteen years.''

"What really happened to her? She obviously didn't die in a car accident with your father.''

"Emphysema. She was sick most of the time I was growing up, but it finally got bad around my fourteenth birthday. She couldn't do much after that. Ray had been in and out of jail for years, and we couldn't count on him for anything but grief. Emma…she'd run away by then, so it was only me and my mother living together when she died.''

"You told your father you don't know where your sister is. Is that true?''

"I haven't seen her since I was twelve. I've searched, but I don't know where she went when she left Springfield. I doubt she wants to be found.'' The confusion in her eyes made him add, "Springfield was where we were living at the time. We moved whenever Ray got into trouble or the landlord wanted the rent. He had a lot of associates, as he called them, friends he met in jail or that he'd pulled jobs with at one time or another. When we didn't have a place to stay, we'd look up one of them.''

Tears rolled silently down her cheeks. The spark of compassion in her eyes gave him hope. "Sounds like a terrible life for a child," she said.

"The worst part was never knowing what I was going to find when I came home, whether Ray would be there or had been arrested again.''

"You called him a thief. Is that why he went to jail?"

"Burglary, theft, running numbers. He did whatever he could to make cash without having to work. I doubt Ray's ever made an honest buck in his life.''

"Why did you call *yourself* a thief? Have you been to prison?''

"No, it never came to that, but I was headed down that road. I knew Ray was pulling jobs long before my mother did. Sometimes…he'd take me with him when he hit a house. Because I was smaller, he'd send me in through a window, or if it was a commercial building, the air-conditioning duct. By the time I was ten, I could pick any kind of lock. It really tickled him that I could do it, and because I was young and stupid and wanted my father's attention, I thought it was pretty cool." He hung his head, shamed by it. "I never got caught, but I knew it was wrong and I hated the way we lived—the lies, the fear… We never had any money, no matter how much he stole. My mom got sicker and sicker. We lived in places no human should have to, where we could look through the holes in the floor and see the dirt below."

"Snakes," Lucky said quietly.

"Yeah, but at least they ate the rats."

A sob escaped her lips. "Oh, Jack…that's horrible. Your sister shouldn't have left you to deal with those problems alone."

"I don't blame her. The situation was even worse for Emma, because Ray had her helping him with his cons. Breaking into a house and stealing from people you never see is hard enough, but Emma was eye-to-eye with the people she stole from."

"What kind of things did she do?"

"Mostly scammed people out of their money. Emma had this uncanny ability to transform herself. She could look younger…older. With a little makeup and a disguise, she could pass herself off as some-one's eight-year-old kid or their eighty-year-old grandmother. She loathed it, though. Finally she couldn't take it anymore. Neither could I. I told Ray I wouldn't help him, that I wanted him to stop and get a real job and buy a house so we could take care of my mother the way she deserved. I wanted…to live for once like decent people."

He swallowed his pain. The conversation had been years ago, but he remembered it as though it was yesterday. Remembered how hopeless he'd felt after-ward.

"But he didn't quit," he said, continuing. "He was afraid he couldn't make it by going straight. Not long after, he got arrested again. We were living in Mary-land by then, the wrong place to get into trouble. They sent him up for hard time—prison. I heard a few years later that he tried to escape and got another ten years.

I figured I'd never have to worry about seeing him again after that, but obviously I was wrong.''

"How did you and your mother get by?''

"Public assistance.''

"And when she died?''

"A guy who owned a hardware store where I had a part-time job pretended to be a distant relative, only he didn't take me into his home like the caseworker believed. He gave me a cot in the back of the store, and I lived there for two years. The deal was sweet for him, because I worked whenever I wasn't in school and he paid me virtually nothing. Those were two of the loneliest years of my life.''

"Wasn't there any other place you could go?''

"A foster home, but the store seemed to be a better option than going to live with strangers. At least I had a dry place to sleep and a little money. And, too, I knew the guy wouldn't physically abuse me in any way. He was a greedy jerk, but he wasn't mean.''

"The devil you know is better than the devil you don't.''

"Yeah, that was how I figured it. I promised my mother that I'd finish high school, so I was willing to do whatever it took to fulfill her dying wish. When I graduated, I joined the army and did my two-year stint. I changed my name, used my G.I. benefits to enroll at Penn State and later joined the police force in Pittsburgh. That seemed like the smart thing to do.'' He smiled humorlessly. "I already had an intimate knowledge of crime.''

"What did your father mean when he said he guessed you'd turned into Marshal Cahill?''

He looked away, embarrassed. "*Cahill, U.S. Marshal* was a movie starring John Wayne. My eighth-grade teacher played it at the end of the school year to keep us quiet while she graded papers. I became obsessed with it. Ray teased me unmercifully. I'm sure he thinks it's pretty funny I chose that name.''

''Great. I'm married to a John Wayne character.''

He grimaced, not knowing how to respond. She must think him a fool.

The baby moved, rolling across her stomach hard enough that he could see the movement through her sweatshirt. She put her hand to the spot.

''That's everything,'' he said. ''I swear it. I love you, and I'm sorry I wasn't truthful from the beginning. Tell me what I have to do to make you forgive me.''

She wiped her eyes with the tissue her mother had given her. ''Hearing about your past breaks my heart. I can't imagine how you survived it and turned out so well. I'm proud of the person you've become, but…a marriage is based on truth and trust. We don't have that, Jack…or J.T. or whatever your name is. And I don't see how we can ever have it after today.''

''We can.''

''How, when I don't even know who you are?''

''You know everything about me, every miserable fault I have. I've told you things today I've never told anyone.''

He leaned forward and took her hand, but she pulled it away. ''No, please don't touch me. That's the last thing I need right now.''

''Then tell me what you *do* need. Whatever it is, I'll give it to you.''

''I'd like you to leave the cabin.''

Fear knotted his stomach. ''Move out? Why?''

''Because I need time alone if I'm going to get past

this. I'm so hurt and angry that just being in the same room with you is difficult. Please, pack some clothes and stay in town for a while.''

''For how long?''

''That's not a question I can answer right now.''

CHAPTER TWELVE

CLOSED UP in the bedroom she'd used as a child, Lucky had plenty of time to grieve, for grief was what it felt like.

After Jack had left, she'd told her parents and grandmother what had happened. They'd been shocked but supportive. Her dad had offered to drive out to the cabin, pick up Beanie and bring her back to the house so Lucky could stay with them, but she wanted to go home.

Once she knew for sure that Jack had collected his things, she'd think about putting her miserable self in the truck and making the trip. Right now, though, she had family to deal with. Against her instructions, her mother had called Leigh, Shannon and Cal and filled them in, and within ten minutes the Mathison siblings had descended on the house.

Shannon commiserated with her. So did poor Cal, who seemed more upset than anyone. Jack's betrayal had hit him hard.

When another soft knock sounded, Lucky knew who it had to be. Leigh opened the bedroom door. "Will you let me come in? I'd really like to talk to you."

"Not if you came here to gloat." She grabbed another tissue from the box on the nightstand and blew her nose. "I already know how stupid I am. A dumb, stupid hick."

"I promise, no gloating. I thought you might need somebody to cry with."

"I'm all cried out." When Leigh continued to stand there, hesitant, Lucky muttered, "But you might as well come in, anyway."

Leigh sat with her on the bed. "I'm so sorry. I mean that. I'd give anything for this not to have happened. And you're not a stupid hick. This wasn't your fault."

"I should've listened to you. Everybody tells me what great intuition I have, but where was it when I needed it?"

"Didn't you suspect just a little something wasn't right?"

"I guess," she admitted, feeling like a complete idiot. "I suppose I didn't want to know the truth."

"You love him. It's easy to overlook problems when love is involved. That doesn't mean you're stupid. It means you're trusting and you have a big heart. Hey, talk about stupid. I've got two university degrees, and Keith was banging his secretary for six months before I even noticed anything suspicious."

"This child keeps me tied to Jack forever, but I don't know how to survive even the thought of it. When I imagine having to see him every day, I hurt so much I want to die."

"So divorce him. You could try suing for full custody and blocking him from your life completely. He entered the marriage without disclosing his full past. A judge would be sympathetic to your side."

"I could never do that. Being separated from his child would kill him." The tears started again as she thought of all the plans they'd made, how he'd painted the nursery and put up the crib, how he'd already bought toys. "He'll be a good father." She sobbed into her sister's shoulder.

"Oh, sweetie." Leigh patted her back. "You'll get through this. I promise."

"I don't want a divorce. I still love him—whoever he is."

"Then stay with him."

"But I don't trust him. I'm not sure he's even telling me the truth now. He could be some con artist. An ax murderer."

Leigh released her and made her wipe her eyes. "I don't think they allow ax murderers in the police academy."

"But how do I know he's really even a cop? He could be like that man they profiled on TV who assumed multiple identities and married wealthy women to bilk them out of their life savings."

"Are you stashing money I don't know about?"

"No."

"Then I don't think you have to worry that he married you for the salary I'm paying you."

"Am I overreacting?"

"Just a teeny bit."

"I don't know what to think or do. My head is telling me I can't trust him and that he'll hurt me again, but my heart is telling me he's worth the risk."

"Give yourself time to sort all this out. Would you like to come and stay with me and Susan? We've got that extra bedroom, and I'd love to have a baby in the house again. Having another one of my own doesn't appear to be an option."

"I appreciate it, but I'm going home. I feel safe and comfortable there."

Leigh nodded. "I understand. If you need me, all you have to do is ask. Day or night."

"I'll be okay."

"You should go ahead and take maternity leave. I know you wanted to work up until the last day, but you're under so much emotional stress right now you should quit and relax."

"I might do that. I'd like to think about it for a couple of days, okay?"

"Whatever you want. I've got another part-time person hired to do reporting, and she has photo and darkroom experience."

"You're not replacing me, are you? Lord, I couldn't stand losing my job on top of losing Jack."

"Kiddo, we could *never* replace you. You're the heart of the whole company. This new person is going to be handling my reporting duties since I've gotten so busy, but she's there to step in and take over for you temporarily whenever you say the word. So don't start inventing things to worry about, okay?"

"Okay."

"What else do you need me to do for you? Anything?"

"Well…there *is* something, but you won't like it. I want you to promise not to confront Jack about what's happened. Don't fight with him."

"Lucky—"

"No, listen to me. I'm furious at him, but he's hurting, too. I don't want him feeling any worse than he already does. That won't help him or me get through this."

"He doesn't deserve compassion. He might be an ax murderer, remember?"

Lucky managed a small smile through her tears. "I remember. But in case he's not…for my sake, don't fight. Please? I can't bear the thought of you and him going at each other."

Leigh didn't want to agree, but Lucky kept after her until she did. "Okay, for your sake, I won't fight with him. Can I at least tell him he's a bastard?"

"That you can do."

Leigh laughed. They hugged again. "There you go. We Mathison girls can still find our sense of humor even in the worst of circumstances."

"I'm lucky to have you. Poor Jack. He has nobody."

Leigh shook her head. "Don't feel sorry for him."

"I can't help it. His mother is dead. He doesn't know where his sister is. And that father of his is a real character."

"Tell me about him. Did you two talk?"

"Not really. I stood there dumbfounded while Jack did the talking. He was furious. He gets this little throbbing place in his cheek when he's trying not to show how angry he is, and it was going ninety miles an hour."

"Not easy, I suppose, having your convict father show up after all these years. I'm surprised he even recognized him."

"Oh, that was no trouble, believe me. They look so much alike it's uncanny. You'd know him in a minute."

"No one in town noticed the resemblance?"

"I'm not sure, but I doubt it. I'd imagine Ray Webster has done his best to avoid the people Jack hangs out with.''

''Cops.''

''Uh-huh. Apparently he was released from prison only a few months ago.''

''What I still don't understand is why he was following *you* if he came here to see Jack.''

''I don't, either, but I plan to find out.''

RAY LIT A CIGARETTE and settled back in a chair on the porch of the boardinghouse to wait. Didn't take long. The boy came screeching up in that unmarked car of his twenty minutes later and stalked to the house.

''Why aren't you packing?'' J.T. asked before he'd even reached the top step.

''I'm not leavin'.''

''I have things to say to you, old man.''

''So say them.''

A couple of the old poops were playing checkers as they did every afternoon, and they were pretty interested in what was going on.

''In private,'' J.T. said.

''Suit yourself.'' Ray got up and went inside, and the boy followed him to his room on the second floor. ''Home, sweet home.''

''It's better than any home you ever gave us.''

''I'm sure that's right.'' Ray sat in a rocker the widow had provided, but the boy preferred to pace back and forth, wearing a hole in the floor. ''Is that why you're here, J.T.? You want to remind me of every bad thing I ever did?''

''That would take more time than I'm willing to spend with you.''

"Bitter. I expected it, but it ain't pretty, son."

"I told you, I'm not your son. You killed whatever feeling I had for you a long time ago."

"I never claimed to be a good father, but maybe I'll have better luck with that grandbaby."

J.T. stopped and yanked him up by the shirt with both hands. "You stay away from my wife and child."

"I only want to get to know them. That wife of yours. She's a pistol. Seems to get herself in more trouble than I do."

"You listen to me. If I even see you on the same street as Lucky, you'll wish they'd kept you in prison." He released his hold, and Ray fell back in the chair.

He straightened his clothes. "I was only watching out for her, boy. No need to get yourself riled up."

"I want you gone." He opened the closet, got out the old suitcase Ray had bought at the pawnshop and flipped it open on the bed. Ray sat there and watched in silence as J.T. pulled his shirts from the closet, stuffed them in the suitcase and emptied the drawers of the bureau.

When he'd finished, he took money from his wallet and tossed it on the bed.

"You trying to get me busted, J.T.? If I leave town, they'll send me back up."

"Now wouldn't that be a shame?"

The boy wasn't going to cut him any slack.

"All right, this is the way it is… I can't take back what I did to you and Emma and your mama, and I know you hate my guts, but I ain't going back to prison just because you can't stand the sight of me. If you want me gone, I'll go, but not until I find me

another place and the parole board says it's okay. I
ain't running again. I did it once and it cost me a
chunk of my life."

"I'll explain the situation to your parole officer."

"And have everybody know I'm your daddy? Fine,
go ahead." J.T. swore. "That's what I thought. Didn't
figure you'd want those cops you work with to know
your daddy's an ex-con."

"Are you threatening me?"

"No, boy, only layin' out the facts so there won't
be any misunderstanding. I'll leave, but I ain't running away. I'm through with running. And I want to
see that grandbaby once before I go."

"No way in hell!"

"I figure you owe me that."

"Owe you! Old man, I don't owe you shit!"

Ray played his trump card. "Yes, you do, son. We
both know you're the one who sent me to prison."

JACK TRIED NOT to show how badly the accusation
had hit him, but it was impossible. The anger rushed
from him like air from a balloon. He sat to keep from
falling. "You tripped the silent alarm that night."

"No, boy. I told your mama that, but the alarm
didn't go off. The owner didn't set it on Thursdays
when he left because he always came back after dinner to write payroll checks. No alarm, and yet those
cops were on me the second I got inside. The only
thing I can't figure out is *why* you tipped them."

Jack swallowed hard. "You knew...all these
years?"

"Why do you think I confessed? If I'd taken my
chances with a trial, your mama might have found out

you were helping me steal. I didn't think she needed that news on top of everything else."

Jack looked at the man he both hated and loved, and fumbled for the words to explain. "I didn't know what else to do but turn you in. You were killing her. I thought if you were out of the picture, we might stay put somewhere and she'd get better."

But she hadn't gotten better.

How young and naive he'd been. He'd believed that without Ray around to drag them down, they get a nice house, maybe even find Emma and bring her home.

But his part-time salary hadn't gone far, and they'd gotten stuck in public housing, a rattrap worse than what they'd given up.

His mother had gotten sicker and sicker. Medicaid hadn't covered all the bills.

"If it means anything, J.T., I don't hold it against you."

Jack sprang to his feet. "It means nothing," he flung at him, and staggered through the door.

He'd barely made it outside to the edge of the porch before he lost his lunch.

Lucky went downstairs when she felt better. Her sisters and Cal had gone home. Her grandmother was in the kitchen heating water. "Where's Mom?" Lucky asked her.

"Oprah's on."

"Oh. Dad?"

"Reading the newspaper in the den. I'm making you some tea with honey. That always makes me feel better when I'm feeling low."

"Thanks, Mema." She got the teapot from the

china cabinet, rinsed it out with hot water and sat down at the table to wait for the water to boil.

Her grandmother patted her hand. "Are you feeling better, Erin?" Mema was the only one who still called her by her given name. "I was afraid you'd cry yourself into a sick headache. You used to do that when you were little."

"I still do now and then. I guess some things you never grow out of. I heard the phone ring a while ago. Was it…Jack?"

"Yes, it was. He called to check on you. Your father says he wants to come over later and sit down with them and talk. Jack's afraid of what we think of him."

"He should be…shouldn't he?"

"Mm."

"You don't think he did wrong?"

"Yes, and I'm terribly disappointed in him, something I'll tell him when he comes, but it's not my place to judge, especially when I don't know the whole story."

"He has this past life I knew nothing about. Did Dad tell you how Jack grew up?"

"Yes, and I can't imagine how difficult it was, caring for a sick mother, having his father in prison."

"If only he'd told me…I would've understood."

The kettle whistled. Her grandmother got up, poured the water into the teapot and brought it to the table to steep. "A tainted past is a terrible thing to drag with you all your life. Give him credit for rising above it."

"I do."

"Can you forgive?"

"His past, yes. His betrayal, I don't know."

"Decide carefully. When you get to be my age, you don't want to look back with regret."

LUCKY WAITED until five, then drove home, not wanting to leave Beanie outside too long in the cool evening air. The dog was getting old, and the arthritis in her hip joints bothered her this time of year.

Jack had promised he'd pack some clothes and check into a motel. True to his word, he wasn't there, but he'd left the porch and outside lights on for her. He'd also left a note on the kitchen table. He hadn't had time to get his files from his office, he said, but would collect them tomorrow while she was at work.

"I love you," he'd written. "I need you and Booger. Please forgive me." The message broke her heart.

Drained of energy, she took a bath. Later, her sisters and Cal called, as did her parents. Jack had stopped by to apologize, her mother said. "I felt sorry for him. He's afraid he's lost you and is just devastated."

"He may have," Lucky told her.

She ate a light dinner, more for the baby's sake than her own, for her appetite had deserted her. At seven, the time Jack usually made it home, Beanie went to the door to wait.

"He's not coming home tonight, girl. You're stuck with me." Lucky tried to coax her back to the rug. She'd walk over when spoken to, lick Lucky's hand, then return to her post at the door. "You're going to have a long wait."

Lucky turned the dead bolt and left Beanie where she was. Ray Webster was probably why she'd felt nervous out here lately, but it wouldn't hurt to remain careful.

Wandering into the baby's room, she ran her fingers across the top rail of the crib. Inside, waiting, were a stuffed dog and a bear with a stitched smile. A mobile of unicorns dangled above.

"Look at what Daddy did for you, Grace."

Everywhere the evidence of Jack lingered—cologne on the bathroom sink, a T-shirt shed after a workout, his running shoes by the front door.

Last night they'd looked through a book of plans, trying to agree on a style for the new house, and it still lay open on the coffee table. She's wanted a log house; he'd wanted something modern with lots of glass. Typical that they couldn't agree.

On his desk was a book about Indian ceremonial bowls. Sitting down, she flipped through the pages. She'd referred him to an expert at the university for the remainder of his questions, and he hadn't bothered to tell her the result.

That was typical, too, the way he closed her out of that part of his life. Was he still working the artifact case? Was it tied to Miss Eileen's disappearance? To Charlie Bagwell's death?

Bending down, she looked under the desk. The box of files was still there. Should she? She'd promised Jack she wouldn't. But did that promise still count after what he'd done?

She battled with her conscience for all of two seconds before she slid out the box and removed the lid.

Inside were clippings and photographs, as Jack had said. Some were about artifact theft. Some were about Miss Eileen's disappearance and the search for her body. Most of this stuff Lucky had seen before.

But also included were the editorials her father had written to try to get Terrell Wade committed. These she'd been too young to read at the time.

"...and confine this individual.

"...known to be violent and uncontrollable."

He'd certainly been convinced of Terrell's guilt. But *she* wasn't convinced. And the more she read, the more it reinforced a worry she'd carried all her life. Clearly the people of Potock—she and her father included—had committed a terrible injustice. They'd ganged up on poor Terrell because he was different. They'd made sure he was sent away.

"Lord, forgive us."

She repacked the box and replaced it under the desk. Beanie was still at her spot by the front door, and Lucky tried once again to get her to move.

"He's gone, Beanie. Daddy's gone." The dog looked at her with the saddest expression, as if she understood. Lucky stroked her hard and started to sniffle. "Oh, not again."

Her purse was on the table by the door, and she searched it for a tissue. In the zippered pocket, where'd she stuck it months ago, she found Terrell's handkerchief. She started to use it to wipe her eyes, then stopped.

What was it her grandmother had said about a tainted past being a heavy thing to drag around? Well, she didn't intend to drag hers around any longer.

Folding the handkerchief neatly, she put it back in the bag. No, she wouldn't use it. She intended to return it.

AFTER JACK MADE HIS APOLOGIES to Lucky's parents, he knew he had another stop before going to the motel for the night—the hardest one. He took a deep breath and knocked on the front door of Cal's house. Cal opened it, the TV remote in one hand and a bowl of popcorn in the other.

He surveyed Jack's rumpled suit and tired face and told him he looked like crap.

"I feel like it."

"Figured I might hear from you tonight."

"I came to say I'm sorry. I should've told you the truth."

"You hurt me, man. You hurt all of us."

"I know. Your family..." Regret filled him again, making it difficult to speak. "I care about all of you very much."

"I can understand why you didn't want anyone to know, but it doesn't make the lying any easier to swallow."

"If you can't forgive me, can you at least accept my apology?" He extended his hand. "You're the closest thing I'll ever have to a brother, Cal. I don't want you hating me."

Cal sighed, stuck the remote on top of the popcorn and shook. "Ah, hell, come in," he said, waving him through the door. "Football's on. And you know how I hate to watch it alone."

CHAPTER THIRTEEN

THE WEATHER REPORT predicted falling temperatures throughout the day and a hard freeze that night. Leona Harrison went out at lunchtime to throw an old sheet over her azalea bushes and cover her herbs with buckets.

"Mrs. Harrison?"

She turned to find a young woman in the yard. Soft brown curls peeked out from under a knitted hat. Her pregnant belly showed beneath her coat where the buttons wouldn't close.

"Yes, I'm Mrs. Harrison."

"My name is…Erin Cahill. I wondered if I might speak to you a moment about your nephew, Terrell Wade."

"About Terrell? What about him?"

The woman dug in her purse and took out a piece of cloth. "A few months ago I hit my head. I was bleeding and Terrell was nice enough to give me his handkerchief. I wanted to give it back and thank him."

Leona looked at the object the woman held and shook her head. "You must be mistaken. Terrell's…ill. He doesn't give young ladies handkerchiefs."

She came closer. "Yes, ma'am, I know he's autistic, but I ran into him one day this summer. I guess he'd walked away from Horizon House again.''

"He was out?''

"Yes, ma'am. Down by the river in a slough near where the old mill used to be. I was in my boat and he was…well, I'm not sure what he was doing. Playing in the water is the best description I can give.''

The center hadn't told her about that instance. "He's fascinated by water. Always has been. You say he helped you?''

"Yes, ma'am. That's why I'd like to thank him.''

Leona still didn't quite understand. Terrell lacked social awareness; he wasn't capable of empathy. Offering a young lady a handkerchief was beyond his known scope of abilities.

"Who did you say you are?''

"Um, Erin Cahill. I was …Erin Mathison before I married.''

"Mathison.'' The name made Leona flinch. "The newspaper Mathisons?''

"Yes, ma'am.''

Erin Mathison. Which of the daughters was… Leona brought herself up ramrod straight. "You!'' she muttered. "You have some nerve coming here after what you did to Terrell. What evil have you conceived now?''

"Mrs. Harrison, I promise you I'm here for exactly the reason I said. I was bleeding and Terrell offered me this—'' she held up the cloth "—to wipe my head.''

"Leave my property.'' She marched up the steps, but the Mathison woman followed.

"I know you dislike me but—''

Leona whirled. "That's a mild word for how I feel

about you, young lady. Do you have any concept of the grief you caused my sister? That you caused Terrell?''

''I'm beginning to.''

''Leave or I'll call the police and have you arrested.''

Leona went inside and slammed the door.

''Please, Mrs. Harrison,'' the woman shouted. ''I believe Terrell is innocent and I'm determined to prove it. Won't you put aside your feelings for me for his sake and listen to what I have to say?''

Leaning against the wall for support, Leona contemplated what she should do. Surely this was a trick. But if it wasn't, she didn't want to send away the first real source of hope she'd had in years.

She cracked the door open a few inches. ''Are you or that editor sister of yours writing some article? Is that why you're doing this?''

''No, this is strictly personal. No one even knows I'm here. And it has nothing to do with the newspaper.''

''We've all suffered enough pain, thanks to you and your father.''

''I understand. And I promise I'm not here to add to that pain.''

''Why did you say you believe he's innocent?'' Leona opened the door a bit wider so she could hear.

''That day at the river Terrell could have hurt me if he'd wanted to, but he didn't. Instead, he was very gentle. He took this out and handed it to me so I could wipe the blood from my forehead. See—'' she pulled back her hair ''—I have a light scar from the cut. The incident got me thinking that maybe I'd been wrong about him. I was a child when Miss Eileen disappeared. Now that I'm an adult, I see things in a different way."

"Terrell wouldn't hurt a fly. No one ever understood that. He sits alone and paints. He doesn't bother a soul."

"I believe you. Please…can I come in and talk for a moment? Hear me out, and if you don't like what I say, I promise I'll leave and never approach you again."

Leona let her stand in the cold while she thought about it. The wind had risen and it whipped up under the woman's coat, making her hug herself for warmth. Her nose was turning red.

"Please, Mrs. Harrison. I want to make things right, if that's possible."

As much as she disliked the woman, she *was* carrying a child and the weather was nasty. "Don't suppose I can let you freeze to death on the porch." She allowed her to enter.

"Thank you."

Leona showed her to the kitchen and told her where to sit. "My husband's not here at the moment."

"He always has a fine garden. I passed this way a few times last summer and saw him working in it."

"Yes, he likes to grow things." She sat, but stiffly. "You'd best say what you came here to say, then leave before he gets back. Terrell isn't a name he much likes to hear spoken."

The woman cleared her throat. "Yes, ma'am. I understand. Seems like we all need to put this behind us. That's why I want to find the truth."

"How do you expect to do that?"

"I'm not exactly sure. I know you believe Terrell was a witness to what happened to Miss Eileen that morning, rather than her killer, and I think so, too. If I can talk to him, I might learn something that will prove it. Only, the center won't let me see him without your permission.''

"Terrell doesn't talk. Seeing him would be a waste of time.''

"I know he doesn't talk, but I felt an odd… connection with him that day on the river. He knew I was afraid and hurt, and he responded. In our own way, we communicated. Maybe I can make that connection again.''

"I don't see how that's possible. He rarely responds to anything outside himself anymore, especially not to people. Not since…that morning the Olenick woman died.''

"Then how do you explain this?'' She held up the handkerchief.

"I can't.''

"Will you let me see him? Please? Even if nothing comes of it, he won't be any worse off.''

Remembering the violent painting Terrell had done of Eileen Olenick a few months back, Leona wondered if that was true. It might not be wise to allow anyone close to him. The woman might do him more harm than good, provide additional evidence against him. Yet what could the authorities do to him that they hadn't already done?

"I'll have to think about this.''

"That's fair. I'll give you my card.'' She took it from her purse and wrote something on it. "I've added my number at home, so call there if you need to. And please, think seriously about letting me see him.''

"I still believe it would be a waste of time."

"Maybe, but we won't know if we don't try."

WHEN LUCKY CAME DOWN the steps to her car, the ancient blue Plymouth that had followed her all morning was parked several houses away. She walked over to it and knocked on the window. The driver rolled it down.

"I have to run by the doctor's, then I'm headed to Turner's drugstore. How about if, instead of following me, you meet me there at noon? I'll buy you a cup of coffee and a sandwich."

"When did you spot me?" Ray Webster asked.

"The minute I left the office. So what do you say, Mr. Webster? Can I buy you lunch? It'll give us a chance to talk. You're obviously as curious about me as I am about you."

"Sounds like a deal." He cranked the car. "I'll see you at noon." He pointed his finger at her. "Don't you get yourself in any scrapes between now and then, missy."

His scolding amused her. "I'll certainly try not to."

Since lunch was the drugstore's busiest time, Lucky went a little early and got the corner booth so they wouldn't be overheard. She ordered sandwiches and pie, but held off on the coffee until Jack's father arrived. He showed up at noon on the dot and slid into the seat across from her.

"I ordered chicken salad for you. I hope that's okay. I think you'll like it." Mr. Webster said it was fine. She motioned for Byrd to pour their coffee. "Would you mind getting those from the counter? Once I sit down in one of these booths, I can't hardly get myself up."

He collected the coffee and sat back down. "When's the young'un due?"

"The first week of January, give or take a week."

"Do you know what it is?"

"The sex? No, not for certain, but I'm pretty sure it's a girl."

"A girl. That would be nice."

"I'm going to be blunt, Mr. Webster. You've given me quite a scare a couple of times. Shame on you. If you came here to see Jack, why are you following *me?*"

"Started out watching him. Wanted to see how he was living, what he did every day, how he was getting along. Thought I'd hang back and check out the situation." He took a bite of his sandwich and chewed as he talked. "When I saw he was doing all right, I had second thoughts about comin' here. Talked to my parole officer and made plans to head out."

"What changed your mind?"

"You swellin' up. Realized I was gonna have me a grandbaby, and thought I'd stick around a bit longer. Didn't mean to scare you. Honest. But you're a whole lot more interesting to watch than that son of mine. Besides, you've needed my help a couple times."

"I have? When?"

"Who do you think took care of that robber a while back?"

"You did something to that man?"

"Had to. You were about to get yourself in a heap of trouble. Coldcocked him when he came flyin' out the door, then skedaddled before anybody saw me."

"When else have you *helped?*"

"That time in the grocery store when your wallet came up missing."

"I remember. I found it later on the floorboard of my car, where I'd dropped it." He shook his head. "That's not what happened?" she asked.

"A creep took it out of your pocketbook in the store."

"Did you coldcock him, too?"

"Nope. He was easier. Picked his pocket and threw your wallet on your floorboard so you'd think you dropped it by accident. You need to be more careful with your things. Thieves like me are all over the place. We're bad people—we'll steal you blind."

Amused, Lucky knew right then and there that she was going to like Ray Webster. But with the knowledge came guilt. He'd hurt Jack so deeply.

"I'd imagine you have better things to do than to follow me. What about your job?"

"Only work Friday, Saturday and Monday mornings, seven till eleven. Got nothing else to do but kill time."

"Please tell me you aren't doing anything…extra that might get you in trouble."

He chuckled at that. "No, missy. That life's behind me."

"Thank goodness. I'd hate to see you go back to jail, Mr. Webster."

"Call me Ray."

"Okay, Ray. My family calls me Lucky."

"Can't understand why. You sure seem to be on the wrong side of luck most of the time."

"I have to agree with you there." She thought of something she'd been curious about since yesterday.

"Have you been out at my cabin watching me? I've felt a presence."

"I thought you had. Wanted to see where you two were living. J.T. didn't know I was there, though, did he?" She said no. "Didn't think so. Followed him for weeks on his job and he never knew it. He sure was a good thief as a kid, though. Could pick a lock faster than anybody I'd ever seen. He a good cop?"

"He's a very good cop."

"Surprised the hell out of me to hear he'd joined the force up in Pennsylvania, but I guess I should've known he'd end up bent that way."

Deaton came in the door, spotted her and waved. Lucky smiled and waved back. He went to the take-out counter, apparently to pick up an order he'd phoned in.

Returning her attention to Ray, she asked, "Did you talk to Jack yesterday after we left you on the street?"

"Wouldn't call it talking exactly. He came over to the boardinghouse and did a lot of yellin'. Wants me gone from here, which ain't surprising, but I'd like to stick around for a while and see the grandbaby. That be okay with you?"

"That's Jack's decision to make, not mine. Do you understand why?" Ray said he did. "The fact that I'm talking to you today would upset him if he knew."

"I won't tell if you won't."

Deaton came over holding a sack, interrupting her reply. "Hey. How are you?" He looked with awe at her stomach. "Wow! You're as big as a house!"

"Gee, say it a little louder, please. I don't think those people over in Georgia heard you."

Always good-natured, he laughed. "Sorry, but it's such a shock to see you with meat on your bones for a change."

"I'll forgive you, but don't you dare say that to me after the baby's born. Deaton, this is—" she wasn't sure how to introduce Jack's father "—Ray Webster. He's new in town. Ray, this comedian is my dear friend Deaton Swain. We've known each other since we were five. He's about the only person around here who can get away with telling me I'm as big as a house."

The men shook hands.

"Nice to meet you, Mr. Webster." He turned back to Lucky. "My mom said to tell you she has a little something to give you for the baby."

"How sweet. Thank her for me."

"I will. Well, I'd like to stay and talk, but I've got to get back. The captain's on the warpath today for some reason. Don't suppose you could sweeten him up in the mornings before you send him off, could you, Lucky?"

"I'm afraid not." She tried to maintain her smile, but being reminded that Jack was no longer there made it hard.

"You take care, kiddo. Don't eat too much." He tweaked her nose and told Ray goodbye.

"Cops," Ray said when Deaton had left. "They've got their own smell."

"Are you telling me you would've known he was a police officer if he hadn't been wearing that radio on his belt and hadn't said something about Jack being his boss?"

"Yes, ma'am, I would've. You can tell a lot about people by how they act and what they say...and don't say. You, for instance, smiled real pretty when he said that about J.T. in the mornings, but your eyes looked sad. Did you boot my boy out?''

''I did.''

''Because of me?''

''No, because of him, because he didn't tell me the truth about you or himself.''

''I reckon I should never have come here.''

''No, Ray, I'm glad you did. Until you and your son can find a way to deal with the past and with each other, I don't think any of us are going to be happy.''

THEY PARTED with an agreement to meet again the following Monday at noon. Lucky knew it probably wasn't wise. Jack would be angry if he found out she'd even talked to his father today, much less made future plans to see him.

The possibility existed that Deaton might mention having seen her and ''Mr. Webster'' eating lunch. But she wasn't going to lie or hide. If Jack found out and didn't like it, too bad. Volunteering the information, though, that was something else entirely. Sooner or later she'd have to tell him, but later suited her just fine.

Her afternoon was packed with assignments, so she called in and said she was on her way back. The receptionist told her Leigh needed to see her in the conference room as soon as possible. When she went inside, she found herself in the middle of a surprise baby shower.

Balloons hung from the ceiling. The staff had bought a cake and made punch. Even the twenty or so employees from the press, insertion and bundling rooms were there. "You shouldn't have done all this." She went through the crowd thanking them, commenting on the decorations. "And all these gifts! My goodness."

"I called your husband and he's on his way," one of the advertising girls said in passing. "Let me cut this cake." She yelled out, "Will somebody go tell Cal to hurry up?"

Leigh took her shoulder and pulled her aside. "I'm sorry—I didn't know what to do. I tried to suggest that maybe Jack would be too busy to come, but they thought it would be a nice gesture to at least ask him. Apparently, the rat said yes."

"Oh, no, please tell me this isn't happening."

"Have you talked to him since yesterday?"

"No, and I don't want to. How do I get out of this?"

"Too late, I'm afraid." She nodded to the doorway where Jack stood.

He scanned the room and his gaze settled on her. She tried to move as he walked over, but her legs were rubbery and her feet felt nailed to the floor. "You shouldn't have come," she told him.

"I wanted to see you, and I knew this might be the only way." He glanced at her sister. "Leigh."

"Lucky made me promise not to fight with you, but she did say I could tell you what a bastard you are. You're a bastard, Jack."

"I know it, Leigh."

"Let's all just get through this, please," Lucky begged.

Someone passed out slices of cake. Cal came in with cartons of ice cream, and Lucky had to go through the excruciating torture of opening all the baby gifts with Jack. By the time the party finally broke up forty-five minutes later, she was about sick from playacting.

"Do you want me to load these presents and take them out to the cabin for you?" Jack asked.

"No, I'll get Leigh to help me."

"Can we talk?"

"I don't know what we have left to say."

"Five minutes? Surely you can give me that."

She relented and they went upstairs to the darkroom. Needing to keep her hands busy, she took down negatives and began filing them in their envelopes. "Where did you sleep last night?"

"At Cal's place. Don't be mad at him about it, though. I'll get a motel room tonight. I don't want to cause any trouble between you and him."

"If you want to stay at Cal's, that's up to you. I don't expect you to cast off your friendship with him just because we're having problems. Is that what you wanted to talk to me about?"

"No, I wanted to see you, ask you to reconsider letting me come home. Being apart isn't going to help either of us. We've tried that before."

"*Home* is a strange word coming from you. You never considered the cabin home."

"*You're* my home, Lucky. Wherever you are, that's where I want to be."

She wavered, wanting to kiss away the hurt in his eyes, to hold him and erase the sadness from his face, but the pain was still too fresh.

Reaching out, he stroked her cheek with the backs of his fingers and the air thickened in her lungs, robbing her of breath.

This was what it must feel like to suffocate.

"Sleeping without you last night was hell," he said.

Her bed had felt empty, too, and she'd tossed and turned all night without his arm around her body to anchor her.

"I was in hell, too. I missed you holding me."

"Then let me come home."

"I don't trust you not to hurt me again."

His hand dropped. "Tell me what I have to do to restore your trust."

"I don't know if you can do anything other than leave me alone to try and get past this. I love you, despite what you've done, but I don't want to have to deal with our problems right now. Can you give me some time?"

"Apparently I don't have much choice."

CHAPTER FOURTEEN

THANKSGIVING CAME, but for the first time in her life, Lucky didn't celebrate it at her parents'. No amount of pleading from her mother would change her mind.

Although she'd patched things up with Leigh, she couldn't bear the thought of celebrating with her family while Jack sat alone in a motel room. Instead of turkey, her grandmother's pecan dressing and Shannon's sweet-potato casserole, she ate chicken noodle soup with a few crackers.

It was one of the most depressing times of Lucky's life. Jack was staying away as she'd asked, although she wasn't so sure now that it was such a good idea. Being alone was proving more stressful than being with him.

Also discouraging was the absence of any word from Leona Harrison. The phone call Lucky had counted on getting from Terrell's aunt hadn't materialized. And without Leona's permission, Horizon House would never let her in to talk to him. If he knew anything about what had happened to Eileen Olenick twenty-one years ago, it seemed Lucky would never have the chance to hear about it.

After the holiday, she drastically cut back her hours at work. She was so big now that her feet stayed swollen most of the time, but the pain in her back, thankfully, had eased since she'd strengthened her stomach muscles. All those pelvic tilts she'd complained about, which Jack had insisted she do night after night, had been worthwhile.

This was her last week at work. Going in to the *Register* part-time, plus her regular lunches with Ray, kept her sane while she waited for the baby to be born.

She tried not to fall back into her old pattern of not bothering to cook and spending too much time talking to the dog, but it wasn't easy with Jack not there.

Until she was alone again, she hadn't realized how much she depended on him emotionally and in every other way. Suddenly she had no one to make her laugh or listen to her problems. She had no one to watch the sunset with or to tell her when she was being grumpy.

He'd come by one day while she was at work and had moved out the rest of his things. Now it was almost as if he'd never lived there at all.

But poor Beanie remembered. She still waited by the door each and every night, hoping he'd walk through it.

"I miss him, too," Lucky told her this night, stroking her head.

The old dog was losing weight, but a broken heart was a poor way to remove her extra pounds. If Jack wasn't living in a motel room, Lucky would have taken Beanie to him and ended her misery.

Maybe she'd ask him to come home and end her *own* misery.

Outside it was still pouring rain for the fifth day in a row, uncommon for December, and the drops created their own strange music on the tin roof. The "freshets," as the locals called the floods, didn't begin until at least January, so this was probably only a preview of the real thing.

In past times, before a series of locks and dams were built, these winter rains were a blessing for the keelboat and light-draught-steamboat captains; they needed them to fill the river and allow boats to get past dangerous shoals.

The river was so rough and high right now that Lucky hadn't dared take her little boat out as she liked to each day. The water was nearly over the pier. She hadn't even been able to fish off it all week.

She asked if Beanie wanted to go out. She went to the screen door and opened it, but the dog took one look at the grim weather and balked.

"I don't blame you. Pretty nasty out there. But you don't hold your bladder any better than I do these days, so how about you rush out really quick and squat under that big tree? I'll stand here on the porch and hold the door."

Finally she persuaded the dog to go. Once back inside the cabin and thoroughly dried with a fluffy towel, Beanie seemed more content. She lay down at Lucky's feet at the kitchen table while she wrapped the last of her Christmas presents.

Lucky hadn't bothered with a tree this year. She'd thought about getting a small one, but she didn't really feel merry. The memories of last Christmas, when she and Jack had still been newlyweds and happy, ruined any spirit she had left.

Christmas was next Tuesday, six days away, and she still didn't know what to do about it. Her mother wanted her there, but... She sighed and rubbed her belly. "What should we do, Grace? Should we stay here or go visit your grandparents? Your daddy will be all by himself, though, and that makes me sad."

And what about poor Ray? Surely the other people in the boardinghouse would visit their families and he'd be alone, too. She hated the thought of that as well.

The telephone rang as she was putting a bow on the package for Leigh's daughter. Struggling to her feet, she grabbed the portable, which lay on the coffee table.

"Hello."

"Mrs. Cahill, this is Leona Harrison."

Lucky gasped in surprise. She'd given up hope that she'd ever hear from the woman. "Mrs. Harrison, how are you?"

"I'm fine, thank you. I'm calling because, well, I've given a great deal of thought to what you asked, and I've decided to let you see Terrell. I don't know if it'll do any good, but like you said, we don't know until we try."

If Lucky hadn't been carrying around thirty-five extra pounds, she would have jumped up and down. "Thank you *so* much."

"I normally visit him on Fridays, but if you happen to be free tomorrow morning, say about nine, we could go then."

"That would be perfect. I can meet you there."

"I'm trusting you, Mrs. Cahill. Please don't hurt him."

"No, Mrs. Harrison, I won't. Trust is something I don't take lightly."

THE FOLLOWING MORNING Lucky pushed the security button at Horizon House, stated her name and was let inside the gate. The heavy rains had finally stopped, and the sky was beginning to clear, but the dissipation of the clouds also brought colder weather.

Her stomach did somersaults as she walked to the door. This was probably an insane idea, but she had to try. She couldn't go on wondering if she'd wronged this man.

Mrs. Harrison was already there and waiting. They were escorted upstairs by one of the male members of the staff, who explained that Terrell was working in his room today.

"Be prepared for a shock," Mrs. Harrison told her, and Lucky's heart accelerated.

The attendant knocked on the door and opened it slightly. "Terrell, you have visitors." He poked his head inside. "It's okay. Go on in," he told the women. "He's decent."

Lucky followed Terrell's aunt, then stopped and stared. Paintings and drawings filled the room. Hundreds of pieces covered the walls, and many more lay stacked in rows by the closet.

"He's so prolific I've had to store a lot of his work at my house," Mrs. Harrison said.

"There's more?"

"Much, much more. Each time I visit he gives me a little something to take home as a present. He's very generous."

Terrell was working at a table by the window, and he didn't acknowledge them.

"Terrell, it's Aunt Leona." She went to his side. "I've brought someone with me today who wants to talk to you." He turned the page of his sketch pad but didn't look up.

Lucky couldn't hide her amazement at the beauty

around her. The drawings were wonderful, the paintings as lifelike as any she'd ever seen. Landscapes. Portraits. Many were scenes of the town or of the river. And people. My God, the people he'd drawn!

She studied the loose drawings pinned to the walls, then looked through the larger ones and the watercolors that had been matted and shrink-wrapped. He'd captured Byrd squeezing lemonade—and he'd done it better with paint than anything she'd ever done with film.

"These are exquisite. I'd heard as a child that he was gifted, but I never dreamed he could do such beautiful work."

"He has an incredible memory for detail."

"I can see that." Her heart wrenched painfully at the thought of this wonderfully talented man being institutionalized for half his life.

"What I find so fascinating is that some of the people he draws he hasn't seen in years," Mrs. Harrison was saying. "Like Mr. Byrd. Terrell was only a tiny child when his mother had to stop taking him to the drugstore. He was terrible about pulling away and getting out in the street, you see. He didn't understand the danger." She pointed to a painting above his desk of an elderly woman. "Oh, and like that one. Do you recognize her?"

"Yes, it's Mrs. Baker-Simms, who used to be the librarian at the elementary school."

"She's been dead for years, yet he painted that last month. I thought it was so lovely I had it matted. When I can afford to, I'd like to have it framed."

"It's exactly what she used to look like when she was younger. Even the expression is perfect."

"He enjoys painting people. I think he does it very

well.'' She turned back to him. ''Terrell, this is Mrs. Cahill. Her name used to be Lucky Mathison. She lived in that big white house over on Brighton Street.''

Lucky bent down to try to see his face. Lord! How old he looked up close. He was Leigh's age, but he appeared forty-five or more.

''Hello, Terrell.'' She took the handkerchief out of her purse, removed it from the plastic bag and held it out for him to see. ''Do you remember giving me this? I was in my boat and I cut my head. You let me borrow it. I've come to give it back.''

He didn't hesitate in his work for even a moment.

''Perhaps,'' Mrs. Harrison said, ''we could stay and visit with you. I'm sure you'd like that. You haven't had any visitors but me since your dear mother passed away.'' Directing Lucky to sit on the edge of the nearby bed, she took a seat next to her.

Lucky chatted endlessly to him about everything she could think of—herself, her family, her cabin, even Beanie—trying to connect.

''I'm afraid it's hopeless,'' Mrs. Harrison said. ''I believe he understands I'm a friend, but I don't think he knows who I am.''

''He knows *me.* Look at what he's drawing.'' He'd sketched a full-length portrait of a pregnant woman. The second piece was a little girl with long, dark braids. ''That's me today. And me as a child.''

''My heavens, it is!''

''He's telling me he remembers me from childhood.''

She took a chance and moved to the chair across from him, where he could see her better. She laid the handkerchief on the table where he could see it, too.

"Yes, that *was* me when I was younger," she told him, smiling. "I had long hair and my mother used to braid it and put bows on the ends. I liked different-colored bows, though, and you've drawn them that way. How clever of you."

He didn't respond. She could only pray she was reaching him.

"Do you remember Miss Eileen?" she continued. "She was your friend. She was my friend, too. Terrell...do you know what happened to her? People think you hurt her, but I don't believe you did. I'm sorry I ever said you weren't her friend. If you saw what happened to her, please, please find some way to tell me. Draw it if you can."

They waited, but nothing happened.

Frustrated, Lucky turned to Mrs. Harrison. "The drawings at your house—are any from back then? Maybe they contain clues about what he saw."

"They don't. At least not that I've been able to determine, and I've looked at all of them very carefully. They're mostly like the ones here, different views of the same spot, various poses of people he's come in contact with over the years or knew as a child. Only once has he painted a disturbing picture."

She told her it was a watercolor of Miss Olenick and described how it showed her dead.

"When was this?"

"A couple of months after he was moved here."

"So when he was *back* in the community. Maybe coming here triggered a memory and he was trying to tell you about it."

"I don't know. To my knowledge, he's never done a portrait of her before. He doesn't like unhappy things. He prefers subjects that are pleasant. See all the bright colors he uses?''

Mrs. Harrison was right. The landscapes were all sunny and vibrant. No storms. No dark clouds. The people were happy and smiling.

Lucky tried again, reminding him that Miss Eileen liked bright colors, too. "She always wore such fun clothes. And her hat—do you remember her hat, Terrell? Do you remember where you picked it up?''

He turned the page and started on a new picture with a pencil, making Lucky's pulse speed up, but as he progressed, she realized the drawing was only of the old railroad depot and couldn't have anything to do with Miss Eileen. That place had been torn down years ago. A shopping mall now occupied the land. Terrell seemed to like old buildings. The earlier versions of his work were pinned above the bed.

They stayed another hour, but it was wasted. Terrell sat and sketched without the slightest indication that he heard her or had anything to reveal.

"I told you this wouldn't do any good," Mrs. Harrison said. "Whatever he knows will be locked forever in his mind."

Regrettably Lucky knew she was probably right.

When they made motions to leave, Terrell got up, went to the wall and took down a drawing. He laid it on the bed.

"My gift," Mrs. Harrison said. "That's his way of telling me he wants me to take it." She lifted it up and showed it to Lucky. A man with a hoe worked among a row of garden squash.

"Your husband?"

"Yes. Thank you, Terrell. It's lovely."

He went to the matted paintings stacked against the

wall, searched and brought one out, laying it on the bed as before.

"I believe that one's for you," Leona Harrison said.

Gingerly, using both hands, Lucky picked it up. The springtime scene was beautiful. Wild dogwood dotted the bank of a pond. The color of the water was a bit off, too bright and blue, but nonetheless, his technique was impressive.

"I'll treasure this," she said, but he'd already gone back to the table to continue his drawing.

She said goodbye to Mrs. Harrison outside. Disheartened by the morning's events, she sat in her car for a long time, fighting tears. The past, it seemed, would always haunt her.

SHE WENT TO THE OFFICE and stayed until four. That was longer than she normally worked lately, but tomorrow was her last day and she wanted to make sure everything was in good shape for the part-time help.

She was about to leave when the police radio went off, reporting suspicious activity at the high school. Closed since yesterday for the Christmas holiday, the school should be empty.

Since it was on her way, she grabbed her camera and left. Patrol cars and unmarked cars were already on the scene. She clicked off a few shots at the barricade, but that wasn't good enough.

"Can I go through?" she called to the officer at the door.

"Let me check." He got on his radio.

As she stood there, her back began to ache. The pain spread to her side, then along her stomach. She

opened her door and sat sideways on the seat to release the pressure.

A couple of minutes later, Deaton came out of the
building and walked over.

"Nothing to it," he told her. "The janitor thought
he heard someone breaking in through the boiler
room, but it turned out to be a stray cat running
around. She has kittens."

"Oh, poor thing. Who'll take care of her over the
holiday?"

"He loaded her and her brood up in a box and he's
going to take them home. He's got four kids, so I
guess they'll have an extra-special Christmas."

"That's good."

"Speaking of broods, you look like you're about
to whelp a litter any minute."

"I feel like it. I'm even bigger than a house now,
huh?"

"A whole apartment complex."

She laughed and it felt good. "Thanks. I needed a
chuckle. I've had a rotten day." She told him about
her visit to Terrell Wade. "I'm sure I connected with
him before, Deaton. If I could spend more time with
him, I believe I could find out what happened."

"Lucky, I wouldn't go within ten feet of that guy.
They didn't put him away for nothing. He got violent,
didn't he?"

"Not really. Do you remember much about when
Miss Eileen disappeared and what happened after?"

"Some, but I was only nine or ten, so what I know
is mostly what I've heard over the years."

"He didn't get violent, he got *disturbed,* and
there's a big difference. If you'd seen somebody mur-

dered and couldn't communicate it, wouldn't you act out?''

''Probably, but you still don't know that's what happened. If I had to bet, I'd say he killed her and hid her body.''

''Well, maybe, but I don't think so. After Christmas I'm going to try talking to him again. I'm sure he remembers something.''

''Does the captain know what you're up to?''

''No, nobody does. And don't you tell a soul. Jack already thinks my pregnancy's made me a little loose in the head, and I don't want him hearing about this. Besides—'' she frowned ''—we're separated again… temporarily. He's renting a room by the week at the Magnolia Motel. He checks on me through my parents. We don't talk directly.''

''Oh, hell, Lucky, I didn't know. When did this happen?''

''Before Thanksgiving. Keep it between you and me, okay? I'm sure he wouldn't want people at work finding out, but you're my friend so you don't count.''

''Hey, I'm really sorry. He's tough as a boss, but he's an okay guy. And of course you know how I feel about you.''

''Yeah, I do.'' She looked at the threatening sky. ''I'd better go. Even though the storm's passing, the roads are still muddy out my way, and I don't like to drive them after dark.''

''How bad's the river up at your place?''

''To the top of the pier. It'll probably crest another foot before it goes down, so I won't be fishing for a couple of weeks. I'm thankful the rain has stopped, though.''

"Me, too. It's been hell working in it."

"I don't know how much more battering my poor old seawall can take. I'd planned to shore it up while the water was down this summer, but I had other things on my mind and forgot."

"I know how that is. Well, you better get going."

"Yes." She pulled in her legs, closed the door and rolled down the window. "Oh, Deaton, I wanted to ask you. Did you and that Conservation officer ever find out who's been digging on federal lands?"

"Captain told you about that, huh?"

"A little. He thought I might help. I'm surprised *you* didn't call me."

"I almost did, but I wasn't sure he'd like it."

"Did you find out anything?"

"Nothing but rumor and hearsay, but that's not unusual in these kinds of cases. Following the leads takes months. I've got three possibly stolen pots, and nobody's sure where they came from or who dug them."

"Mississippian pots?" He nodded. "That's my speciality. I'd be glad to help. And I'd love to look at them—on the sly if you think Jack wouldn't like it."

"Thanks. After we get past this holiday, I'll give you a call." He leaned in and kissed her. "You take it easy. If I don't see you again before Christmas, have a good one."

"You, too. Remember, you can't tell Jack what I did today."

"You can trust me."

"I know I can."

THAT NIGHT Lucky moved one of the lamps and propped her painting on an end table so she could study it. Incredible. She felt as though she was in the scene.

Beanie growled and Lucky jerked, making a pain shoot along her right side from her back to her stomach. She put her hands under her belly and held her breath until it went away.

"What is it, girl?"

Flipping on the outside lights, she looked through the kitchen window toward the driveway. The moon had come out to splash the storm clouds with silver, but it barely penetrated the dark woods below.

A low growl rumbled in Beanie's throat. This time the fur on her back stood up.

Lucky cracked open the window. "Ray, is that you?" she called out. When Ray didn't come forward, Lucky's uneasiness heightened. "Terrell?" A shiver ran through her body as old fears surfaced.

She checked to make sure she'd bolted and chained the door, then settled on the couch again. Not two minutes later a hard knock sounded on the screen door and Beanie went wild. Lucky peeked out.

"It's Leigh. Let me in."

Relieved, she unlocked the door, but then remembered the painting. Quickly she put it out of sight in the closet. Then she hurried back to release the eye bolt on the screen. "Hey. What are you doing here this late?"

"Mom sent me out. She's fretting about Christmas. She asked me to talk to you in person."

"Come on in. I was about to fix some hot chocolate. Um, did you just get here?"

"Yeah, why?"

She shrugged. "Beanie thought she heard something a few minutes ago. Must've been a coon after the trash. Where's Susan?''

''She's spending the night with one of her friends. They're out for Christmas vacation.''

Lucky heated the milk and they sat down at the table. ''About Christmas…you have to come, Lucky. That's all there is to it. Mom's making herself crazy about it and driving everyone else crazy. And you don't really want to stay here brooding all day, do you?''

''No, I—'' Another pain hit her side. She winced and, in a reflex action, put her hand there.

''What's wrong?''

''My back again.''

''I thought your back had quit hurting.''

''It had, but today, for some reason, I keep getting these sharp pains. They don't last long, but they run along my side and double me over.''

''Ooh, that sounds like labor. It often starts with lower back pain.''

''No, it can't be labor. I'm not due for another two weeks.''

Leigh laughed at that. ''Babies don't have calendars or watches, silly. They come when they want to.'' She stood. ''Pack a bag. You're coming home with me tonight, just to be on the safe side.''

''No, I'll be okay.''

''This isn't up for debate. You're going home with me and that's final. I'll drag you out of here if I have to. In fact, I think you should pack enough for several days and stay with me until the baby's born. You shouldn't be alone out here.''

''But Beanie…''

''Bring her food and bed. We'll take her with us.''

Lucky gave in, and an hour later she was comfortable in the frilly bedroom of Leigh's daughter. They'd put Beanie's pallet in the kitchen and blocked the doorway with the baby gate Leigh still had from when Susan was little.

"She'll be okay," Leigh reassured her for the fifth time.

"You must think I'm crazy, but she's old and gets confused. I don't want to upset her."

"I'll check on her before I go to bed. Don't worry."

Lucky snuggled into the warmth of the quilt. "This is nice. I like how you've redecorated the room."

Leigh put an extra blanket at the foot of the bed in case she needed it. "Susan thinks she's too old for baby stuff, so I tried to make it look more feminine."

Her baby deserved a pretty room like this. "Will you help me finish the nursery? Jack and I started it, but—" Memories overwhelmed her and she burst into tears. "I'm sorry," she said, swiping at them with one hand. "I just miss him so much. Even saying his name makes me cry."

"Oh, Lucky…" Leigh sat down on the side of the bed and hugged her. "I've never seen you more miserable than you've been in the past few weeks."

"It's like…like someone has ripped me in half."

"I know. But it gets easier. I promise."

Did it? How, when she hurt more every day?

Leigh left and came back with a box of tissues. "Quit crying before you give yourself a headache. We'll have no sniffling in this house tonight. It's nearly Christmas and you have a baby about to be born. This is a happy time. Chin up."

"Yes, ma'am." She blew her nose.

"Any more pains?"

"No, I think it really was my back."

"Well, I'll leave the door open, so if anything happens during the night and you need me, call out."

Lucky hugged her again. "I'm so glad you're my sister."

"Me, too. Now get some rest. You look exhausted."

Lucky turned off the light and within minutes she'd fallen into a troubled sleep. She dreamed she was in the water, but a strange kind of water, so thick she could hardly move her arms to stay afloat, and the bright blue color of it was wrong.

In every direction the water stretched out around her like an ocean, but she somehow knew it wasn't really an ocean, just a huge pond without a visible shoreline. She was in Terrell's painting, but not as a person, rather, an insignificant speck, so tiny that a foot was like a mile and every ripple was a huge wave.

Miss Eileen was there, struggling against the current. She had on her funny hat with the petroglyphs and her pretty rock earrings.

Her pretty *blue rock* earrings.

Lucky awoke with a start and sat up in bed. Not blue *water.* Blue *rocks!* Blue mica beneath the surface that made the water look falsely blue.

"Oh, my God!"

Terrell *had* communicated with her through the painting. And he'd told her where to find Miss Eileen's body.

CHAPTER FIFTEEN

"I'VE MADE YOU some breakfast, and I've already let the dog out," Leigh said. She stood at the stove in her robe and slippers. "Sit down and I'll fix you a plate."

"Thanks, but I've got to run. I'll eat something later."

Awake most of the night, she could hardly wait to get out this morning. There were two important things she had to do today—solve a murder and get her husband back.

Somewhere last night, in the midst of her pain and strange dreams, she'd accepted the truth: she'd never be happy until she reconciled with Jack. The choice to forgive him, be happy and go forward with her life was within her power. All she had to do was act.

She pulled on her coat and hat and grabbed her camera bag. She scratched Beanie under the chin.

"Where are you going? It's still dark outside."

"To work. I'm always in by seven."

"If that's true, I need to give you a raise. You're worth more than I'm paying you."

"Yes, I am. Remember that when we open the new complex with my photographic studio and you have to contract for my services, instead of paying me a flat salary."

That brought Leigh around. "You've decided?"

"Yes, I think it's a great idea and I'm the perfect person to run it, but I want one change to the renovation plans."

"What kind of change?"

"I'll go over it with you and Cal later, but right now I have a ton of film to process and I want to get started so I can finish early."

"How are you feeling? Any more pains?"

"No, all better. In fact, I'm feeling wonderful."

"You shouldn't go into work today. You're way too giddy." She got the milk and poured a glass. "Drink this if you're not going to eat any breakfast."

Lucky kissed her on the cheek. "You drink it. I love you, big sister, but sometimes you're more like a mother hen. I'll come by later and pick up Beanie, so leave the spare key in the usual place."

"I thought you were going to stay with me a few days."

"As much as I appreciate your offer, I have other plans. I realized last night that it was time to let go of the past. So today, no matter what happens, I'm shedding it and starting fresh."

"I don't understand. What do you mean, 'no matter what happens'?"

"I'll explain later. Oh, tell Mom I'm definitely coming for Christmas dinner *with my husband,* and ask her if it's okay to bring his father."

Leigh had just taken a swallow of the milk and nearly choked on it.

"You and Jack are getting back together?"

"If I have to beat him over the head and drag him home. And after this...well, he'd better not leave again if he knows what's good for him."

"My God, what happened between last night and this morning?"

"I woke up," Lucky said, smiling at her play on words. "Bye."

She hurried to get all the prints done to meet the deadline for the Sunday paper, but had to keep stopping to sit down. The pains had begun again, a dull ache in her back and her abdomen. They weren't sharp, though, more like an upset stomach.

The part-time person came in at ten and finished the printing while Lucky sat. That made her feel better, and at eleven-thirty, when she went over to Turner's to meet Ray, she felt sure that whatever had caused her earlier problems was gone.

"Have you been waiting long?"

"Only a couple minutes."

"I'm sorry I'm late. This is always my busiest morning of the week and my last day before maternity leave, so things have been a little crazy."

"You're looking pretty chipper."

"I have so much to tell you I don't know where to start."

They sat in their usual booth and ordered the luncheon special of homemade beef stew and corn bread, along with iced tea. Lucky only spooned the broth and gave Ray her corn bread.

"Not hungry today?" he asked.

"My stomach's a bit queasy."

"Never known you to pass up food, sweet pea," he said, and the endearment made her smile. "Sweet pea" was Ray's new nickname for her.

Over the past few weeks she'd grown very fond of her father-in-law, and she understood where Jack got his sense of humor. Ray wasn't a bad person; he was a misguided one who'd done bad things. She didn't excuse the harm he'd done his victims and neither did he, but she understood his desire to make a fresh start.

Like Jack—who also deserved another chance. He'd never meant to hurt her by withholding the truth. He'd only been trying to put his terrible childhood behind him. She accepted that now.

And like her. She'd failed to understand that it was the here and now that mattered. Possessions—like her cabin—weren't important. People were.

Last night, lying in bed after her nightmare, she realized she couldn't go on living the way she'd been, always tethered to past events, past hurts. Family traditions were wonderful, but not when they interfered with living in the present.

She loved Jack, and didn't intend to spend another day without him.

"So what's got you so fired up?" he asked. "Your face is glowing like Fourth of July sparklers."

"Remember the story I told you about the autistic man, Terrell Wade, and that I was trying to persuade his aunt to let me talk to him?" He said he did. "She and I went over there yesterday."

She gave Ray a quick version of what had happened and told him about the painting.

"I came away disappointed, thinking I'd failed to communicate with him, but I *did,* Ray. The painting was a message. He was leading me to a specific spot on a stream that feeds the river, a hidden place I doubt too many people know about. I only stumbled across it by accident a couple of years ago."

She'd been up the stream before to what had been its most navigable point, but that particular year the water was unusually high for a couple of weeks and

the mouth had widened to some twenty feet across.
Once past the bottleneck, it had opened into a small,
stream-fed pond.

"The rock there was a strange blue mica, and that
made the water look blue––like in Terrell's painting.
I've never seen that rock anywhere else on the river.
Initially I didn't recognize the location because I only
saw the place once, and the painting is slightly different from the real thing. In it, the trees are smaller
and there's no dense undergrowth, but that's because
he was drawing it as he remembered it from 1980.
Plus, I saw the scene during winter when the trees
were bare. Terrell's painting depicts it in the spring
when Miss Eileen disappeared."

"How do you know it's tied to this lady comin'
up missin'? Maybe he drew a pretty picture of the
place because he'd seen it before and that's all there
is to it."

"Because I remembered something else." She
stopped suddenly, fighting off what this time was a
small but definite cramp.

"You okay?"

"Yes, fine. Excuse me a minute. I have to go to
the ladies' room."

There, she was surprised to find she'd spotted a few
drops of blood. Okay, that was a definite sign of labor,
but she still had plenty of time.

Leigh had taken two days to have Susan. Poor
Shannon had gone to the hospital on Wednesday,
been sent home, gone back on Thursday and hadn't
had her first child until Saturday morning.

Lucky's bag with clothes for her and the baby was
still at the cabin, so she'd better get that. She'd meant
to take it with her to Leigh's, but had forgotten. And

she wanted to retrieve Terrell's painting and take it with her when she went to see Jack.

Splashing water on her face, she wound her way back through the tables to Ray, deciding not to say anything to him. If she *was* in labor, she wanted to tell Jack first.

"Sorry. You know how often I have to go. What was I saying? Oh…when Miss Eileen came to church that last Sunday before her death, she was wearing a pair of earrings she'd made. I told her how pretty they were. They were small pieces of blue mica. Don't you see? She either knew about the pond and had been there, or someone else who'd been there gave her the stones."

"Maybe this Terrell gave 'em to her. And he still might've killed her."

"No, I don't think so. I believe he was on his way to the river that morning, cut through the woods and came upon her at the pond. He saw who killed her. If he'd done it, he wouldn't have told me where to find her."

"You don't know for sure that he *has* told you."

"I feel it, Ray. Miss Eileen's body has to be in or near the pond or the stream. Probably in the water, since the killer disposed of the car." She gasped and became even more excited as another possibility hit her. "All the land around there is federally owned! Maybe there *is* a connection to the artifact thefts like Jack suspected."

"You've lost me now. I ain't got the slightest idea what you're talking about."

"I'm sorry, it's complicated and involves other cases Jack's been working on, but he'll know what it means."

"You two talking again?"

"No, but that's something I plan to change this afternoon. I need to run home first and get that painting, then he and I are going to sit down and straighten out a few things."

Ray brightened. "You gonna take him back?"

"If he wants to come back."

"Don't think there's much chance he'll turn you down, sweet pea. If he does, I'll come live with you."

She smiled. "Maybe I'll tell him you said that."

Ray snorted, knowing better.

She patted his hand. "You're a sweet man. Oh, and you really have to stop skulking around, though."

"I ain't."

"Now, Ray. The house. Last night. If you want to visit me, all you have to do is knock on the door."

"I wasn't out at your place last night."

"You weren't? But I thought..." She shook her head. "Must have been my sister I heard. Leigh drove up about that time." She checked her watch. "I've got to cut our lunch short. Is that okay?"

"Yeah, but hang on a minute. Want you to do something for me." He dug in his pocket, came up a couple of bills and shoved them across the table. "I'm buying your lunch, but I want you to take these up there to pay."

"You don't have to buy my lunch."

"My treat today. Don't fuss with me, gal."

She let him have his way this once, telling him she'd buy his lunch next time.

At the cash register she had to stand in line for a couple of minutes. When she turned around, she found that Ray had slipped out without saying goodbye. Odd. And he hadn't bothered to wait for his change.

THE ROAD WAS STILL MUDDY and the Blazer slid a couple of times before Lucky slowed down to engage the four-wheel drive. The going was easier once she got to her driveway, because the driveway was covered in gravel that packed well and gave her better traction.

She pulled up to the cabin and parked. The river had turned chocolate-brown and was still a churning mass of mud and debris. Even from here she could see tree limbs racing by.

Taking out her key, she let herself in and listened to the messages on the answering machine. Jack had called last night after she'd left with Leigh. His words sounded slurred.

"I know I said I'd let you call me when you were ready, but…ah, hell, I miss you. Pick up the phone. You can yell at me if you want, 'cause I deserve it, but I need to hear your voice." A long silence followed. "Please, baby…" After another pause, he'd mumbled an expletive, but it seemed directed at himself and not her. Then he'd hung up.

"Oh, Jack…" He'd thought she was at home but refusing to talk to him. How miserable he'd sounded. And she knew exactly how he felt.

Now she was even more determined to set things right between them. Never again did she want to hear his voice filled with such pain.

A contraction—it had to be—doubled her over. Taking shallow breaths, she was able to get through it, but she was sweating now and thinking she might not have as much time as she'd estimated. "Grace, please don't be in a hurry. Give Mommy an hour to get back to town and see your daddy...."

Her hospital bag was stashed in the baby's room. She started to reach for it when a noise startled her, a light creak of the plywood floor in the living room. Her heart hammered. Every nerve ending fired.

Stepping softly to the door, she stopped and listened. An eerie stillness filled the cabin.

There was nothing in this room that could be used as a weapon. She slipped into the storage room and picked up a boat paddle. Raising it like a baseball bat, she crept into the hall. If this turned out to be Ray, she was going to hit him, anyway, for scaring her.

Bracing herself for an attack from the kitchen, she whipped around the wall...and found no one. She lowered the paddle and laughed at herself.

Suddenly a man came at her from behind. She screamed and whirled, hitting him on the shoulder with the paddle, but it didn't stop him. He plowed into her, knocking her down, and sent the paddle flying from her hands.

He was on top of her now, and she fought him with all her strength, clawing at his face, poking at his eyes with her thumbs as Jack had taught her to do. The bulk of him was pressing on her stomach, intensifying her pain.

Did this man intend to rob her? To rape her?

Jack had said to go for the nose if she was ever attacked, so she did, pushing the heel of her hand into it as hard as she could.

He yelped and rolled away, giving her enough time to get up. She retrieved the paddle and hit him on the head, hard. He cursed, but came quickly to his feet to face her. Running to the back of the cabin would be useless, because she had no door there. He blocked her escape through the front.

She gasped, recognizing him. This wasn't some random burglary attempt. Shannon had pointed out the man that night at the funeral home—the ranger, Paul Hightower.

Now she knew why he was here, and her fear turned to terror. He intended to kill her.

He pulled a gun from his pocket. "You couldn't let it alone. You had to go digging into things that weren't your business."

"I don't know what you're talking about. Who are you and what do you want?" She tried to act cool, but she was shaking all over and her fear was evident in her voice.

"Don't play coy. You know who I am. And *I* know you went to see Wade yesterday."

"You've been following me?"

"I'd have taken care of you last night if that sister of yours hadn't shown up."

Oh, God! *He'd* been the presence she'd felt outside in the dark, watching her, waiting to kill her. Leigh's visit had saved her life. But today no one would come to save her.

Desperately she tried to think of a way to escape. She was truly isolated. No one except Ray knew she was here.

He nodded at the paddle. "Put it down on the floor—nice and slow, or I'll kill you right here. Kick it toward me." She did as he said, buying time.

When she was unarmed, he grabbed her and roughly yanked her around. The muzzle of the gun touched the back of her head as a deadly reminder of what was to come.

"Please, don't hurt me."

"Oh, I'm going to do more than that." With his free hand he clamped down on her shoulder and steered her forward through the front door. "You're going to have a tragic accident, Mrs. Cahill."

He made her walk down the steps and toward the pier.

"But why? I don't even know you."

"Because you know what I did—or at least Terrell might've found some way to reveal it to you if you kept visiting him."

"*You* were Eileen Olcnick's married lover, weren't you? And you killed her."

"That's right. She found out about the artifacts I was digging and threatened to tell."

"And Terrell was in the woods and saw you do it."

"Yeah, but I didn't know it until later when he showed up with that stupid hat. Figured I was done for. But Rolly Akers convinced himself that Terrell had done the killing. And since the kid couldn't dispute it…"

"You got away with murder."

"Yeah. Rolly always did have a sweet spot for Eileen. Just like your daddy."

"What do you mean?"

"Exactly what I said." He laughcd. "Neither one of 'em knows the favor they did me by demanding swift justice for her killer."

"You're lying. My father wasn't… He couldn't have been."

"Suit yourself. Won't matter to you in a couple of minutes, anyway."

They reached the pier and he pushed her forward.

Icy water ran over her shoes and soaked the hems of her pant legs.

"How could you have killed someone you supposedly cared for?"

"Easy. The bitch threatened to turn me in if I didn't leave my wife and marry her. She had the nerve to toy with me about it, wore that damn hat to church with the Indian stuff on it to show she was serious about going to the cops. To shut her up, I pretended I'd asked for a divorce, had her meet me the next Sunday morning at a little pond where we'd sometimes go. I told her I had a ring I wanted to give her. I promised her we'd go to church together so everyone would know."

"You bastard! That's why she'd decorated her hat with a wedding theme that morning. She thought she was going to be a bride."

"The whore thought I'd actually leave my wife for her. Instead, I hit her with a tire iron, stuffed the body in the trunk of her car and pushed it into the water. Nobody knew about that pond but me and Charlie."

"Charlie Bagwell?"

"We had a nice little sideline going."

Miss Eileen. Mr. Bagwell. The artifacts. Everything was horribly clear. "Oh, my God! You and he were partners!"

"Poor Mrs. Cahill," he said with fake sincerity, shoving her toward the end of the pier and close to the dangerous water. "She went out on her pier and somehow stumbled and hit her head. She fell into the river."

"Please don't do this."

He grinned, gesturing at the river. "The water was so turbulent and cold that she couldn't swim to safety, and her body was swept downstream. Both she and her unborn child were lost. How sad.''

She began to cry, to plead for Grace's life. ''Please, you can't do this to my baby. None of this involves her. She's innocent.''

''Quit sniveling,'' he ordered. The water swirled around their feet, nearly knocking her over.

''Mr. Bagwell got scared when Terrell came back to town, didn't he. You killed him, too, because you were afraid he'd go to the police and confess what you two had been doing all these years.''

''Oh, I didn't kill Charlie. My wife and I were in Atlanta visiting my mother, just like I told the cops.''

''His death was an accident?''

He laughed. ''Let's say he *accidentally* got himself murdered by a train.''

''But I don't understand. If you didn't kill him, who did?''

''That would be —'' he turned her head toward the bank where a second man stood with a gun, grinning ''—him. Meet my partner.''

''Hello, friend,'' Deaton said.

CHAPTER SIXTEEN

"DAMMIT!" JACK SLAMMED down the receiver of his desk phone, then regretted it when the sound reverberated through his head. Never again would he try to drink away his troubles.

Lucky wasn't at work and she wasn't at the cabin. He'd left messages on her cell phone, and she hadn't called him back. He wanted to talk to her, *needed* to talk to her, if he was going to keep his sanity.

Work was piled on his desk twenty folders deep, and all he could think about was his wife.

Grabbing his jacket from the back of the chair, he stalked through the division room. "Where the hell is Swain?" he asked Rogers. She stood at the copy machine. "He was supposed to give me a written progress report on his cases."

Across the room Domingo answered for him. "He's off, Captain. Personal business."

"Yeah, that's right. I remember." Jack pressed his throbbing temples with one hand. "My head feels like it's trying to unscrew itself today."

"I have aspirin," Rogers said.

"Thanks, I could use a couple."

He followed her to her desk, where she opened her top drawer. "Here you go." He shook two tablets into his hand and returned the bottle.

A broom handle minus the broom stood propped

against the wall, and he picked it up out of curiosity. The point of a nail stuck out from the end.

"What's this?"

"Chief rooked me into volunteering for that highway-trash detail tomorrow," she explained. "I borrowed that so I don't kill my back bending over. Makes it easy to spear paper, then dump it in the bag."

Jack momentarily forgot about his headache as he examined the piece of wood and the protruding metal. A nail had been hammered into the end, then the head was clipped off and filed into a point. *A double-ended nail.* This spike—or a similar one—was what had punctured Charlie Bagwell's tire and disabled his car.

"You borrowed this from the chief?" he asked, wondering if Rolly had done more than make a few case files disappear.

"Oh, no, that's not the chief's. It belongs to Deaton."

Jack wasn't so befuddled by his hangover that he lost the significance of that piece of information. His brain began to process and sort, filling in gaps, examining possibilities. He laid out all the pieces:

The crank call that morning to the box factory that had tied Jack up and kept him away from the scene of Charlie Bagwell's death. Deaton? Probably. And if so, it also explained why the voice was mechanically altered. The dispatcher and fellow officers would have recognized it otherwise.

The screwup with procedure at the train track that Jack suspected had destroyed crucial evidence. *Deaton.*

The cases of artifact theft the department had

worked in the past couple of years, but never solved. *Deaton.*

And *Deaton* had volunteered to go to Bagwell's house that morning, where he'd probably emptied the shed of artifacts he and Bagwell had stolen...or made sure he hadn't left evidence of his earlier burglary.

"Damn! I'm an idiot! The truth was in front of me all the time."

He told Rogers to bag the broom handle, that it might be evidence in a murder case, and asked Domingo to pull all the artifact thefts Deaton had investigated for the past five years.

"Murder, sir?" Rogers asked.

Domingo rose from his chair and came over. "What's this about?"

"I want you to get on the phone and find Deaton," he told Rogers. "Don't say anything about a murder. Tell him only that I want him back in the office. If he asks what's going on, tell him you don't know."

"Yes, sir, but I still don't understand."

He started to explain when a uniformed officer came in, holding Ray by the upper arm. "Captain, this man was causing a stink out at the desk. Says he has to talk to you immediately. He insists it's an emergency."

"Get the hell out of here, Ray. I don't have time to deal with you right now."

He'd only seen his father once since that morning he'd caught him following Lucky. Jack had gone by the car wash and reminded him he wasn't welcome in town.

"You listen to me, boy." Ray jerked out of the officer's grasp. "You better *find* time. It's Lucky I'm here about. She may have gotten herself in a pack of trouble, and I ain't leavin' here until you hear what I've got to say."

The officer asked if Jack wanted the man removed from the building.

"Hold on. What are you talking about, Ray? What about Lucky?"

"She's been investigatin' behind your back, talkin' to that aufisic...that man with the brain problem, and she thinks she's figured out where the body of the Eileen woman is stashed."

"Eileen Olenick?"

"That's the name. But she done stirred herself up a hornet's nest over it. I think somebody was out to her place last night watchin' her and sneakin' about. And just now, two men in a black truck followed her from the drugstore." He handed him a piece of paper with a license number on it. "Didn't know the one drivin', but I recognized the other. That Deaton fella who's supposed to be a friend of hers."

"Oh, hell!"

"Never liked the looks of him. Smiles too much."

Jack handed the paper to Domingo. Although he was pretty sure he already knew who the owner of the truck was, he told Domingo to run the tag, anyway.

"Ray, you're right. She's in danger. Do you know where she was headed?"

"To her house."

"Rogers, follow us in your car and arrange for backup. Come on, Ray. You're riding with me. You have some explaining to do."

"No, DEATON...not you." Lucky wept, the betrayal more than she could bear. "Why?"

"I couldn't let old Charlie mess up a good thing. He'd gotten scared, with Terrell back in town, started whining and wanting out of the partnership. I simply obliged him."

"But you were only a child when Miss Eileen disappeared. You couldn't have been involved in her death or the thefts from that far back."

"I wasn't. I didn't even know until a couple of years ago, when the chief asked me to assist in a case, that anyone could make money from Indian relics. When I found out Paul and Charlie were responsible, I cut myself in for a third of the action. Now with Charlie out of the way, that percentage has gone up a whole heap."

"But you're a police officer."

"A poorly paid one."

"A few pots and implements aren't worth someone's life!"

He shrugged, not seeming to care what he'd done. "A guy's got to make a living."

She felt damp suddenly and realized her water had broken. Another contraction started and she tried to grab her stomach, but Hightower jerked her upright.

"Please don't do this, Deaton. We've been friends all our lives."

"Sorry, Lucky. I like you. I really do." He clucked his tongue. "If only you hadn't told me about your visit to Terrell and how you thought you could communicate with him…"

"You can't believe you'll get away with this."

"Already have. That husband of yours thinks he's some hotshot investigator, but he hasn't got a clue about what's been going on. I've been screwing things up right under his nose, and he doesn't even suspect."

"You're wrong. He'll figure it out. And if you kill me and his child, I guarantee there's nowhere on earth you'll be able to hide from him."

"Well, then, maybe I'll just kill him, too."

"No!"

He walked down the pier and took Hightower's place. He grabbed her by the hair, nearly pulling it out by the roots. "Time to go in the water, sweet cakes."

"Deaton, please! My baby!"

"Ah, now, Lucky, don't be a girl."

JACK DROVE THE ROADS like a maniac, sirens blaring, searing the blacktop and fishtailing through the gummy mud of the unpaved roads. The cabin was less than five miles from the police station, but he feared they might already be too late.

Ray sat in the passenger seat, clutching the dash with one hand and Jack's cell phone with the other, trying to reach Lucky. Rogers followed in her car.

"Keep calling," Jack ordered his father. "Try the house." He barked out the number.

"Nothin'," Ray said. "I'm gettin' machines."

Dispatch said that three patrol units were on their way for backup and that the sheriff's department had also been alerted. Domingo had run the tag of the black truck, the operator said, and it belonged to ranger Paul Hightower.

"Is that good or bad?" Ray asked.

"Bad. Very bad."

As they raced ahead, Ray quickly filled him in on what Lucky had told him that day, including the details of her visit to Terrell Wade. Jack wondered what Lucky and Ray were doing having lunch, but that could wait until later.

"Dammit!" he yelled in frustration. "She should have come to me."

"She was going to. Told me she'd lay it all out for you this afternoon, but wanted to get that picture first."

"I mean earlier. She has no idea what she's gotten herself into. They'll kill her!"

Sirens in the distance made Deaton hesitate.

"Cops!" Hightower yelled. "Let's get outta here." He took off toward the drive.

"Come back!" Deaton screamed at him.

"It's Jack," Lucky told him, praying it was and not some fire truck headed in another direction. "You'd better run, too."

"Shut up!" He jerked her hard by the hair, nearly making her lose her balance.

"He outsmarted you. If you give up now, you might get life in prison, but kill me and you'll go to the electric chair. He'll see to it."

"I said shut up!"

He raised the gun to strike her, his face contorted with rage at being thwarted, but this time Lucky wasn't going to be so easily subdued. She grabbed his hand with both of hers and fought for her life and her child's.

At the last curve before the driveway branched off, Jack saw a black truck backed into a power line right-of-way in the woods. He got on the radio. "Rogers. Black truck coming up on your right. Stop and check it out. Remember Deaton is a suspect in a murder. Consider him armed and dangerous." He turned to Ray. "We're almost there. I want you to stay in the car and keep your head down. Is that clear?"

"No way." As in every squad and unmarked car, a pump shotgun stood mounted against the seat. Ray pulled it out. "This will do."

"Like hell it will!" Jack took it away and snapped it back in the brackets. "You're a convicted felon. You can't be running around with a gun."

"I ain't stayin' in the car if my sweet pea's in trouble."

"Dammit it, Ray! I can't help her if I have to worry about you getting hurt."

"You ain't never worried about me before, so don't start now."

Jack swore again. There was so much between them that he couldn't forget—or completely forgive—but Ray was wrong if he thought Jack had never cared. "Back seat," he snapped. "Black box. Inside it are several stun guns."

"Well, now you're talkin'!" Ray reached over and grabbed the box.

Jack was certain Deaton had used such a device to immobilize Charlie Bagwell, thus the paired marks on Bagwell's neck.

"Get the one with the orange handle," he told Ray. "You don't have to be close enough to press the muzzle against the body. It shoots from a distance and uses tethers to fire the charge. The voltage will keep a man down for thirty minutes or more."

"Gotcha," Ray said, pulling it out.

"*Don't* play hero. Watch your back. And, Ray, after this is over, the two of us need to settle some things.''

''Glad to oblige.''

Jack swallowed hard. Despite everything, he still had feelings for the old coot. ''I'm glad you're here.''

Ray looked at him in surprise, then grinned. ''Me, too. Kinda like old times, ain't it? Me and you. Partners again.''

''Don't press your luck, old man.''

Ray chuckled. ''I hear you, son.''

Jack took the turn without slowing, nearly hitting a tree, and barreled down the quarter-mile driveway. At the end he slid to a stop behind Lucky's truck, hitting Hightower, who bounced off the hood, rolled to his feet and kept running toward the road. Jack could hear the sirens of the approaching backup vehicles.

''I got this one!'' Ray yelled as they both jumped out.

Ray flew one way and Jack the other. As Jack rounded the corner of the cabin, he saw Lucky struggling with Deaton on the pier. Terror nearly stopped his heart. He raced forward with his gun drawn. Deaton hit Lucky hard in the face, and Jack roared with rage. ''Leave her alone!''

''Stop!'' Deaton yelled as Jack reached the pier. He had no choice but to obey.

Deaton now had his forearm around Lucky's throat and his gun to her side. She coughed and gasped for air as he pressed against her windpipe. Her eyes were wide with fright. Blood ran from her lips.

''I'll kill her!'' Deaton screamed at him. ''I swear it!'' He forced her to the edge. Holding on to her only by the back of her sweatshirt, he let her hang precariously over the dangerous water.

The sirens of the arriving backup units drew closer. Behind him Jack could hear doors slamming and radios squawking, could hear the other officers approaching. But his eyes were riveted on the two people in front of him.

"You're a smart guy," Jack said slowly, trying to express calm. "You know how these things always go down."

"Yeah," Deaton said, and Jack didn't like the look in his eyes.

"Let her go."

"Sure thing, boss."

Deaton fired. And let Lucky fall into the river.

THIS TIME IT WASN'T a dream and the water wasn't blue; it was the color of cocoa. But unlike cocoa, it was so icy that Lucky could barely feel her arms and legs. The only warm place was on her right side, where the pain seared her like a hot poker.

Instead of floating like in Terrell's painting, she was carried along by the swift current, forced to go where the water dictated. Her only thought: survival. If she couldn't save herself, then Grace was lost. She had to stay conscious long enough to be found, and will herself not to think about the damage the bullet might have done to her child.

Something bumped up against her. She reached out and clung to it with every bit of strength she had left.

BEFORE DEATON COULD FIRE again, Jack was on him. The horrifying sound of the gunshot, the sight of Lucky's body falling into the water, robbed him of reason. Out of control, he hit Deaton again and again with his fists until the man lay limp on the pier.

Four officers rushed forward to pull him off. When he tried to dive into the water after Lucky, they held him down, shouting that he'd only be risking his own life. But he didn't care. Without her, he was a dead man, anyway.

Rogers had arrived to command. "Captain, listen to me!" she yelled. He still lay prostrate, his arms and legs pinned by the men. Rogers was beside him on her knees. "We need you to get control of yourself. She may still be alive. Do you understand? Help me coordinate a search."

The words penetrated his rage. *Alive. Search.* Rogers was right. He had to keep hoping.

"Let me up!" He struggled against those who held him.

"Can you be calm?" Rogers asked. "You're not helping this way."

"Yes," he said, ceasing to resist. "Tell them to let me go."

Rogers had Deaton removed first, out of Jack's reach, and placed in a squad car. "Okay, release him."

Jack stood, trying desperately to clear his head and think what to do. "Lucky's boat," he said, glancing around for it. He cursed as he saw it on the trailer, up on the ramp. She'd probably asked Cal to put it there, to keep her boat safe from the floodwaters.

"Too small, Captain. I've called the water-rescue squad. Help me coordinate a ground search of the bank. She may have made it to shore."

"Good idea." Thank God someone had remained sane.

"We need maps."

"Lucky has navigational maps in the cabin. On the bookcase. Have someone get them. Get the Walker and Jefferson County sheriff's departments out here to help. Round up all the volunteers you can."

"I've already put the word out, sir. "

"Hightower?"

"In custody. When backup arrived, they found him lying in the driveway with your friend sitting on his back, lecturing him about the evils of crime. That old guy's something else."

"He's not my friend, Rogers. Ray is my father. But you're right, he's one of a kind."

In a matter of minutes volunteers from other agencies started to arrive. They fanned out and began a search of both banks. Jack manned the command post they set up in the front yard, feeling helpless and more desperate with each passing minute. Lucky had been in the cold water for more than thirty minutes.

She was a strong swimmer. But if she'd survived the gunshot and was still conscious, she'd be bleeding and battling hypothermia. He couldn't let himself even think about the baby. The grief of that loss would overwhelm him.

Jack stood on the pier and stared out into the turbulent water. "Hold on," he whispered, as if Lucky could hear. "I'm coming for you."

A cheer alerted him that something had happened. "Captain! They found her!" Rogers yelled.

THE EMERGENCY ROOM at Riverside Community Hospital was a chaotic mass of hospital and law-enforcement personnel. Leigh and Cal had arrived shortly after Jack. Shannon showed up minutes later, and Lucky's parents and grandmother followed on her heels, alerted to the unfolding drama by Ray.

No one knew anything other than that Lucky was alive when they'd brought her in. Found clinging to a log three miles downstream, she'd fallen into unconsciousness the moment they'd put her in the boat.

That had been four hours ago. Jack sat apart from everyone as he waited, not wanting company in his misery. And he feared, too, what Matt and Ruth thought of him now that he'd endangered their daughter and probably killed their grandchild.

At some point he'd overheard Rogers say that Deaton and Hightower were already screaming to testify against each other in exchange for immunity from prosecution.

But Jack no longer cared about them.

A dull ache had started in the center of his chest and spread to his entire body. Grief. Hopelessness. The baby couldn't have survived. He hung his head and prayed for Lucky's life now, unable to bear the thought of losing them both.

God, please don't take her from me.

"Cahill?" called a man in a white coat.

"Here," Jack said, quickly rising. Lucky's family rushed over.

"I'm Dr. Chopra. Your wife is in serious condition, but stable. The bullet glanced off a rib and came out her abdomen without hitting any major organs."

Jack held his breath, waiting to hear the bad news.

"Her body temperature is critically low and she swallowed a lot of water, but..." The doctor scratched his head. "Actually the cold water helped. It slowed her circulation and the blood flow from the entry and exit wounds. I'd say falling into the river may have saved her life."

A murmur of disbelief went through the crowd. Leigh and Shannon cried and their parents hugged.

"Thank God," Cal said, kissing his grandmother.

Jack's knees felt weak. "Wait…are you saying she's going to be all right?"

"With rest, she'll be fine," the doctor predicted.

"The baby's alive?"

"Yes."

"And Lucky will be able to carry it to term?"

"Because your wife was in labor when she was shot, the baby had already moved into the birth canal and away from the path of the bullet. She wasn't injured."

"She?"

The doctor smiled. "Your wife delivered a baby girl not long after she came in."

A cheer went up.

"I'll send a nurse out to let you know when you can see your daughter. We want to continue warming her, but we've checked her thoroughly and she seems healthy. She's of normal weight, and we have every reason to believe she'll be fine." He patted him on the shoulder and told him congratulations. "Let's give your wife a couple of hours to rest before you go in there. She's recovering from surgery."

Jack tried to restrain the tears, but couldn't. His legs would no longer support him. He barely made it back to the bench before he collapsed. Leaning over, he put his face in his hands and wept.

The bench creaked with the weight of someone else. He recognized the woman from her shoes, but still felt surprise when Leigh's hand rubbed his back in comfort.

She encircled him in a loving embrace. He clung to her, needing what she had never before offered him.

And together they cried.

CHAPTER SEVENTEEN

WHERE IN THE WORLD was Jack?

Lucky pushed the button that raised her hospital bed so she could look at the newspapers her father had brought with him, but her mind was on her wayward husband.

After two weeks in intensive care and another in progressive care, doctors had ordered her moved into a regular room three days ago. Everyone had taken turns seeing her—parents, grandmother, sisters and brother. Even Ray had popped in for a minute to say hello.

But missing was the one person she wanted to see most.

"This is the article from the *Register*," her father said, holding it up. The issue date was the Sunday after she'd been shot. The headline read:

Lucky Mother And Baby
Survive Ordeal In River

"That's cute, Dad. It mimics the article from 1973."

"I thought you'd like it. I'm having a copy framed so you can put it up in *your* office hallway when we renovate the building."

"Thank you." She made him lean down so she could kiss him.

"You look almost healthy today."

Her right side hurt when she talked or moved too much, but she could walk to the bathroom now, and they'd taken out all her tubes. She was even wearing her own nightgown.

"Leigh helped me shampoo my hair and wash and that made me feel much better. How's Grace today? I hope she's not giving you and Mom any trouble."

"She's fine. Cries some, but that's probably because she misses her mother."

"I miss her, too. I can't wait to see her again."

Grace Emma Cahill, dark-eyed and dark-haired like her father, hadn't suffered any lingering effects from her traumatic birth and had been released a week earlier. But with her mother recuperating and her father stupidly living in a motel room, she'd gone home with her grandparents.

Doctors had advised Lucky not to allow Grace to be brought back for a visit, since the hospital was full of flu patients. Lucky had only seen her once for a few minutes and ached to hold her.

"Does Jack still come by every night to see her?" she asked, finding it painful even to say his name.

"Like clockwork at six and stays an hour. He gives her a bath and puts her to bed. He's really good with her."

"I knew he would be." At least he was visiting his daughter. "Did you talk to him? Did you tell him I want to see him?"

"I did. He won't come, sweetheart. He feels responsible for what happened to you."

"That's crazy! Nothing was his fault."

"I know. But he has this fool notion that he put you and Grace in danger because you weren't able to trust him."

"Oh, that's ridiculous. *I'm* the one who put us in danger. He did his best to keep me out of the case."

He shrugged. "Only passing along what I was able to pry out of him."

"Can't you reason with him for me? I've left messages at the motel and at the station, and he hasn't returned them."

"I've tried. Your mom even asked him to move to the house until you get out of the hospital. She thought that might make him understand that we're his family and we don't blame him."

"He wouldn't consider it?"

"No, he's distancing himself from Cal, too."

"That's not good. The two of them have always been so close."

She sighed heavily, and he patted her hand. "Don't worry yourself about it. Give him time to get past what he witnessed that day. He thought he'd lost you and the baby."

"So when he finds out I'm okay, he deserts me? What kind of idiot have I married?"

He chuckled. "When you get out, you can set him straight."

"I certainly will."

She cursed under her breath. He'd sent roses every day with a card that said simply "Love, Jack," but it was *him* she needed, not flowers. As soon as she saw him again, she'd kill him for staying away.

"Daddy, every time I ask the doctor when I can go home, he won't tell me anything. What has he told you?"

"Nothing definite. A week or so. Maybe more."

"Another week?" She couldn't go another week without clearing this up with Jack.

"When you get out, we'll have our family Christmas. Nobody felt much like having it before. Had to take down the tree of course, because it dried out, but we haven't touched the presents. Everything's sitting there waiting for you."

"You all should have gone ahead without me."

"We had a small dinner. That was enough."

"What did Jack do Christmas Day?"

"We asked him to eat with us, but he spent a couple of hours with the baby, then said he had to go. Ray told me later that he showed up out of the blue and wanted to take him to dinner."

"He and Ray spent Christmas together?"

"That's what Ray said."

"Oh, Daddy, that's wonderful!" The news made her brighten a little, but she wouldn't be happy until Jack was standing in front of her. "Um…is Leigh still outside? I forgot to ask her something when she was in earlier."

"I think so. Want me to get her?"

"Please."

"Okay, and then I'm going to run back to the house in case your mother needs help with the baby. Unless you need me to stay."

"No, I'm fine. You go on. Oh! In these newspapers, are there any articles about the Indian mounds? Leigh mentioned the university had found them."

"Sixteen. Seems it's turning out to be a significant historical find. Interesting, too, because they're farther from the river than researchers usually see."

"The natives probably did that to keep their town

out of the rising waters during the freshets. The stream would have given them access to the river without having to locate the town directly on its banks.''

"That makes sense."

"Have the mounds been badly vandalized?"

"Several have, but the thieves kept their operation low-key to avoid detection, which means many of them haven't been touched."

The thieves. Deaton among them. Her eyes watered. She didn't know if she'd ever be able to accept that her oldest friend had tried to kill her.

"Leigh's written several article about all this," her father said. "You'll find them in the stack."

"Okay, I'll look through them. What about Miss Eileen's car? Have they found it yet?"

"They've given up searching. They examined every inch of the pond and stream and found nothing. Floodwaters over the years must have carried it off down the river. I doubt it'll ever be recovered."

"Will not having her body affect the case against Hightower?"

"Probably not, since he confessed to you, but it doesn't seem right that Eileen may never be properly laid to rest."

He leaned over again and kissed her goodbye, and she remembered what Hightower had said about her father and Miss Eileen. Could he have had an affair with her teacher?

"Daddy?"

"Something else, sweetheart?"

"Yes, I..." She looked into the eyes of the man who'd always been there for her, who loved her mother deeply—and realized it didn't matter. Anything he might have done was part of the past. "I love you very much."

He smiled. "I love you, too, sweetheart. You try to get some rest today. Don't overdo."

A minute or so after he left, Leigh came in. "I was about to head back to work. Do you need something before I go?"

"Yes—clothes and a ride. I *have* to see Jack. Get me out of here!"

"No! I told you this morning, I'm not helping you. And I've already warned Shannon and Cal not to do it, either, so don't even bother to ask them."

"Leigh, please! I have to talk to him. You must've messed up when you explained to him what I said."

"I didn't. I told him about that morning, how you intended to ask him to come home. He thanked me for the information, but that was it."

"Then I need to see him face-to-face. He has to hear it from me to believe it."

"There'll be plenty of time when you're better."

"But—"

"No! None of us are going to help you, so quit asking."

Lucky growled in frustration. Her whole family was against her. Well, maybe not her *whole* family.

She resisted the urge to grin as a plan began to form. All she needed was a getaway driver who also knew how to pick the lock on her cabin door. Good thing she knew just the person for the job.

Shooing Leigh back to work, she picked up the phone and dialed Ray. Sweet pea was breaking out.

WHEN HE DROVE back to the motel that night after visiting Grace, Jack felt more drained than he ever had in his life. He wished he could spend more time with his daughter, but clearing up all the loose ends on the cases involving Deaton Swain and Paul Hightower had taken practically every waking hour.

At Deaton's house Jack had found artifacts, the purloined case files on Olenick and a stun gun now being tested by DFS to see if it matched the marks on Bagwell's body. Jack had uncovered more stolen items in Hightower's garage and a substantial amount of hidden cash. The cases would go to a grand jury when Lucky was well enough to testify.

Lucky. In the messages she'd left, she'd sounded both angry and hurt, and it had torn him apart. But he was determined to stick to his decision to stay away.

He wouldn't abandon his child, and he hoped Lucky would allow him to be part of Grace's life, but she'd been right about the marriage not working. A woman needed security and protection. He hadn't given her those. She needed to know she could trust her husband. He'd proved himself untrustworthy.

After taking a hot shower, he slipped into a pair of sweatpants and socks and sat up in bed to watch TV. Wasn't much else to do here. When he moved out, he'd thrown all his books and tapes into the locker he and Lucky had rented earlier to store their bed.

Pretty soon he'd have to find a permanent place to live. The weekly rent was putting a big dent in his finances. His stomach couldn't handle much more take-out food.

He yawned, his exhaustion emotional, as well as physical. Occupying himself with work had kept him busy, but it hadn't prevented his mind from constantly reliving the terror of that day on the pier.

A soft knock sounded. When he opened the door, he was stupefied to see Lucky standing there. He couldn't make his mouth work. "Wha…?" He sputtered a few times before he finally got out his questions. "What the hell are you doing out of the hospital?" He looked past her to the parking lot. "How did you get here?"

"Ray brought me. I had him break into the cabin and get me some clothes."

"I'll kill that old coot." He let her in and closed the door. Grabbing a flannel shirt from the end of the bed, he put it on, then found his running shoes. "I'm taking you back," he said, sitting in the chair to put them on.

"I'm not going anywhere. When you moved out, you took something of mine."

"Lucky, you've been shot, nearly drowned and just had a baby. Whatever it is, it can wait."

"No, it can't. I have to know it's safe."

He stood and threw up his hands, unable to imagine anything of hers he'd packed by accident. "What? What did I take that's worth risking your life over?"

Walking to within couple of feet of him, she stopped. Her face appeared bloodless. She favored her right side and held on to the dresser for support.

"My heart," she said. "I need to know what you're going to do with it."

"Baby, this isn't the time for games."

"Why wouldn't you come see me? Are you leaving me?"

"We can talk about it when you're well."

"I'll *never* give you a divorce, so get that into your hard head right now. I was in pain when I asked you to move out, but I was wrong. I don't care who you are or what you call yourself. I don't care about your past or what you did. The only thing that matters is that we love each other. Please…forgive me. I'll never make you unhappy again. I swear it.''

"Forgive *you?*" He shook his head. "I'm the idiot who made all the mistakes.''

"No, I've made them, too. I didn't understand why it was so important to you to have a normal home and family, but now I do, and I want you to have that dream, Jack. I want us to be a family—you, me, our daughter, other daughters and sons, Ray.''

"It's too late.''

"No, it's not! You forgive my mistakes and I forgive yours. That's what people who love each other do. They put past hurts behind them and start over.''

"We already had our second chance, and I blew it.''

"So take a third.''

"I can't. You deserve better.''

"Jack, please. I need to be with you.'' She raised her arms, but he slipped out of her reach.

He cleared his throat nervously. "I need to get you back before you catch a chill.''

She ignored him and came forward. Again he moved away, climbing over the bed to do it.

This time, instead of looking at him with confusion, she laughed. "Oh, I get it. You're afraid to let me touch you. One touch and you're powerless against me. One kiss and you're under my spell, willing to do any naughty thing I say.''

"What makes you think that?''

"Because that's the way I feel about you.''

"You're wrong.''

"I suppose I—" She coughed and grabbed her side. "Oh, Jack, help me!"

"Lucky!"

He grabbed her before she could hit the floor. Sweeping her up in his arms, he laid her on the bed. He reached for the phone to dial 911, but she threw an arm around his neck and giggled. "Gotcha."

"You little faker." He tried to pull away, but stopped when she yelped.

"Oh, don't move, really. It hurts when you fight me. Bend to my will." She pulled him closer, until their faces were only inches apart. "Mm, yes, that's much better. Now—I order you to say you love me."

"I love you. You know that already. I'll always love you."

"Then promise me you'll come home and never leave again."

"No, I won't do that."

"Ray said if you didn't agree, he'd be happy to move in. I kinda like that idea. Imagine Ray and me on the loose together. I'm thinking he and I might even go into partnership. We could start our own private-detective business."

"Hell, no."

She giggled. "Then come home and keep me out of trouble. I can't promise you'll have a normal wife, but I can provide the family. We'll build a house, buy a house, whatever you want. Grace and I will even move to Pittsburgh so you can take that job, if it makes you happy. We'll sell the cabin and the land."

"You'd leave your home and the river?"

"You're my home, Jack. Where you are, that's where I want to be."

His eyes watered. How he deserved this woman's love, he didn't know. "Do you mean that?"

"With all my heart. Say yes to your dreams," she pleaded, "and to mine. You'll never be happy without me. You might as well face it."

She was right. Without her, happiness would always elude him. "If I turn you down, are you going to have one of those hissy fits?"

"Oh, the biggest one ever pitched in Alabama. I'll scream and kick and whine and get us both thrown out of here."

"Then...I guess I'd better come home."

She grinned. "We'll start over and make it work this time."

"Do we have to go through another engagement?"

"No, I don't care about courtships anymore, or being engaged or having a big wedding. I'll settle for a marriage. But a *real* one, with all its problems and joys. Can you give me that?"

"Sweetheart, if it takes me a lifetime."

EPILOGUE

Sixteen months later…

THE HAMMOCK ROCKED gently in the warm spring breeze, reflecting the lazy mood of its two inhabitants. Contented, Lucky hated to get up, but she had a hundred things to get ready for tomorrow's opening of the gallery wing of her new studio.

"Stay with me," Jack said, pulling her back down.

"I can't. Could you watch Grace for a while? I need to run in and check a few last-minute details."

"Do you have to go now?" He slipped his hand under her shirt. "I thought we might work on giving Grace a little brother like we talked about last night."

"Sounds intriguing, but I really have to go. Ray's meeting me at three to recheck the system."

"You shouldn't have hired that old swindler." The affection was apparent in his voice.

"I love that old swindler, and stop pretending you don't. He did a great job putting in the burglar-alarm system, and I think I have some more business lined up for him. He has a real talent for security."

Jack snorted. "He should. He's disarmed enough systems. Just watch him and make sure he doesn't steal everything out from under you."

"You know he wouldn't do that. He's put his former life behind him—like you have." She patted his leg. "How's the search for your sister going? Learned anything new?"

"We have a lead."

"A promising one?"

"We'll see. I turned everything over to that private detective my old boss recommended. Wes says if anyone can find Emma, it's this guy. I sure hope so. I'm beginning to worry I might never see her again."

"Don't run out of hope, sweetheart."

He wanted desperately to find Emma. Ray did, too.

"It's hard to keep hoping when she's been gone so long," he said. He let Lucky rise and sat up himself. "Go on to the studio. I'll watch Grace."

"Thank you." She kissed him. "I'll only be a few hours. When I get home, I promise we'll work on that little-brother idea."

He nodded toward the baby, gurgling happily in her swing nearby. Beanie sat gazing at her with expectation, waiting for her to drop her cookie as she would inevitably do. "Watching her is no problem. I have a built-in baby-sitter."

"And to think you were once the man of Beanie's dreams."

"She gets more food out of Grace than she does me."

Lucky chuckled, then took a deep breath of the pine-scented air. She sighed with happiness. The sky was a brilliant blue dotted with puffy clouds, and sunlight twinkled on the water at the edge of the yard, making it seem jewel-like.

From where she stood on their new dock, she could see both up and down the river. Nowhere could there be a more spectacular view. ''Are you ever sorry we didn't move to Pittsburgh?'' she asked.

''Not a day.''

''Me, neither. I love it here.''

They'd found the perfect spot to build, a hill that kept them close to the river but above the threat of rising water.

The house was an eclectic combination of modern and country styles. Jack got everything he wanted—city services, a grass yard, a large family room. The rustic log structure also suited Lucky. Her feathers, shells, driftwood and other items looked wonderful displayed on the rough timbers inside.

A wall of glass faced the water and let them enjoy the sunset every evening. At night they went out on the deck and studied the stars through Jack's telescope.

They'd moved in two months ago, just in time, or so it had turned out. The biggest flood in fifty years destroyed the cabin a week later, cutting a new water channel. Her land was now an island.

She'd cried over the loss, but had accepted it. The river was a wild thing, unpredictable and free. Every once in a while, even *she* needed to be reminded of that.

''What kind of turnout are you anticipating tomorrow?'' Jack asked. He picked up the baby and followed Lucky to the Blazer.

"Huge. We have collectors flying in from all over to look at the other pieces not on exhibit. And I think curiosity will bring a lot of people to the opening."

The renovation of the *Register* building included the day care and studio as planned, but Lucky had also insisted on a gallery to display and sell the works of local artists. The first show opened tomorrow—the landscapes of Terrell Wade.

Substantial offers on the selected pieces had already come in, thanks to a cover story done on him by a national news magazine. The money would go into a trust to provide for Terrell's needs the rest of his life and to fund an art program in his name in area schools.

"Does Terrell understand all this?"

"Yes," Lucky told Jack with confidence. "He may not understand everything, but he knows people are looking at his work and liking it. He's very happy about that."

"You've done a good thing."

"It hardly seems enough to make up for what I did to him all those years ago."

"Lucky, most people with the level of autism Terrell has end up in institutions. His own aunt admitted that. Even before all the business with Eileen Olenick, his mother was getting ready to give him up. She couldn't take care of him at home anymore."

"I know."

"You've got to forgive yourself. Terrell has."

He was right. Above their fireplace was a painting Terrell had given her as a present, of Lucky and Terrell sitting side by side at the river, both smiling. He *had* forgiven her. Now she had to do what Jack said— work on forgiving herself. This exhibit was a start.

And seeing Deaton Swain and Paul Hightower punished for what they'd done would help, too. Deaton had pleaded guilty to murder and attempted murder and was serving a life sentence.

Hightower, though, had decided to fight his charges. Based on the inability of the state to produce the body of his victim, Eileen Olenick, that case was still pending. He'd gotten twenty years for the attempted murder of Lucky, but she prayed he'd also be made to pay for the cruel murder of Miss Eileen.

She kissed Jack and the baby, and put her key in the ignition. Jack squatted to talk to her through the open door, setting Grace between his legs. Beanie pushed in next to him. "Be careful. Got your cell phone?"

"Yes, worrywort, I do."

"Call me if you have any trouble."

"Now don't start with me."

"Don't start with you?" He shook his head in disbelief. "Do the words *bank robbery* ring a bell?"

"How was I supposed to know some fool would pull the first stickup in Potock history while I was cashing a check? Besides, that was months ago. I haven't been in trouble since."

"That's what worries me. You're long overdue."

"Bye. I promise I won't get into trouble."

"Don't forget. When you come home, we work on a little brother. Right, Gracie?" He bounced her up and down, which always made her squeal. "See, she said, 'Yes! Yes!'"

"You're too funny."

"That's why you love me."

"That and a million other reasons. Now let me scoot. I want to take a few more shots of the flood damage on the way."

Once out of the drive, she turned right, heading downriver. The receding waters had left a blotted landscape of unrooted trees, thick mud and scattered personal belongings from destroyed homes and businesses. The area still resembled ground zero after a bomb.

She slipped her feet into tall rubber boots and loaded her camera.

An hour later, with two rolls completed, she engaged the four-wheel drive and cut through a series of abandoned mining roads—a shortcut along the river.

She was about to get back onto the blacktop when an object caught her eye. Reloading the camera, she plodded through the trees and across the dried, cracked mud to where the river had deposited debris several hundred yards inland.

The object was devoid of paint, but the shape of the funny little car—jutting fins and a blunt nose—was unmistakable. With certainty, Lucky knew she was looking at a 1960 Metropolitan, the missing car of Eileen Olenick.

She went back to the Blazer to dial the house. Jack picked up. "You're never going to believe what I just found."

"Yeah," he said without hesitation. "I'm sure I will."

* * * *

Watch for Emma's story in 2004.

Emma Webster ran away from home at fifteen to escape her larcenous father. She has changed her name, covered up her past and turned her gift for disguise into a profitable—and legal—business.

Years later, she is close to having the respectability she has always craved for herself and for her teenage son, Tom.

But when a private investigator hired by her brother finds her, Emma's past threatens her future. Especially when she starts to fall for the PI… Whitaker Lewis is everything Emma doesn't need—and everything she wants!

▼ SILHOUETTE®
SUPERROMANCE™

AVAILABLE FROM 18TH APRIL 2003

ALL SUMMER LONG

DADDY'S GIRL Judith Arnold
HOME, HEARTH AND HALEY Muriel Jensen
TEMPERATURE RISING Bobby Hutchinson

Three fabulous stories from three of your favourite authors, all with a summer theme!

A CONVENIENT PROPOSAL
CJ Carmichael

The Shannon Sisters

When police officer Kelly Shannon is forced to kill a father of two in the line of duty, his brother Mick Mizzoni is left looking after the children. Kelly feels the only way to cope is by helping to care for them, so she makes Mick an offer he can't refuse…

THE BABY GIFT Bethany Campbell

Nine Months Later

One perfect thing came from Briana and Josh's brief marriage. But now their daughter, Nealie, needs a transfusion from a sibling to survive. To save her daughter's life, Briana must do the unthinkable: contact Josh and convince him to father another child…

HIS PARTNER'S WIFE
Janice Kay Johnson

Three Good Cops

Single father and policeman John McLean feels duty-bound to help his late partner's widow, Natalie Reed. So when a body is found in her house, he realises the safest place for her is with him. It seems the honourable thing to do…until he realises he's falling in love with his partner's wife…

0403/

NORA ROBERTS

Time *&* Again

Two enchanting and intriguing tales about passion so powerful that it transcends time itself

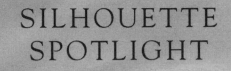

SILHOUETTE® SUPERROMANCE™

is proud to present

THREE GOOD COPS

by

Janice Kay Johnson

The McLean brothers are all good,
strong, honest, men. Men a woman
can trust…with her heart!

HIS PARTNER'S WIFE
May 2003

THE WORD OF A CHILD
July 2003

MATERNAL INSTINCT
September 2003

0503/SH/LC64

SILHOUETTE®
DESIRE™

is proud to introduce

DYNASTIES:
THE CONNELLYS

*Meet the royal Connellys—wealthy,
powerful and rocked by scandal,
betrayal...and passion!*

TWELVE GLAMOROUS STORIES IN SIX 2-IN-1 VOLUMES:

February 2003
TALL, DARK & ROYAL by Leanne Banks
MATERNALLY YOURS by Kathie DeNosky

April 2003
THE SHEIKH TAKES A BRIDE by Caroline Cross
THE SEAL'S SURRENDER by Maureen Child

June 2003
PLAIN JANE & DOCTOR DAD by Kate Little
AND THE WINNER GETS...MARRIED! by Metsy Hingle

August 2003
THE ROYAL & THE RUNAWAY BRIDE by Kathryn Jensen
HIS E-MAIL ORDER WIFE by Kristi Gold

October 2003
THE SECRET BABY BOND by Cindy Gerard
CINDERELLA'S CONVENIENT HUSBAND by Katherine Garbera

December 2003
EXPECTING...AND IN DANGER by Eileen Wilks
CHEROKEE MARRIAGE DARE by Sheri WhiteFeather

2 FREE

books and a surprise gift!

We would like to take this opportunity to thank you for reading this Silhouette® book by offering you the chance to take TWO more specially selected titles from the Superromance™ series absolutely FREE! We're also making this offer to introduce you to the benefits of the Reader Service™—

- ★ FREE home delivery
- ★ FREE gifts and competitions
- ★ FREE monthly Newsletter
- ★ Exclusive Reader Service discount
- ★ Books available before they're in the shops

Accepting these FREE books and gift places you under no obligation to buy, you may cancel at any time, even after receiving your free shipment. Simply complete your details below and return the entire page to the address below. *You don't even need a stamp!*

YES! Please send me 2 free Superromance books and a surprise gift. I understand that unless you hear from me, I will receive 4 superb new titles every month for just £3.49 each, postage and packing free. I am under no obligation to purchase any books and may cancel my subscription at any time. The free books and gift will be mine to keep in any case.

U3ZEA

Ms/Mrs/Miss/Mr ....Initials.....................................
BLOCK CAPITALS PLEASE

Surname ....

Address ....

....

....Postcode...............................

Send this whole page to:
UK: FREEPOST CN81, Croydon, CR9 3WZ
EIRE: PO Box 4546, Kilcock, County Kildare (stamp required)